The

Utopian

Michael Westlake

The

Utopian

Michael Westlake

Verbivoracious Press

Glentrees, 13 Mt Sinai Lane, Singapore

This edition published in Great Britain & Singapore

by Verbivoracious Press

www.verbivoraciouspress.org

ISBN: 978-981-07-9387-6

Printed and bound in Great Britain & Singapore

First published in Great Britain by Carcanet (1989).

Contents

Note on chronology:

The Utopian was conceived and written in the early 1980s, contemporaneously with the world in which Mesmer undergoes his analysis, but was not published until 1989, after the publication (also by Carcanet Press) of my later novel *Imaginary Women*. The Supplement, written shortly after the novel itself and as a commentary on it, was not included in the original publication, and appears here for the first time. Andrew Collier's review article, an extract from which forms the Afterword, was published in the journal *News From Nowhere* around 1992. Finally, Toril Moi's Foreword, written expressly for this reissue, provides both an introduction to the novel and a fascinating personal account of the feminist milieu of the 1970s and 80s. I am profoundly grateful to Toril and to Andrew for their perceptive and thought-provoking readings.

Michael Westlake
January 2016

Foreword

TORIL MOI

1.

The Utopian consists of two intertwined storylines unfolding in two radically different settings. First there is the story of a young man called Mesmer, who in 2411 sets out on his Journey, a rite of passage which is to last a year and a day, in a gloriously pansexual, matriarchal, and feminist utopia. The second storyline is set in Britain in 1979, and concerns Dr. Reed, a patriarchal and self-obsessed psychoanalyst, and his analysand, a young man called Mesmer Partridge.

Mesmer's 2411 Journey is told in the third person, by a gentle and guileless narrator. Dr. Reed, on the other hand, who writes in the first person, comes across as a spoilt, sarcastic, hostile curmudgeon. The two narratives entertain a complex, twisting relationship to one another, moving in all kinds of configuration, in which they intermittently appear to parallel, oppose, double, and subvert one another.

To the reader, Mesmer's compelling vision of the post-communist, matriarchal and feminist utopian world of 2411 is as real as Dr. Reed's 1979. To Dr. Reed, who keeps interrupting Mesmer's blissful utopia with his own negativity, Mesmer's utopian world is not real at all, but simply a symptom of his madness. Every time the reader wants to immerse herself in a world containing wondrous cities such as New Stoke and Bright On, Dr. Reed's grinding voice pulls her back to 1979. In this novel, utopia is never allowed to forget its roots in the real.

What kind of name is "The Utopian"? Is "The Utopian" the pseudonym given to Mesmer Partridge by Dr. Reed? If so, the novel as a whole would be Dr. Reed's narrative, a story modelling itself on Freud's famous case studies. Maybe the odious doctor hopes that "The Utopian" will make him famous, that the names of Reed and The Utopian will go down in history, forever linked like those of Freud and Dora, Freud and Little Hans, Freud and the Rat Man. ("The Rat Man" in fact appears in the novel as a ghost singing the praises of psychoanalysis to the young Dr. Reed.)

But *The Utopian* doesn't let itself be pinned down to the case history format. While Dr. Reed freely admits he is writing a case history, he never calls his analysand "The Utopian." Mesmer's story, moreover, is told in the 3rd person, in a style that is nothing like Reed's death-dealing sarcasm. Maybe this is Mesmer's own voice, accurately noted by Dr. Reed. Or maybe not. Who tells Mesmer's and Reed's stories? Who gives the novel its title? We don't really know. The narrator may be neither Reed nor Mesmer. Perhaps it's Michael, Dr. Reed's driver, said to be an "excellent raconteur," and whose last name, for all we know, might well be Westlake.

In the context of psychoanalysis, "Mesmer" is not an innocent name, for it takes us back to Franz Mesmer (1734-1815), a man who thought he could cure hysteria and other nervous illnesses by "animal magnetism." In the German doctor's first famous case, he made a woman swallow a drink containing iron, and then placed magnets all over her body. Apparently, her hysterical symptoms disappeared. In 1979, Mesmer Partridge too swallows iron. Or to be more precise: he swallows a TV aerial cable, so that he can watch the evening news with his own body as an intermediary between the outside aerial and the TV set. In this state he can finally watch the evening news in blissful contentment. To him, the aerial-swallowing stunt was logical. To his society, it was a symptom of madness so severe that it lands him on Dr. Reed's couch.

The historical Mesmer eventually set up an ultra-fashionable practice in Paris, attracted competitors and followers, and provoked so much controversy that, in 1784, the French King established a commission to investigate "animal magnetism." The meetings of the commission must have been quite astonishing, for among its members we find the chemist Antoine Lavoisier, the doctor Joseph-Ignace Guillotin (inventor of the guillotine), and the US Ambassador to France, Benjamin Franklin. Eventually, the Commission concluded that "animal magnetism" didn't exist, and that Mesmer's and his colleagues' cures were due to the imagination.

In *The Utopian*, the imagination is the source of good. Mesmer Partridge uses his utopian imagination both to free himself from the symptoms produced by his own dystopian society, and to escape from Reed's clutches. In his mind, 2411 is a sexually satisfying utopian world, filled both with magic and with high tech devices. In 2411, phallic father-figures still exist—Mesmer is joined on his Journey by the ancient Very Light, a reincarnation of Lenin—but they don't win. *The Utopian*, then, is the story of how an oppressive society can make people sick, of how the dream of a utopian world can at once be a symptom and a cure.

But would Mesmer have told his utopian story—a story of a rite of passage from youth to adult maturity—if it hadn't been for his analyst? Who would have made him talk, if not Dr. Reed? Just as we can't pin down the narrator, we can't decide between genres. *The Utopian* is at once a utopian novel, a vision of a matriarchal, feminist society in 2411, and a dystopian vision of Britain in 1979, a society so crushed by negative forces that the only way to watch the television news with some degree of peace is through one's own anus.

Of course, we don't really know that Mesmer is cured at the end. But we do know that Dr. Reed, gone crazy, fails to kill him, and instead mysteriously dies from his own poison. In the world of the real, the evil doctor dies. In the utopian world, the old trapeze artist and phallic symbol Very Light disappears on a dragon, leaving Mesmer free to return home as a mature adult. In *The Utopian*, 1979 and 2411, reality and fiction, critique and utopia, constantly insist on their interconnections, insist that we can never have the one without the other.

2.

As I immersed myself in *The Utopian*'s braided worlds, I began to realize how deeply this novel speaks to my personal experience. I moved to the UK in 1979, a few weeks after Margaret Thatcher came to power. She was still in power when I left for the United States in 1989, the year of the original publication of *The Utopian*. I recognize all too well both the dystopian vision and the yearning for utopia those years gave rise to in young people on the left.

But this is not the only connection. I actually spent the late 1970s immersed in feminist visions of the ideal society. During my first year in Britain (May 1979–May 1980)—which happens to be the exact time period of the novel's dystopian plot—I was finishing my thesis for the University of Bergen, on the feminist utopias of the French writer Christiane Rochefort. I was not alone in being interested in utopias at the time. For many feminists and socialists, the radical spirit of May 68 was most memorably summed up by the famous slogan *Sous les pavés, la plage!* (Under the cobblestones, the beach!). Much of the culture and politics of the 1970s remained suffused by the glowing tail-end of that idea.

In the late 1970s, I wanted to write a feminist thesis on a topic relevant to feminist politics. The utopian novel attracted me because it is an inherently political genre. Moreover, it seemed to me then—and it still does—that feminism can't just be about critique. A political movement needs its utopias—its visions of an ideal society—as much as it needs its critique.

If my thesis taught me anything, however, it was that my initial understanding of the opposition between critique and positive vision, between the negative and the positive, was too simple. The utopian vision, I quickly discovered, always springs from a felt horror of its own contemporary society. Even in its most positive moments, the utopia preserves the shape of the critique from which it springs. Utopia is positive, but only because it is the negation of a negation.

Because it constantly intertwines critique and utopia, the very structure of *The Utopian* makes the same point. Mesmer's feminist vision of 2411 would be unthinkable without its grounding in a feminist critique of 1979. In the novel, the world of 1979 is constantly present in the form of the twisted personality of that culture's stalwart supporter, Dr. Reed, but also in the form of Mesmer Partridge's "Blue Prints," his long lists of the horrors of the 1970s, established after intense reading of the decade's newspapers. Some of Mesmer's dystopian horrors are time specific (Chilean Junta, Sus laws, *Berufsverbot*), but most are still with us (racism, vanishing fish species, ministerial lies). And some are more salient than ever (Islamic fundamentalism, diesel fumes, the art market).

The decade after the uprising of May 1968 (a revolt which the novel's Dr. Reed experiences in the jaded company of a French analyst called Jules, a dead ringer for Jacques Lacan) witnessed the publication of many feminist utopias. The best, and most lasting, feminist utopian vision of the post-May period remains Monique Wittig's *Les Guérillères* from 1969, a deeply poetic and theoretically challenging account of the war of the sexes, its resolution and the birth of a new, free society. In France, Christiane Rochefort's dystopia, *Une rose pour Morrison* ("A Rose for Morrison," 1966) uncannily anticipated the youth revolt of 1968. In 1972, she followed up with a classical utopian novel, *Archaos ou le jardin étincelant* ("Archaos, or the shining garden"). In Scandinavia, Inge Eriksen's *Victoria og verdensrevolutionen* (Victoria and the world revolution), published in Denmark in 1976, had a huge impact. In the English-speaking world, Marge Piercy's *Woman on the Edge of Time* (1976) is the obvious precursor to Mesmer Partridge's 2411 (let's note that Marge and Mesmer share the same initials, which can't be a coincidence in a novel which makes those very initials a matter for extensive discussion). Before Marge Piercy there was Ursula K. Le Guin, whose *Left Hand of Darkness* from 1969 provided a radical vision of a world in which people periodically change sex. The radical implications of Le Guin's vision of fluid genders and sexes, however, were not fully integrated in the feminism of the 1970s.

What were the concerns of the feminist utopias of the 1970s? In general, they were at pains to negate the vision of sex, gender, sexuality and the family that had cemented bourgeois society since the French Revolution. At the dawn of the bourgeois era, philosophers such as Rousseau and Hegel had insisted that the family was the essential building block of society, that the father was the head of the family, the only one who could represent it in public. Confining women to the private sphere, these philosophers saw the public sphere as a male preserve. One implication was that women could never be full ethical (or political) subjects, for they had no direct relationship to or responsibility for society as such. Their only ethical bonds were to their own family members. A traditional woman was not an individual, but mother, daughter, sister. The achievement of 1970s feminism was to show that the classical distinction between public and private was untenable, that the private was as political as the public, and that the bourgeois family was the prime mechanism for the oppression of women.

1970s utopias take as their starting point this feminist critique of the family. They are overwhelmingly preoccupied with sexual freedom and the destruction of the nuclear family. Their key themes are reproduction, sexuality and child-rearing, which happen to be three of the four structures Juliet Mitchell, in *Women's Estate* (1972), singles out as fundamental to women's condition. In these utopias, old taboos fall (the incest taboo, the taboo on same sex relations), and the traditional patriarchal family disappears. Women give birth proudly and publicly, with other women as co-parents, or with multiple men as possible fathers. Children are reared collectively, freely, and without sexual inhibitions. So also in Mesmer's 2411. Missing in Mesmer's utopia, as in other feminist utopias of the 1970s, is an account of working life (production was Juliet Mitchell's fourth structure).

In the 1970s, French feminists did not primarily express their visions of freedom in the form of the classical utopian novel. (Rochefort was the exception, not the rule). Yet historically, late 20th century feminism in France is the child of the post-May moment. (The first French feminist groups were formed by women students fed up with the sexism of male student activists.) Post-May utopian elements surface everywhere in French feminism of the 1970s: in feminist theory, essays, novels, and in feminist experiments with everyday life. In France, at the time, all these strands converged in psychoanalysis. (*The Utopian*'s focus on the analytic situation is no coincidence.)

I don't mean to say that all French feminists of the 1970s were in favor of psychoanalysis. I particularly don't mean to say that the specific strand of French feminism called "Psych et Po" (short for "psychoanalysis and politics") represented all French feminists. On the contrary: at the time "Psych et Po" was at once influential and deeply divisive. I just mean to say that the feminist intellectual and political climate in France after 1968 was more open to psychoanalysis, in theory and practice, than in most other countries. US feminists influenced by Betty Friedan (*The Feminine Mystique*, 1962) and Kate Millett (*Sexual Politics*, 1970), saw Freudian analysis as a patriarchal conspiracy against women. Such views had also been widespread in the UK, until Juliet Mitchell's *Psychoanalysis and Feminism* (1974) helped to change the situation. For me, as for many other women readers immersed in French culture at the time, Marie Cardinal's best-selling 1975 novel *Les mots pour le dire* provided an eye-opening account of a woman's use of psychoanalysis to find her way to freedom. (The English translation, *The Words to Say It*, was published in 1984.)

For many of us, the decade of the 1980s—the decade during which *The Utopian* was written—marked a political retreat. This was the decade when we immersed ourselves in the finer details of French feminist theory, French psychoanalysis (all those passionate debates about the phallus!) and other French theories.

The Utopian incorporates all these theoretical trends, and can be read in the light of them, as I think its author brilliantly shows in his own original "Supplement" to the book. Its striking theoretical sophistication marks The Utopian as a child of the 1980s. Nevertheless, its playful mobilization of the genre of the feminist utopia owes everything to the 1970s. When we know the historical and literary background for this novel, The Utopian becomes legible as an intricate intertwinement of critique and utopia. As such it exemplifies a form of political expression characteristic of the left in Western Europe in the aftermath of 1968, a form which still resonates with our present preoccupations.

THE UTOPIAN

I

GOLDEN GATE

Mesmer awoke, his dream falling away from him with the dawn mist shrouding the Mersey this first of May, New Year's day, 2411. Dreaming, he'd been, of times long gone, before the Californian Redoubt, last stand of garagism, had surrendered without a bolt being fired and the Revo made worldwide. If it pleased the flux to tickle him with what was no more the last night before his Journey, that was fine with him. There'd be time enough in a year and a day to tease out its every meaning, should the fancy to interpret take him. Just now, an early start was what was needed, off and away with a minimum of fuss.

He eased himself out from between his sleeping sisters, fair Lois, poised on the edge of the clitoral-littoral, a haze of peach below her belly, a bloom of flesh at her breast, and raven-haired Marushka, loved throughout the commune, a source of continual joy. He'd bade his goodbyes in the nicest way in last night's guttering fireglow, memories to warm him in the chill of dawn, Lois' purr, Marushka's deep-throated spinal-vaginal, his own spilled juice. Standing over them in his nakedness he made the sign of universal sisterhood, palms outward, thumbs and index fingers touching at the tips, unmistakably cunniform. Already they'd moved towards each other to close the gap he'd left, like two lips no longer separated by a tongue.

He swiftly put on his shirt and trousers, woollen socks and soft boots, clipped his allcock to his belt and slipped on his headband sporting the single eagle primary he'd found beneath one of the Pennine eyries.

A couple of logs on the fire would give the girls a good blaze to wake to, and he added some pinewood to the embers in the hearth.

With one last glance over his shoulder he stepped out into the courtyard where the sun was just breaking clear of the stable roof. As he approached the double doors he was greeted by a familiar neighing from within.

Gently rubbing the mare's soft muzzle, he said, 'Easy, Golden, a big day for you and me both.'

*

Should I introduce myself at this juncture? Indicate, with a muffled cough, that our boy will not be alone in his travels? Tempted, I resist. My resplendence must await a more opportune hiatus. The cough, putatively muffled, is discreetly stifled. I note only his association from this Golden, the rather obvious gate, and discard my own far richer rule, mean and oldie.

*

The clatter of Golden's hooves on the cobbles sounded loud enough to wake the whole commune. Not that any would be likely to invade his solitude, after his stated wish to make his departure alone, but to do so while all were unconscious would be that much more appropriate.

He was tempted to peer through the window of his breast-mother's house, at her and Old Jack, curled up in the bed where he'd been born, when Jack had been just one of many and not as now the favourite. Perhaps, in earlier times, before the Matriarchy had become established, Old Jack would have been something of a father to him, for he'd been to hand at two out of three of his infantile initiations. And he'd contributed a genetic half-twist to Mesmer's endowment, that much everyone acknowledged through an indelible likeness. Golden, bless her, had been raised and trained by Old Jack. His best, he'd said, and ready for Mesmer whenever he felt like beginning his Journey. Mesmer knew there was no better mount in the whole of Stock Port, for since his administration of Lake, Dale and Peak had gradually passed on to younger comrades, Jack had devoted himself to horseflesh, with wonderful results. 'Thanks, Old Jack,' he murmured, as he passed by the familiar ivy-covered front of his mother's house, 'thanks for the horse and thanks for the lore.' Many were the stories Old Jack had told of his own Journey, eighty years before.

'And thank you, mother, for bringing me into this world and for giving me the breast whenever I wanted it.' Only yesterday, while he'd been fondling her breasts, she'd run a finger through his hair and told him she'd miss him. And he her, he'd acknowledged, for no bond was stronger, prior to Journeying, than the breast-mother child, even in this age of multiple mothering and occluded fathering.

But this morning even her dear presence would not have been welcome, such was his sense of necessary solitude.

The sound of Golden's hooves diminished as he led her on to the grass fairway leading out of the commune courtyard. Then, with a cry of 'Away' he leapt into the saddle, thumped his heels into her glossy flanks, and man and horse together bounded forth into the great wide Communist world.

*

Yerse. An introduction is decidedly called for, lest my silence be interpreted as approval, or worse, its opposite. My hippocratic oath and astounding benevolence rule out anything but the disinterested pursuit of cure. If, however, at times, my enthusiasm takes me along forest paths far from the macadamised highway laid down by the master, let the signature Reed legitimate such divertissements. Yerse? Did I call? It must be your imagination, my dear Miss Thingum, bells in your head as well, if I may say so, as upon your toes. This female sex is a wonderful addition to our culture.

How I love to lubricate an opening.

Now, the facts of the case, one at a time.

(1) Mesmer Partridge. The product of a union between Mr Partridge, garage proprietor, of Stockport, in the county of Cheshire, latterly Greater Manchester, and his wife named, for want of evidence to the contrary, Esme. Born 14th October 1959, a date of no significance except to make him 20 years old today. Childhood unexceptional, likewise puberty. Blessed with two siblings, female, his juniors by three and seven years. Time for another?

Be so good as to tell Mrs Minceberger I shall be ready for her in five, no six, minutes.

(2) Aged seventeen and some weeks, at the wheel of his mother's car, alongside the lovely fourth placed Miss Junior Stockport, he announced, It's boiling. I've heard that before, it may be assumed the young lady thought, and readied herself for what was coming. I know just what to do, said Mesmer, lowering his left hand to his trouser zip. With his right hand he opened the car door, got out, walked to the front of the vehicle, released the catch, raised the bonnet, circumspectly unscrewed the radiator cap, waited for the steam to subside, completed the unzipping of his fly, removed his organ of generation and urinated a well-judged bladderful into the dessicated innards of the cooling system. His homage to Dovzhenko's Earth, seen the previous week at a local Film Society, where the collectivised peasantry perform the same service for a stranded tractor. This symbolic consummation he followed with an altogether more carnal one on the backseat of the car, enabling Miss Junior Stockport to notch up one more to her unwitting score of male deflorations and he to think of himself thenceforth as a Socialist and as a man, in that order.

*

The spires of the University gleamed as he cantered over the suburban turf towards the Mersey. Any other day he'd have popped in for breakfast with the curators of the Library, a scholarly trio always ready for a natter about the past. Theirs was one of the best in the region, fully restored to its late twentieth century condition, before the Great Crisis began to bite, converting its books to microfiches and its archives to ceefax. Even as a child he'd shown an interest in pre-history, especially its final years of turmoil, and his innate curiosity had led him to ask many a question about that fascinating era, along with the more usual ones on sexual difference. He recalled an occasion when he and his little friends had dropped in on one of them, old Elmsfootloose III, in her nearby cottage, to listen to her stories, which everyone agreed were the best-told around. Afterwards she'd asked them to stay the night and watch the badgers at their set. During their vigil, he'd suddenly asked, 'What was it like before the Revo?' Without a word, Elmsfootloose had taken hold of her famous broomstick in both hands, and with a mighty tug had pulled its shaft clear away from its head. Nodding at the one she'd whispered, 'Socialism', and at the other, 'Democracy'. Just then a badger had pushed her head out of her set, and in his excitement he'd forgotten to take this his first lesson in pre-history any further. The memory made him smile. No doubt about it, Elmsfootloose was a great teacher.

A herd of roe deer clustering at the river's edge near the bridge trotted a few paces away before turning and eyeing him with a genetic wariness still not abolished by the absence of danger from Woman. In the middle he reined to a halt, and gazed over the balustrade into the crystal depths, as so often in the past. Still too early in the year for the tide of salmon returning to spawn, more abundantly each summer. He loved to fish of a summer's morning, with the sun warming his back and the air humming with insects, perhaps a flash of a kingfisher, then the sudden tug on the line, a whirr of spinning reel, and the struggle between man and fish, ending in a lost hook or twenty pounds of succulence for the commune kitchen.

He'd take the greenway rather than the pike, preferring its long deserted pre-revo curves to the bustle of the highroad. Hard to imagine now how once its grassy banks and sheep-cropped carriageways thundered to the machine imperatives of its garagist heyday. From the bus, ten miles up, the greenway network appeared as a tracery of pale green veins criss-crossing the seasonally varied shades of the forest park.

It was set fair for another perfect day, thanks to the weather-woman who hardly ever got things wrong now meteorology was a fully fledged science. A couple of hours of gentle rain in the small hours, days such as made you thrill to be alive, bright and sunny with sufficient breeze to take the heat out of an afternoon. Sometimes, for a change, an electric storm, or a leaden grey sky softly drizzling, or even a good old-fashioned downpour when least you'd expect it. Plus real springs, sad exhilarating autumns and short dry frosty winters, all in accordance with the theory of Regional Difference.

The only indications of fellow consciousness were a couple of bus trails high overhead and once the whoosh of a tube passing over the treetops a mile or so to the east. Not that he'd have chosen those highroads for his Journey, for all their ease, views and speed. Each according to her pace, and no devil to take the hindmost, that was the spirit of things nowadays. Take Elmsfootloose III, rattling over the Snake Pass in all weathers in her reconstructed Hispano-Suiza, or leaping on to her broomstick for the sheer fun of buzzing the ruminants grazing in the south Man Chester pastures.

*

No martinet in matters of the clock, I always allow my patients to finish their sentences, however heavy, while not going so far as some of my laxer colleagues in letting whole paragraphs eat their way into our ten minutes of recuperation. Time is money, and money is what you make of it, such predications being axiomatic.

I shall postpone an analysis of his allusions to senility, two so far I note, first Old Jack, now this sylvan and wandervogel third generation hybrid, Elmsfootloose III, whose eccentricity verges on the certifiable. Another, therefore, on a principle I am loath to account for, cannot be far behind. Then and only then shall I pounce, and now content myself with his evident transportation mania. I assign the aetiology to the boy's misfortune in getting born into the motor trade. From infancy the gurgle of the pumps, the hiss of sprayguns, the whine of the salesmen, all contributing to Partridge père's climb up the long ladder from the shed beneath the railway arches to the imposing frontage on the Stockport Road. One can comprehend the choice of metaphor, the telling garagism, for the times we live in, he and I. And appreciate the residues, those ineliminable traces of an earlier age, that even he seems reluctant to eradicate entirely. My own well-lined Silver Cloud would I readily admit be no match for the crone's Hispano-Suiza were it not for the indubitable clunk of my doors and the hypothetical click of hers. As for Mesmer's tubes and buses, they may be his notion of a mobile heaven, but before I handed my token to St Peter I would be inclined to enquire of the service and cellar in the restaurant car. Even the charm of a free automat could barely compensate for the absence of a discreet murmur of advice on the merits of the pricier clarets. Mesmer's dreams are irredeemably petit-bourgeois, prole though he would doubtless prefer them to be, and in them is. My syntax functions as a digestive.

And now, taking good care to make the necessary adjustment to my impeccably creased trousers, I get on all fours and place my ear to the ground, so as not to miss the slightest tremor of traffic approaching along the royal road.

*

Unexpectedly, on the far loop of the overgrown cloverleaf M6-M56, a figure hove into view, bumping along on a donkey. Mesmer reckoned if he cut across the centre rather than take the long way round he'd be able to intercept him, stop for a chat, even ride alongside for a while if they were going in the same direction.

'C'mon Golden' he urged, and the horse responded with her customary energy, so that they reached the bottom of the far ramp while the donkey was still jogging down it.

The rider, an old man of somewhat unusual appearance, gave no sign of having registered Mesmer's presence. Thinking perhaps he might be inserted into the noble-global, or doing some yogic mind-bodywork, in either case oblivious of his surroundings, Mesmer called out, 'Our paths cross, hail!'

Still the old man made no response. Only when Mesmer shifted Golden out of the way to avoid a collision did the other bring his donkey to a halt, open his eyes, and say in a surprisingly loud voice, 'Very Light, from Wick. Some call me Verry, some Veery. Either way I'm a Light, so please yourself. Who are you?'

'Flux, Very,' said Mesmer, taken aback by the suddenness of the introduction, but plumping instinctively for the short e. 'I'm Mesmer, born and raised in Stock Port, heading south, on a Journey, riding with the possibilities as they arise.'

Very Light fixed him with a gaze of startling blue, cocked his bald and sunburnt head to one side, and said, 'I am a trapezist, from the circus in Wick, the greatest, some say, in the northern hemisphere. Watch me flying through the night, spinning like a little top in the big one, defying gravity and the imagination, balancing on the brink, teetering on the high wire, and more, much much more. Hence the outfit, hence the style.'

And that, Mesmer had to admit, he'd got. Even for 2411, when three centuries of communism had ironed out the wrinkles of the socialist mode, and opened up a whole new set of differences, non-antagonistically and a delight for all, Very Light's dress, manner and bearing all bespoke the unusual. That much was clear from the snow-white beard falling from the berry-brown face in a billow over his chest before dividing into twin hanks, one on either side of the donkey. Add to that the diamante pantaloons of variable spectrum synthetic, rope sandals and a lemon coloured silk ribbon wound around the otherwise naked torso in two converse spirals, and you'd got the makings of a second glance anywhere from the Californian outback to the Alma Ata Soviet.

*

Mesmer, it would seem, has dreamt up a clown, however much he may phallicize him with piercing gaze, bald head and aerial brilliance. I note the berry-brown face and ask what ilk of berry calls forth that particular colour adjective, while tendering my regrets that all that glisters is not gold. No, the be-donkeyed idiot evokes not a hee-haw from this end of the couch. If he imagines he can sabotage my impartiality with attempts at collusive mirth then he reckons not with the fees his father feeds me. My reputation has not been lightly acquired, not will it be lightly surrendered.

Yerse, Miss Petersen? Did I make a proposal? Ah, lunch, one of my favourite repasts. Five minutes, no longer. Please be so good as to adjust the damask antimacassar on the couch, and while you're about it pick up the pencil I seem carelessly to have dropped. Excellent. One more thing, Miss Petersen, before your charming posterior crosses the threshold, never question the motives of your master. What he says goes, as will you if you do.

A wholly delightful addition to my vestibule. Let us hope she lasts, so many seem to fall by the wayside of my discontent, or theirs, three in as many months is too rapid a turnover. Her name bodes well, and makes a welcome change from the standard Irishisms I have to get my tongue around. Miss Murphy was a fine beginner but became increasingly disinclined to pass the time of day, Miss Watt I am afraid lacked posture and lasted but a week, and Miss Malone, of Miss Malone the less said the better, except to record I warned the agency in the strongest terms that if they sent me any more ready to drop dead at Mrs Skywide's feet at eleven in the morning they'd best look elsewhere for their clientele. It worked, hence Miss P. She was at first reluctant to accept the stipend I was offering on the grounds it fell short of the norm negotiated by the union. Did I reply that my stools are invariably well-formed if inclined to dryness, my sphincters having been trained in the grand manner of my class? No, I met her cool stare with the suggestion that if she served me well I would find it in me to reward her with a bonus. We seemed to understand each other. How much I admire intelligence in a woman.

*

'May I match your pace, stride for stride, my mount Golden alongside yours?' Mesmer asked, delicately.

'Bert.'

'Your pardon?'

'Bert. I sit on Bert. My ass's name is Bert. A truncation of I forget what, so long have we been together.'

'Perhaps Albert,' Mesmer suggested.

'Absolutely not,' Very assured him.

'Or Bertrand.'

'Most improbable.'

'Bertolt, then.'

'Possibly. Of course you may, dear lad, our meeting was not indeterminate.'

Though somewhat surprised by this reversion to his earlier request in the midst of so interesting an enquiry, Mesmer thanked him for his kindness.

'What is more,' Very continued, 'Bert ports an excellent luncheon, at least enough for two. So let us ride till then, if not thereafter.'

As they trotted along, Very spoke of life in the circus. By the time the sun had reached its zenith Mesmer had heard all about the Flying Fortinis, Very's greatest rivals in the ring, his closest friends outside it, of whom Viola could lay claim to have tuned the high wire to a pitch of perfection, enough to bring tears of joy to one eye, of sorrow to the other. Was familiar, too, with the dynamics of the quadruple somersault, that figure in the air that had had to wait until the Revo to find its realisation. Knew all about the sublimated power lust of Angus Bar-Higgins, the lion tamer, and about his celebrated solido projections from Ngorongoro Crater, complete with dust and fleeing zebras. He'd learnt of Very's debut on the trapeze at the breast of his beloved mother Candle, an act billed as 'Candle Light from Wick, with little Very on too', and one they'd repeated until a not so little Very had become rather too heavy for Candle to bear. And he'd listened to the tale of her death, in front of a massed audience, when she'd dived into a tank of gasoline with a lit torch between her teeth.

'But why?' Mesmer cried, aghast.

'Because,' Very explained, 'she wanted to go out like a Light.'

Mesmer could hardly deny the logic of her last wish, put so, yet it still seemed somewhat abrupt. He wondered what effect such a violent end might have had upon the young Very. It was possible his eccentricity stemmed from such a loss, one that the rituals of mourning might only partially have made good.

'Did you know she was going to kill herself?'

Very said simply, 'It was I who lit the torch!'

This was as startling a confession as Mesmer had heard in his two decades of existence. Strange enough that one in life's prime should choose to euthanase, stranger still the choice of method, but that the son should collaborate in the destruction of his own mother was almost unbelievable. An image came to him of his own breast-mother, back home, tending the animals while making her dear presence felt in the noble-global.

'How could you do such a thing?' he blurted out, his voice trembling with emotion.

'Only by surrendering myself to her desire. It was what she wanted. I was the instrument, not the cause.'

So shocked was Mesmer by the old man's story, he found himself unable to say anything further, while Very evidently felt there was no more to be said on the subject.

They therefore rode on in silence until Very pointed and said, 'Look, sprout, there's a likely place for lunch, down there by the brook, beneath the crackwillow. Sit yourself down by yon butterbur and I'll dish you up some truffled chicken in aspic, and to wash it down, a Meursault '97, nicely chilled from Bert's saddlebag.'

*

What a pleasure to encounter a case so ripe it spills its seed at the slightest touch of the horticulturist! I speak not of the donkey's appellative origins, though Bertram would be my choice, after the past master of the ring, B. Mills. Nor do I speak of the imitative hence flattering discourse of the wine and bird, noting only in passing that I'd stake the contents of my humble cellar against any technical trickery in matters of oenology, and as for the cuisine I remain unconvinced any automatic jigger can replace a practised wrist when dealing with the higher sauces. Still, bon appétit, I can afford to be generous with a memory-full of taut silk across Miss Petersen's gluteus maximus superbus and comparable mammaries. The combination of that specular and this professional advance renders me almost too good to be true, but I shall do my best. Of what I speak is the precipitate collapse of the maternal idyll into one most murderous, the flaming mother, on the first day away from home. This signal departure from matriarchal mores calls forth the conjecture that the name of the father, unlike the donkey's, is not so easily forgotten. From his prehistorical grave he may reach out a hand and claim his due, as I will from mine, if I chance to enter it before the case is through.

And now, as befits a case study, a fact or, if time, two.

(3) At University, to and from which he commuted daily, Mesmer fell in love with his tutor, a quietly spoken member of the Communist Party. He kept his passion to himself until a Spring Term tutorial when emboldened by desire he proposed that her finely tuned sense of the possible was a betrayal of the working class, and was able to substantiate

his rash claim by pointing out certain inconsistencies in her recently submitted doctoral thesis, having read it with more than academic interest during the vacation. It would seem Mesmer's critique provoked Dr X's curiosity, for a coffee in the refectory led, via a comradely discussion in a pub, back to her flat, so bringing to an end the celibacy he had endured since his initiation. She broke off the affair before the end of term on grounds which, although considered, having to do with her non-academic reputation, were hardly just, so it seemed to Mesmer, under her spell as he was. In retrospect he allows he learnt much from her of the theory of politics and practice of love, a configuration which was reversed when he took up with a dour nurse he met at a college 'disco', how I loathe the upwardly displaced comma, though less, I admit, than the unquarantined neologism. The price of his weekly bout of solace was ward politics in one ear and the perfidy of a certain medico who could be seen shooting around the hospital grounds in a sports car paid for largely out of her hard-earned savings in the other. The arrangement with Brenda lasted until the week before his Part One examinations when a post-coital discussion on the possibility of a peaceful transition to socialism intensified to a pitch of accusation and counter-accusation such that in a very few minutes he was up, dressed and out in the rain-sodden street in front of the nurses' residence, never to see her again. His expected Comfortable Pass turned out to be an Irredeemable Fail, unrescinded even after the intervention of Dr X whose guilt over her own part in his premature exit from higher education culminated in a determination to hand in her resignation, an option she was talked out of only by the silver tongue of her silver-templed latest beau. These last clauses are inferential.

*

After lunch, Mesmer lay back against the bank of the stream and watched the early afternoon cumulus build up in the western sky, far away over the Welsh hills. He'd not been able to put the story of Candle's demise completely out of his mind, and so it was with relief he heard Very ask if his allcock was programmed to show old movies.

'It certainly is,' Mesmer replied, 'more than three hundred stored in its innards.'

Reaching down to his belt, he unclipped the intricately etched cylinder and passed it across to his companion. It was, he knew full well, as pretty an allcock as one could expect to find, and capable of just about anything. He'd taken the advice of the whole commune in its design, though he'd heeded none more so than that of Mandy Rocket, as good an electronicist as any between the Mersey and the Irwell. While his breast-mother had taken care of the marquetry, Mandy had helped him with the inside. On his fourteenth birthday, when he'd worn it for the first time, she told him she'd put a surprise or two among its powers, because all the best allcocks had something to them their bearers didn't know about. But whatever that might be it wasn't movies. Mandy and he had passed many a happy hour ransacking the archives, watching this and that, before making their selection. They could, of course, have simply inserted every movie in the library, but that would have precluded choice and promoted surfeit. Each of the three hundred then was a personal favourite, or a treat in store, or a classic.

'What do you fancy?'

'Do you have Man with a Movie Camera?' the old trapezist asked.

Not only did Mesmer have it in stock, but it was among his ten alltime best, and he'd enjoy nothing more than to see it yet again.

It didn't take long to find a suitable point of projection, an abandoned sand-martin's hole in the bank above their heads. Carefully Mesmer inserted the allcock, having instructed it as to what they wanted to watch. As the man and boy settled back the light dimmed in the cone of projection and the optical discontinuity comprising the screen some ten feet in front of them began to flicker with the opening shots of the Soviet classic.

*

Lest it be assumed my contribution is to be entirely reactionary, forever following in the traces of the other, I must make it clear that Dr Reed is as lusty a geriatric as Comrade Light. My life shall not go unrecorded in these notes. It is, I freely admit, not one to inspire the lyricists, with what good I may have done tempered by a temperament as abrasive as the stridulation from Miss Petersen's stocking tops. Oh yes, the sartorial insistence of my consultancy does not stop at surface phenomena, the infrastructure too must be just right. No tights here, I told her, and she told me she never wore them. Her way of easing a tired back compels my admiration as well as ensuring my ease, and there is more to her smile than money can buy, of that I have latterly been convinced.

His allcock, by the by, does not impress. More telling is the screen it constructs, behind which something hides, as ever. No cinephile, I've yet to see the film I'd not award a U certificate, X-worthy though their perpetrators imagine them to be.

By way of justification for the coming 'autobiopic', yerse, I unfurl the safety net of the dialectic, catch-all for slippages from the highwire of strict necessity, and relish my metaphoric melange. This new high mood is Miss Petersen's doing, of that there can be no doubt.

Rich, was I, at birth, and have been ever since. My father made his pile in defiance of the imputed tendency for the rate of profit to fall, and I watched him do it with the all-seeing child's eye, formed when my gaze fell upon the miraculous geography of nanny's lower half, aged two. Aged twelve, objectively beautiful and as anxious as my sire at the threat of Bolshevism, I was sent to a jail on a hill noted for the quality of its air where I was to acquire character and the rudiments of a classical education. This institution, not Eton but the Other, was mastered by sadists and matronned by a tribe of such malignancy that my adoration for their garb underwent a temporary decline. Here, in case it be assumed I am joining forces with the wretched of the earth, is the extent and limit of my radicalism, the wish to blitz the site of my pubertal years. The lavatories were the focus of social life, our schoolboy trinity defecation, micturation, masturbation. There were two boys I liked and one I worshipped, a narrow-headed athlete with a protruding upper lip, who conceded me but four furtive epiphanies, once, in the darkness, during a school performance of Richard III, twice in similar ditches on different Field Days, and once more, the only time I have voluntarily swallowed semen, during a housematch, when we two, alone, were confined indoors with coughs. Games were compulsory and brutal. The food was disgusting, and what was not was made so by the necessity of spitting upon one's own to prevent its theft by stronger or hungrier inmates. When at last I passed through my Old School's portals I vowed I would never again allow myself to suffer.

Since then, despite my immense claims upon the economic resources of our globe and upon the labour of its less fortunate inhabitants, I have failed to achieve the degree of serenity I aspired to, not only, I must stress, because of the inescapability of lust that can have me chasing a hint of a perambulating perfume or make me happy to lick the ground bearing the imprint of a treasured heel, but also through a willingness, more, a compulsion to take on the burdens of others, however leaden. The series of accidents leading up to my choice of profession was not, I now realise, as fortuitous as it appeared.

*

With the movie over and Mesmer's allcock back at his belt, Very said, 'Methinks one good turn deserves another. Be so kind as to seat yourself down on yonder willow stump and wait for what's coming.'

While Mesmer did as he was asked, Very rummaged deep in Bert's saddlebag. After removing and replacing an inordinate number of items, he pulled out a violin case, and from it the venerable and lustrous instrument.

'You like music?'

Mesmer could only nod, for of all the performing arts music in its many guises ancient and modern was that which reduced him to silence.

'Excellent. Allow me to introduce my fellow performers.'

Conjuring up three ring speakers from patient Bert's amazing saddlebag, Very set them spinning, each one turning into a shimmering sphere some three feet above the ground and half as much again from its neighbour.

'Violoncello, Angus Bar-Higgins, lion tamer and, on those rare and happy occasions when he can be persuaded to abandon his beasts, aesthete. Viola, Viola Fortini, my rival on the rope, my companion in the strings, who kindly allowed me to tape her wildest phantasy before my departure in order to respond the better to my musical mood.'

Respectfully, for ring speakers had the sensitivity if not the intelligence of their originators, Mesmer inclined his head at each one as it was introduced.

'First fiddle, dear Candle, lamentably fallen out of the world through her own choosing, happily still with us through the excellence of trans-Caledonian recordings.'

A mother, however attenuated, was not to be greeted from ground level, and Mesmer leapt to his feet the better to open his face. His action seemed to delight the old man, for he hopped around in a small circle indicating with his bow that Mesmer should reseat himself. When Mesmer did so, he immediately came to a halt and announced, 'And I, verily, will complete the quartet on second fiddle.'

After checking the harmonics and making sure the harmonic box was resonating to his liking, Very tucked his beard into his pantaloons and picked up his violin.

'Ready, young Mesmer?'

Again, Mesmer could only nod.

Very gave an authoritative tap with his bow on the nearest ring speaker, and the quartet was off into the contrapuntal intricacies of Beethoven's middle period, the perfect sound, Mesmer had time to think before he surrendered his consciousness to its spell, with which to place a signature on this the first day of his Journey.

*

The first day, he says, while it seems to me, and is according to the external time consciousness of our corporate order, the third week of these twice-weekly hours. Such discrepancies are to be expected in the early stages. His and my times are by no means the same, separated as they are by four hundred years of unalloyed progress for him and for me the knowledge that the fluidity of night-time mentation, however logicised by reportage, coincides but tentatively with the digital accountancy of waking life. In time, his rhythm and mine, if such mine can be called, staccato punctilio more like, will match, fire, flare and dwindle, him cured and I richer by one studied case, plus the fees.

I find this talk of time more wearying than most of what I listen to, though I applaud his choice of quartet when so easily he could have made the buffoon perform some treacly waltz or worse, a syncopated horror in four four, three eight, five nine.

Let me be precise, for I'm too old to tender generalities when facts are at hand. I have been quite impotent these last twenty years, or some say twenty-five, despite the mouth to mouth resuscitation I have persuaded my employees to administer, an exercise which does nothing but disgust the would-be rescuer and exhaust the drowning man. Other remedies, like the cumulative revelation of pudenda, or the engorgement of dozens of molluscs, or the assumption of masks, have all failed, utterly. As for my talk of the whip and thong, it is only talk, and perhaps not even that, I forget. In any case, I am sure I would only bleed. My inability, regrettably, does not deter the toad of desire from squatting in the middle of my Bokhara carpet, the last avatar of the handsome prince who once so charmingly preened himself thereon. This warty beast, genus Bufo, species vulgaris, always manages to stay just out of reach, eyeing me over his poorly-defined shoulder, evading my exterminating intent. I am literally beside myself for Miss Petersen, latest in a line of near-replicas, stretching away into the mist, towards the one theory not memory tells me must be the first, she who sailed forth from the shores of my young life before I ever knew her. I have as little chance of finding satisfaction with the newest as with the vanished prima donna, odds that will not stop me trying any more than the centuries of difference between my time and that of Mesmer puzzling his way through the maze of his dreaming will stop me trying to restore him safe and well into our conjoint present. This preliminary confession done, I think I shall allow myself a dram. How thankful I am that it is he not I who must board the 19.17 out of Euston this evening, to travel north, or is it south?

New Stoke, said New Stokers, was a ripe fig of a town. They'd rebuilt it up-river from the fused silica of the old town, in sight of the memorial for those lost in the Great Rage, when the colonels had unleashed their sniffer bombs and a third of the nation had been jellified in the course of a single night. In Stoke, only two go-go dancers and a transvestite potter had escaped the lethal rays, and it was these three, reconstructed in thirty foot high skyblue Wedgwood, who stood over the glassy waste, linking present to past.

Let the people decide, had been the cry from the co-ordinating committee, when the idea had been voiced to once more have a city straddle the Trent, let us be the architects. So it was, some three hundred years back, that the dynasty founded by the potter and the go-go dancers gathered together in the great TV concourses of the time, thrashing out the possibilities. Many had been the differences to be worked across before the concept was mature. It would be in the form of a pentagram, with five gates at the apices, five great thoroughfares with the Trent as one of them, and five distinct neighbourhoods, variously suited to the passing life-moods of the population. Perm revo, the Trots had exulted, as they began to lay the foundations. A cosmic crossroads, the witches and warlocks had declared, funnelling their supply quotas into the production network. Simply sublime, the aesthetes had murmured, hard-hatted and shovelling with their diggers. All, in short, had approved the idea, and as it became reality, their excitement turned to the steady joy of being in the right place at the right time.

Much of this Mesmer had heard from Elmsfootloose, who'd taken the final syllable of her name in New Stoke to celebrate overcoming the last vestiges of rootedness. The rest Very had supplied, in his cheerful and extravagant manner, studded with nuggets of detail such as even his allcock tuned into the Man Chester archive might be hard put to provide.

They'd bade their goodbyes, Very and he, on the greenway after his musical performance. Very had insisted Mesmer should not be slowed by Bert's pace, being so young and into the first day of his Journey. So Mesmer had thanked him for his company, for lunch and for playing so beautifully for him. His last glance back down the greenway as he'd cantered off had revealed Very wagging his finger in Bert's face, as if lecturing the donkey on a point of major import.

That had been yesterday, and today, refreshed from a night's sleep under the stars in his transparent eco-tent, Mesmer was as ready as anyone for a ripe fig of a town.

Round a bend in the highway, the fabled pentacular city came suddenly into view, some half mile away, at the end of a broad avenue. As they rode down the gravelled road, flanked by wide lawns, flanked in turn by a profusion of cherry trees in blossom, Mesmer and Golden entered a cone of silence, causing the beat of her hooves to be muffled to near inaudibility. No restraining hand was needed to slow Golden to a walk, then, as the silence deepened, to a halt, for horse was as sensitive as rider to the protocols of entry. The passage into a pentacle via one of its apices was not the same as bussing into its centre. If the collective wisdom of New Stokers required a rite of initiation for riders, then Mesmer was only too happy to oblige. Journeying was nothing if not the acceptance of difference.

In front of him, dividing the avenue into two loops, was a lozenge-shaped lake with its long axis aligned towards the gate beyond it. In its waters there cruised great carp, some so huge that their lifelines might conceivably reach back even to before the Revo. One of these, larger than the rest and a deep carmine in colour, was swimming through figures of eight, as if to catch the attention of the young human in his different element. Mesmer dismounted, coming close to the water's edge. With a shoreward swerve, close enough to the silver-sanded beach to risk its shining integument, the fish flipped itself over to reveal a nacreous belly, on which was inscribed, to Mesmer's considerable surprise, the word ATTEND in reflecting lettering. Never had he heard of signifying fish, but nor had he heard of Very Light till yesterday. With no qualms, then, did he follow its instruction, whether in English or High French, and squatted down on his haunches to see what would follow.

Whereupon there erupted out of the lake a jet of white, up and up to a hundred feet or more, until at last gravity's persistent pull broke its cohesion, mushrooming it to spume, spray and a curtain of rain falling back to the lake, transforming its glassy surface into a cross-hatch of ripples, all in complete silence.

'Boy!' exhaled Mesmer, ever appreciative of the spectacular. Immediately the single column split into five, each jet assuming an inclination ten degrees to the vertical and taking on a different colour of the rainbow, blue, green, yellow, red and violet.

'Girl!' now came Mesmer's exhalation, a measure higher in appreciation, and the fountain began its polychromous fiveplay. Through angle, spread, force, direction, colour, the changes were rung, harmonising pattern after pattern, ever more complex, until his wide-eyed pleasure became strained with the effort of keeping pace with their unfolding. Still the complexity intensified, towards the realm of the insoluble fourth degree, when it seemed all sense must disappear in a chaos of disconnection and he would have to foreclose on the protocol by shutting his eyes. All of a sudden, across his field of vision, in a tremendous arc, a roseate carp leapt, quite clear of the water. On its underside Mesmer read the word RENDER.

As he absorbed its meaning, the pain of trying to comprehend eased, and the complexity of the fiveplay seemed as straightforward as a moment previously it had been tortuous. The fountain was taking him via the cryptic-elliptic, where sense was not so much thought as felt. The ways of the city were thus revealed. How New Stoke fitted into the region in accordance with the demands of difference, how its fifty thousand inhabitants lived out their lives and made their contribution to the sifting-shifting, how the ironies implicit in the endless knot of the pentacle made it a truly magical town, and more besides.

Eventually the fiveplay came to an end and the turbulence of the lake's surface settled back to calm. In its depths Mesmer could once again see the carp, of which one, brightly orange and smaller than the others, rotated on its back to flash the word PERSIST. Mesmer needed no further bidding. He knew he could enter the city whenever he wished. There was no reason to delay. He got up off his heels and turned to Golden who neighed loudly, proof that the cone of silence had also lifted. Behind him, unseen in the smooth waters of the lake, the carp swam majestically on, as innocent of language as fish ever were.

*

There are some, in my profession, who would find his lurid symbolism and creeping mysticism fine progenitors for their hybrid practice. Rather, I would say, expect more fertile offspring from Bert and Golden, whether hinny or mule, I always forget the order of the sexes in these miscegenations, than this most loathsome conjunction. The fountain, the lake, the five-gated city awaiting the pilgrim, is this not the stock in trade of the saint-analyst promising lifelong futurity and the most amazing series of coincidences which are, of course, not coincidences at all? It is a short hop from the pentagrammaton to the mandala, from the swish of fish to the hum of om. I'd be inclined to detect the unscrupulous hand of my rival down the street, the unaccredited Dr Schwitzelstik, who's not above pinching a promising patient given half a chance, except that no half chance or any lesser fraction has been given. I must assume therefore Mesmer's gleaned enough bilge from his reading of the encyclopaedia to slop a bucketful in my direction, just to annoy. The odour of marsh gas is so intense hereabouts I'm reluctant even to strike a match. Miss Petersen, could I beg you to open a window? I am aware I detest the noise of traffic, but it is preferable to Schwitzelstik's conceptual flatus.

Breathing more easily, I can release another fact of this fascinating case.

(4) Unqualified and unemployed, Mesmer joined a sect devoted to the instantiation of socialism should the current crisis of capitalism prove to be its last, as was profoundly held to be so by the party theoreticians. Does socialism grow on trees? cried its Secretary, a man of colossal and arguably paranoic energy. And in answer to his own rhetoric, he continued, Down with all reformism, parliamentary roadism, third worldism and tail endism!, this, I have been given to understand, from left to right disposing of rival parties from right to left. As a raw recruit Mesmer underwent the regime of proletarianisation deemed to be necessary to rid him of his petit-bourgeois ways, in the course of which he thickened the accent his mother had taken such pains to eliminate in her children and attended the party's summer camp. For six months he drew the dole and lived politics, acquiring a reputation for doctrinal orthodoxy such that he was asked to speak at the forthcoming annual conference. Three days beforehand he contracted a bout of hiccoughs that no known remedy had the slightest impact on. In the swaying lavatory of the train bearing him towards the great event, hiccoughing every twelve seconds, Mesmer gazed at his reflection in the mirror and said, If they're on the road to socialism then I'm a tree-frog. Whereupon the spasms ceased, and he left the train at the next stop. Subsequently, he worked mornings in his father's body-shop, spraying for the most part because he liked the smell, though he found himself prey to a fear of retribution from his former comrades and botched more than one job.

Fact rendered, duty done, I can return to the latest instalment of his dreaming to put the question that should not come amiss to any reader-members of the organisation he has specifically asked me not to initial. Why, in his ultra-world, no plebs? True, I have toyed with the ideal of a planet populated by none but myself and the beasts, perfectly Pliocene, with not even an Eve to sweeten my mornings on the principle that the presence of one would soon call up the absence of another, but that Mesmer should encounter just one fellow traveller in a month of analysis hardly squares with his avowed mass psychology. Perhaps my suspicion of misanthropy will prove to be unfounded when he passes through the Western Gate and becomes one of fifty thousand, a fair-sized football crowd, I'd say. I must ask him what team he supports. And express my gratitude for his summary despatch of the verbal-gerbil, if I may be allowed to make a contribution to his schizoid lexicon, due to be elaborated under the heading of White Heap, in the terminal case fact. Even the dimmest eyes can tire of too much Light. Lastly, I should record I ate garlic at lunch and my digestif was flavoured with asafoetida, so I shall have no difficulty whatsoever in pursuing him into the pentacle, if he had foolishly imagined he'd keep me out.

*

He needed to go no further than the Western Gate to find accommodation for himself and stabling for Golden. The inn, The Cheery Wryneck, straddled the gate, so that traffic entering and leaving the city passed through the middle of it. Its two wings formed part of the city wall, and all its rooms faced two directions, outwards over the carp-filled lake to the garden forest beyond, and inwards to the tessellation of roofs comprising the archaic fifth of Old.

Mesmer luxuriated in the vast agate bath in the centre of his room and considered how he'd spend the rest of the day. To explore the neighbourhood was the obvious possibility. He knew he'd have no difficulty in meeting New Stokers, for everyone he'd encountered so far had been as charming as his friends in Stock Port. The landlord of the inn, for example, had shown him all the vacant rooms, so as he might choose the one he liked best. And the group of young horse lovers now busily rubbing down Golden in the courtyard beneath his city-facing window had straightaway invited him on a trek through the wilder big game country beyond New Stoke. He'd have accepted had he not just arrived, for he greatly enjoyed taking photos with his allcock. Then there had been the chef, at work in the kitchen preparing a confection involving much sugar and a little hashish, something she'd perfected in her native Sahara. She'd told him he'd be welcome in the kitchen any time, to cook whatever he fancied, or make a contribution to the menu, or give her a hand. He would indeed, he'd said, and he'd got some salmon recipes as would make the driest mouth water. And there'd been the two oldsters, planting rare alpines in their fabulous hanging garden on the outside wall of The Cheery Wryneck. If he felt like a trip to the Eastern Pyrenees, they'd said, they were off in a week to find the insects to establish an authentic eco-balance. He'd thanked them for their kind invitation, wishing them good climbing, but he would be staying for a while here in New Stoke.

Refreshed by his bath and ready to like all New Stokers as much as those he'd met so far, he set off on foot through the narrow streets of Old towards the boulevards of Downtown. These were filling up with folk emerging from their siestas, as elegant a throng as you'd find anywhere between the Black Country and the Marches.

A pub, with terraces tumbling down to the Trent and canopied over with an ancient vine, proved to be the ideal vantage point from which to take it all in. He drew himself a pint of the house bitter and found himself a seat in the corner of the uppermost terrace. Across the river there was a fabulous view of the twenty second century architecture of Town, with its translucent minarets and sweeping curves, while beyond, in the distance, he could just make out the cedars and stately mansions of Park.

His first pint slipped down almost unnoticed, so involved was he with the view and the folk drifting in and out of the pub. He was about to return to the bar for a refill, when an unmistakable voice called out his name.

'Allow me, young sprout. Rounds aren't what they used to be, but reciprocity still extends to fetching and carrying.'

'Very! Where on earth did you spring from?'

The flamboyant old trapezist placed a pint mug in front of Mesmer, sat down at the table, and took a deep draught of ale before replying.

'From the station, is the answer.'

'You came by tube?'

'Bert's legs and my arse, don't like to abuse either of them.'

'So you missed the fountain and the fiveplay?'

Very confessed he had indeed, so Mesmer recounted the story of his own entry into the city, though for some reason he felt disinclined to mention the words inscribed on the fish. It was as if they had been written especially for him, and to speak of them to another, even one as worldly as Very, would be to divest them of their significance.

He went on, 'So you missed out on all the protocols, what with your tubing in.'

'Not exactly,' Very chuckled, 'even ol' Very doesn't get into a pentacle without a key.'

By this, of course, he didn't mean that there was any restriction of access. Ever since the last passport had been ritually burned in the twenty fifth year of the Revo, everyone was free to go anywhere and remain anywhere.

'Oh,' said Mesmer, wondering what Very might be referring to, but not wanting to pry after he'd kept his significant fish to himself.

Very dug him in the ribs with a sharp elbow. 'Wondering what it is, eh, sprout?'

'Well, yes,' Mesmer admitted.

'This'll answer your question, methinks.'

Very pulled aside his beard. On a chain circling his neck there hung a curved pointed object some three inches in length, of indeterminate material, with a burnished sheen as if it had been exposed to high temperatures.

'Take a look at it,' said Very.

'What is it?'

'Here, take it.'

Very undid a clip, slid the object off its chain, and passed it across the table.

As soon as its curiously warm weight pressed against his palm, Mesmer found himself subject to an indescribable sensation of unease, while from nowhere a whole array of questions, the like of which he'd never met before, presented themselves to him.

Had not Very assured him when they'd taken their leave, one from the other, on the greenway, that he was heading for Wales, intending a sojourn among the bards in order to improve his own balladic re-enactment of Candle's happiest hours? Could it be, hard though it was to imagine in these days of no ulterior motivation, that Very was following him? If so, why, when all ends, however discordant, could be satisfactorily reconciled through feeding them into the nearest kiosk of the noble-global? And why might he wish to by-pass the noble-global unless, inconceivably, to interfere with Mesmer's place in the world? And didn't that imply he was entertaining, all unwittingly, a temporal succubus straddling a time fault? Even, possibly, one from before the Revo? In which case . . .

Abruptly the flow of questions ceased, and with them his feeling of unease. What a moment before had seemed of the greatest importance, now seemed trivial, and, a moment later, meaningless. Opening his eyes, which he'd involuntarily shut, he saw Very had removed the strange object from his grasp, and had placed it on the table.

'I'll tell you what it is, and then you'll know.'

'Yes, do tell.'

As pleased with himself as if he'd done a triple somersault from a standing position, Very said, 'It's a dragon's tooth.'

*

Were my training not present in my every thought and deed I would embrace the patient at this most beneficent of transferences. The dragon's tooth, so precisely warm and weighty to the touch, from which sprang the ancient city of Thebes, signifies the recognition of my presence in his futurity. Such, the unveiling of the authentic phallus to replace the altogether overplayed allcock of the opening scenes, must be obvious to the meanest intelligence, among which I do not rank my own.

And obvious, too, the subseqent disavowal. First the chain of questions leading inexorably towards the glove flung in the face of the probing analyst, next the happy consciousness that comes with forgetting what he knew a moment before. As yet he is fearful to make his challenge explicit. But he cannot fail to expect I will take note, and react, as is my wont and only option. His revolution versus my reaction, how neatly the terms fit, how well he has established the rules of the game. One suspects the aged fool will figure in our struggle as mount for me, as Bert for he, allowing me to release on to Mesmer's world-stage all those denied a speaking part, snuffling and gibbering their way from the dark of the wings towards the limelight which one more hideous than the rest stumbles into, firing stage and theatre, the whole to burn to ashes in a matter of minutes. Yerse. Beyond such preliminary schematism I ought not to go, though my blood is up.

The tempo of my pulse has more than one sufficient cause, or is, as the young monkeys of my profession for whom I confess a certain liking even while administering well-deserved cuffs might prefer it, overdetermined.

Miss Petersen has consented to accompany me to an hotel, in a forest, where I know the chef and where the management knows me. I dare to hope she will extend her favours beyond the professional intimacies it has been my happy though frustrating lot to receive. Her tactful parrying of more leading suggestions has earned my respect, when so often such ploys have resulted in diatribes in brogue or churlish calculations as to how much it might be worth. She has, with an inward smile, contrived to make it appear that my advances have been of the same order as those of a much younger man, to whom premature response would do less than justice to what might be. May such hubris go unpunished. One can only brief the hotel staff from night porter to commis waiter, and trust the gods are sleeping. The former is done, the latter in process, my hands are actually trembling, it is only a woman, albeit one so rare as to make the inmates shuffling along the corridors of my mind howl at the moon in their agony at not being able to pluck it from the sky, silence ye mad, we'll have you better yet, and do I hear the swish of Michael in the Rolls outside my window, attendant too on the whim of Sonia to be ready? The gift of a sable knick-knack gracefully received along with her last salary cheque has earned me the right to thus caress her forename, an exchange of commodities for which I make no apology or excuse, only the passing remark that if Mesmer imagines he can abolish the way stations of love in his after-world he'll need more powerful magic than he's so far mustered. Which brings me to ask, while we wait, Michael and I, wherefrom this witchcraft springs, when history as he sees it has been progressively burying it for a thousand years? That I have little use for such rubbish is hardly unexpected when I have known from childhood money weaves the strongest spells of all. I must conclude he wishes to confound me with what he cannot possibly believe. I ask therefore of those who might be in the know, *Are* there Marxist-Leninist magicians? Sonia has just popped her head around the door and smiled a yes, causing me to leap, or totter, to my feet and bring to a close this week's study of the case.

*

'You should have seen us. Me, Candle, a raconteur to conjure it up, a farlook sensitive to hold on to it, and a stabilising medium to keep the way back free from astral traffic, the five of us plugged into an IBM Werewolf with a power pack big enough to energise from here to Wick. The dragon manifested for less than a second, but plenty long enough to give me a nasty burn when I grabbed hold of a tooth and hung on for dear life. Still, it was worth it.'

Fondly Very fingered the stolen molar.

'Extraordinary,' said Mesmer. He was on the point of enquiring about the properties of the tooth, for the memory of his unease was still with him, though he couldn't recall exactly what had been the cause of it, when he was cut short by the arrival at their table of two little girls, who introduced themselves as April, aged eleven, and May, twelve.

'We heard you from afar,' said May.

'And we couldn't resist,' said April.

'Welcome, welcome, sit your pretty selves down,' cried the high flier, 'and examine me trophy if that's what brought you.'

April, not so dark she hadn't a crop of freckles across her turned up nose, sat to Mesmer's left, and May, not so fair she wasn't tanned a biscuit brown, to his right, leaving the vacant space of the five-sided table between her and Very.

'Can I?' April asked Very, who bowed his encouragement across the century separating them.

Hesitantly, she reached across to where the dragon's tooth lay in the middle of the table, prodded it once or twice, then with a quick decisive move, closed her hand around it.

'It's . . .' She fell silent, even as Mesmer's heart suddenly thumped. 'It's . . .'

'Yes?'

'*Nice.*'

She flicked her eyes towards Mesmer who received, in the instant their gazes locked, an image of her, naked as a bird, standing on the table before him, with her vulva exposed, and of him, the same age as her, and as naked, kneeling before her, on the tabletop, each of them perfectly motionless.

Then she looked away, and the image was gone, leaving only the certainty it had been shared. She replaced the tooth where it had been before.

Without touching it, May leaned over and began looking at it carefully. Mesmer noticed that the points of its root had been cut short, leaving twin oval flat surfaces at its base, on which were inscribed the initials May was reading out.

'Vee Ell. What does that mean?'

Pleased to have something he could make sense of, Mesmer chipped in before Very could answer, 'Very Light, no less, famed throughout the Northern night for his feats on the trapeze.'

The trapezist coughed. 'My initials are no accident.'

'Spoken like a dialectical,' April murmured, perhaps a trifle absent-mindedly, for her forefinger was again straying towards the lustrous molar.

'Dialectician,' May corrected, then, of Very, she enquired, 'In what way?'

'No sooner had I grabbed this little item from the flux than I discovered who I was, in a manner of speaking.'

With a sidelong glance at Mesmer April replaced her finger on the dragon's tooth, presenting him with an image of such verisimilitude he could easily have mistaken it for reality, had he not known for certain she was sitting at the table to his left as fully clothed as he was. The image he so forcefully received was of himself, doing a headstand facing April who was supported by her forearms on the tabletop and by her upper thighs passing between his own slightly open legs. So much could he deduce from the point at which he was inscribed upside down in the geometrical figure. And, from the logic of their position, if not from the undeniably delicious sensations emanating from that part of his body, he must also assume that clever April was massaging his pre-pubertal penis with her open vulva.

'The soul reborn of him whose theory and practice made possible the first of the last Revos, none other than Vladimir Lenin himself.'

'Oh boy!' said April.

'Oh girl!' said Mesmer.

May thumped both her fists on the table in delight, causing the dragon's tooth to jump into the air, to be snatched by April's quick hand.

News travels fast around a pub in a pentacle, and in no time at all the four of them were surrounded by a crowd drawn by the reincarnation in their midst. Not that all were prepared to be believers, for after-politics was a topic on which folk were still likely to disagree. Some, like the grizzled programmer seated at the bar, were in favour of a once and for all time quicker-flicker with no chance at the end of it, while others held just as strongly to the notion of the wheel of life, forever throwing up incarnations according to the thistledown law of karma.

Mesmer edged a little closer to the table, so that the attention of the gathering crowd would not be drawn to his physical state, responsive as it had been to April's beautiful imagery. Although public manifestations of sexual arousal were, in 2411, quite acceptable, he rather felt that the erection pulling tight his trousers was in defiance of the gravity of Very's revelation. April, he noticed, was tapping the dragon's tooth against one of her own, and smiling to herself.

'Do you remember much about it?' May asked.

'As through a glass darkly. Times are when it's pitchy black, like when Candle snuffed it, flux rest her flicker, others like daylight.'

'How's now?'

'So-so. Give me a cue and I'll see what I get.'

'How about the Second Party Congress?'

'Madman.'

'Surely not,' objected May, as ready as the next to enter into debate, even with one who had made history.

Very's brow wrinkled in an agony of recollection until April, reaching across the table, caught hold of one of May's hands and pulled it over on to the dragon's tooth. Immediately Very's face cleared, even as May's jaw dropped.

'Sorry, sorry, sorry, what I meant to say was this. The madman, dear friends, was something Krupskaya found in Tolstoy. A man walking along a road sees a figure in the distance, on his knees, flailing the air with his arms, obviously a fruitcake. It's only when he gets up close he sees there's a rational explanation for the fellow's behaviour. He's sharpening his knife on a strop. That was us, crazy to some, whetting the blade of the Social Democratic Party on the strop of theoretical difference.'

'Don't stop,' said May faintly and with a flush reddening her tan. 'I'm just catching up with my little sister.'

But Very needed no further encouragement. Out it poured, as Mesmer kept his eyes strictly on the tooth passing backward and forward between the two girls. He would allow no further diversions to come between him and historical truth. Thus armed, he heard of the shift from Brussels to

London in the midst of the Congress, the question of the Bund, the ratification of the Iskra editorial line, Martov's disagreement, Plekhanov's tactlessness, the decisive vote, the split of the Party, Bolshevik determination, until an athletic lad who'd climbed the vine to gain a vantage point called out, '1905, tell us about 1905.' Mesmer, forgetting, cast his eyes upward, and encountered the dual look of April and May.

He heard Very cry out, 'A mighty revolutionary upsurge, a time of life,' then came the image the girls had ready for him. A triangle in a pentagon. A simple notion for this age when elementary geometry was understood from the Oedipal-schmoedipal, but one easier to imagine than construct. His own younger body comprised one line, on his side across the tabletop, making one angle at the intersection of his head and the notch of May's thighs, another by the envelopment of his little organ in April's mouth, the third angle being formed by the conjunction of May's tongue and April's ruby-red labia, a fitting tribute to a childhood spent basking together on the clitoral-littoral, the whole forming an equilateral triangle. The sensory details were so finely crafted as to defy description. What else could Mesmer do but tongue-tickle May's clitty, stop his ears with the silk of her inner thighs, and enjoy April's nibbling his willy?

When at last the girls released him from the power of their imagery, he discovered he'd missed all but the bitter aftermath of the failed Revo, with the Czarist forces in the ascendancy and the exiled revolutionists in thorough disarray. So close and yet so far! Thank flux there'd be a next time, and next time he'd make sure he kept his ears free, however much the rest of him might enter into the spirit of the girls' revolutionary geometry. He didn't want to think what mischief lay behind their secret smiles. Taking advantage of the respite he addressed himself to Very.

'But your philosophical studies, were they not important for the Revo, during those bleak years in exile?'

'Never made up my mind on that one, sprout,' Very replied, expansively gesturing his unconcern to the admiring crowd, now three deep all around. 'One thing for sure, it was a time for thought, not action.'

At this, even ebony-eyed April and honey-rose May looked pensive, with the dragon's tooth suspended between the tips of their outstretched forefingers, waiting for times to change. Which they soon did, what with war in the offing, all of Europe mobilised, millions on the march from Flanders to the Don, and the parties of the Second International rallying to their national flags.

'Even Kautsky,' said Very, shaking his head sadly.

'The renegade,' added Mesmer, glad he'd studied the beginnings of history at Elmsfootloose's knee.

'It was the end of the autocracy, though none of us guessed it. 1917, and the Revo seemed years away. Then came news of unrest in Petrograd, mutiny in the Imperial army, excited despatches from Trotsky, in the thick of it as always, the Putilov workers out on strike, the government tottering, the Czar about to abdicate and there we were in exile while the Revo built up without us. February,' cried Very in anguish, 'and I was stuck in Switzerland.'

Was April whispering something to May? A tilt maybe of the dragon's tooth in his direction?

'Negotiations, negotiations, and yet more negotiations.' May giggled, whispered something in return, and nodded. 'The sealed train through Germany. Finland. At last Petrograd!'

From New Stokers young and old, seated, standing or hanging from the vine, there came a deep murmur of excitement.

'My April theses!'

Whereupon that little girl jumped up and planted a kiss on Very's visage, causing him to blush and momentarily stammer.

'N-not b-bourgeois d-democracy, but socialist Revo!'

From all around came the voices of New Stokers, silent no longer.

'The end of economic anarchy!'

'The beginning of our true history!'

'The real become rational!'

'Leisure, pleasure and progress!'

'To each according to his need!'

'From each according to her desire!'

These and other cries ringing across the Trent that summer afternoon found Mesmer dumbstruck and lost in the last of the theorems concocted through the agency of Very's dragon's tooth. Surrendering himself to the girls' geometry, once more the triangle, now upended and revised, he found himself lying on his back, April's dusky-musky brushing his eyes, nose, lips, tongue, May sliding like glycerine up and down his electric erection, each astraddle, kneeling, facing the other and kissing with the passion of blood sisters. Their only concession was to leave him his ears, into which poured the very stuff of history, struggle, hope, decision, indecision, the days of dual power, the vacillation of the Provisional Government, continuous debate in the Soviet, the growing strength of the Bolsheviks, the growing confidence of the workers, the threat from Kornilov which evaporated like his cossacks when the proletariat stood against them, the last retreat into hiding with the bourgeoisie desperate to assert itself before it was too late, the return from which there could be no turning back. Very's words rolled on, unstoppable as the dialectic they were but the tiniest part of, while in his tri-dimensional pentagrammaton Mesmer moaned out the cadences of his want and its first ever satisfaction, nearer, even nearer.

'All power to the Soviets!'

Deep inside him Mesmer felt something melt . . .

'The storming of the Winter Palace.'

. . . flow . . .

'Victory!'

. . . and burst forth.

With a clatter the dragon's tooth fell on to the table. April and May were staring at a point above and behind Mesmer's head, out of his field of vision. He was about to turn, to see who it was who'd so effectively caught their attention at the instant of their return from geometry to reality, when April, her face glowing, called out, 'Momma! You couldn't have come at a better time!'

*

My innate frivolity allows me to ask, before getting on to higher things, whether a Yiddish variant might not have been more apt. Thus: Momma? You couldn't have come at a better time? Trotsky, at any rate, would appreciate it. Also, in the face of so much ejaculatory enthusiasm, one is reluctant to enquire too deeply into the precise order of events, the coming of Mesmer or of the mother, whether even they are conceptually distinct. The most ardent researcher may on occasion find cause not to put his pent-up question to recalcitrant nature.

My own weekend was a more modest success, predictably crowned with failure. In the sitting room of our hotel suite, with two sherries between us and the sun obligingly setting in a sky of roseate magnificence over her left shoulder, she told me she had never worked for a more interesting man. I told her she shouldn't look on me as an employer, more as a . . . She regarded me quizzically, while I rejected a trio in f, friend father physician, as entirely too Platonic and a quartet in some other key as rather too Machiavellian. Equal? She suggested, snapping a dry biscuit between her exquisitely manicured fingers and inspecting the rim of her glass as if in search of a blemish. Sonia, I enquired, seized by a dark suspicion, are you by any chance a feminist? Do I look like a feminist? she asked in return, while I, gazing at her auburn hair, at her green-eyed oval face, at her assured pose tilting her chair an inch off the carpet, wondered. Another sherry? But she would not.

I could eat a horse, she said, as we were shown to our table by the head waiter who managed without allowing his eyes to drift towards her breasts to express that variety of silent appreciation characterising the best of his breed, and I, I concluded after inspecting the menu, a morsel of foie gras, then brains. She settled for beefsteak, bleu. We talked of tennis until the pudding, then of youth, a cruel topic that, yet one I persisted in despite her gallant efforts to steer me off it. I spoke of its folly, illustrating my thesis with examples taken from Mesmer's baroque politique, though without of course naming him, before drawing her attention, as had been my purpose all along, to what many might call the folly of her own, seated opposite my drooling dotage. She said, There are things more important than the way people look, it's what they are that counts. At times I suspect she cultivates a deliberate naïveté in order to enhance her second thoughts. And what they want, she added with a look that sent my pulse surging into the dangerous nineties. Without further speech we abandoned our coffees for the sanctuary of our adjoining rooms, of which mine, that night, was the site of our incomparable performance.

Of her body I shall say but that she possesses a cunt unparalleled among those many I have squandered my life on, in search of one such as this, which now that it is found I am unable to possess. Youth's folly, I repeated, as she tried with many a wile, some surely cooked up for the occasion, and with the full force of a generous disposition, to enable me to do what alone could have made me happy. Nor was she without her climaxes. At last she slept, curled up beside me, while I lay awake, on my back, thinking that my hell was after all preferable to many heavens, and listened to the dawn chorus, in order of appearance, blackbird, robin, willow warbler, spotted flycatcher and crow.

I must have surrendered my consciousness to their happy territorial tune, for I awoke to the sound of breakfast and the sight of Sonia in a cream peignoir despatching a kipper. Hope you don't mind, she said, my starting without you, but I was ravenous. Ravishing, I said, and not at all, I think I may take a bite myself, your ministrations appear to have improved my capacity to eat, if nothing else. It was then, as she wheeled the trolley towards my bedside, that I told her I loved her, words I had last used in high seriousness when I flung them at the departing back of the wife of the Danish chargé d'affaires at an embassy ball more than a quarter of a century ago. She said nothing, but smiled before passing me the eggs. Afterwards, and for the day and a half that followed, we shared strolls in the garden, a memorable sole she was wise enough to order against my advice, jokes, at her suggestion her bed when I'd hesitated to compound a fiasco, and a mood I can truthfully describe as carefree, broken only by the driving of Michael on the way home, an uncheckable eighty miles an hour. I'd fire him were he not an excellent raconteur when traffic conditions or my ruffled psyche calls for it.

And now, with a new week hardening into a certainty, for it is already Tuesday, I am faced with the other face of what I am obliged to call my life, the rantings of the mad, of which none madder it seems this rainy après-midi than those of the heir to the Partridge estate. Yet there is, in the midst of it all, something to compel my admiration. No easy task, for example, to harness together two such incompatible nags as sex and pol, as my esteemed Reichian colleague Dr Beanbag will attest. You see, he says, nervously running his hands over the sweptback hair he affects in the wake of his master, it's all a matter of dissolving the metal of character armour in the aqua regia of genital sexuality, elementary hygiene from which wells up, thank you Beanbag, we shall be delighted to hear from you another time, but now there are more important matters in the offing.

*

'Do you mind if I ask you a question?' The speaker was June, April and May's breast-mother, who'd sat down at the vacant fifth place at their table.

'Go ahead, dear lady,' replied Very. 'Where there are no questions, there are no answers, as we say in Wick.'

'It's about your successor, the man of steel.'

'Ah, yes,' said Very, with a frown.

'Naughty Old Stalin,' said April and May excitedly.

'None other. What I want to ask is this.'

What June wanted to ask, and what Very replied, Mesmer never knew, for no sooner did her straying finger make contact with the dragon's tooth lying on the table than Mesmer fell into deep enchantment. Mindful though he'd been of Elmsfootloose's warnings, he'd never have guessed he'd find himself bound by a spell of such power that he could barely pay attention to his most immediate surroundings let alone the sense of what was being said. He'd have called Elmsfootloose on his allcock, or his breast-mother, or Old Jack, or any one of a hundred Stock Porters, and asked them their advice, except he had not the slightest inclination to do so. To gaze freely on June, to hear the cadences of her voice, to smell the perfume wafting from her as she moved, to note each gesture and change of expression, to marvel at her every splendour, was to experience something he'd never known through any one of the many things he'd grown up doing, all of which made life in 2411 as marvellous as one could imagine. This new found entrancement made him feel faint with ecstasy and, strangely, a suspicion of nausea.

*

Yerse. I shall not permit such summary evasion of what was on the agenda. There are places within cases when the mask of indifference must be dropped and the healer appear in all his awesome curative majesty. This substitution of June for Djugashvili, a transparent ploy to hush up the repressed of his dream. It was she who asked the question, and I who must therefore provide the answer, despite the sudden dive of my patient into the stomach-turning elevator shaft of love, a decoy a lesser analyst would be inclined to scurry after.

This memoir, then, may cast light where Comrade ditto has not been allowed to do so.

Naughty Old Stalin, or The Ally, as my employers had cheerfully known him even since he'd disposed of the remnants of the Old Bolsheviks, was my pigeon. We want, they said, after a letter from the Admiralty offering a commission I was pleased to accept on condition my office overlooked St James Park and I wouldn't be burdened with decorations when it was done, the Dirt. We want to know all about his father's beatings and his mother's kisses, we want to know what boyish pranks he got up to, we want you to tell us just how he found out about the birds and the bees and whether he pulled the wings off flies, tell us about his life in the seminary and why he didn't become a harmless priest, give us the lowdown on what young Koba did in Tiflis when he wasn't plotting revolution, find out about his thoughts on Lenin, on Trotsky, on the Jews, the Germans, the Czar, in short, Reed, we want an Analysis. Wild, I replied, it'll be as wild an analysis as even Groddeck could wish for. They revealed their incomprehension in true Whitehall fashion by agitating their teacups in their saucers, so I explained further, Persuade him to leave the Kremlin and visit my consultancy one hour a day, five days a week, for shall we say five years, and I'll give you a hand that'll outplay the straightest flush the rascal can muster. Five years, howled one, forgetful of the greater difficulty, but the war will be over by then, he'll be The Enemy. I held up a hand to still their protests. Nevertheless, I told them, I will do what I can.

Throughout the War, then, I devoted myself to the Word of The Ally and suffered stylistic agonies from the official requirement to Capitalise, a practice I have subsequently recognised as a compensation for feared losses of other capitals, both administrative and financial. That such outcomes were avoided, then and later, with a happy return to lower case, was in no small part due to my own efforts in interpreting dictats, speeches, pronouncements, orders to the front, minutes of meetings, letters, so-called theoretical writings and scribbled menu backs bagged out by Our Man in Moscow. By the Fall of France we were well embarked, he and I, upon an unproblematic castration complex. Pearl Harbour found us pushing into the barely mapped wastes of the pre-Oedipus with all its hallucinatory geography of absence and presence, mother and self, world and language. When Stalingrad began we were uncovering traces of a birth trauma complicated by his mother's fears that this, her fourth, would go the way of the other three into premature oblivion, and by its end, even as his troops poured through the conduits of the shattered city, we relived the first deep breath of the infant animal who was to grow into Uncle Joe. If he'd been with me, I could surely have pronounced him cured of whatever ills he may have suffered. As it was I could only advise, when called upon, which was rarely and in the utmost secrecy. Before Teheran, I said, Have Winston present him with a sword of honour, from our King, for the city that bears his name, a gift he will be deeply moved to receive, and a moved man is a weakened man. Before Yalta, Foreground him in the official photographs, have them taken from a low angle, in order to increase his stature which is small, no doubt from malnutrition as a child, and may well be something he'd like to forget if his dwarf henchmen Yezhov and Yagoda are anything to go by. Before Potsdam, Slip a teaspoon of arsenic into his vodka along with the red pepper he customarily takes.

Whether they heeded my advice I know not and care less, though students of history can no doubt find the answers in their rewritten texts, if such niceties of outcome seem important.

And now, having been provoked into historical indiscretion by the absurdities of Mesmer's Utopia, having therefore rumpled the fabric of my mind, I shall allow it to launder itself in the interstice of the movement I'm about to bring to an end and that following which as yet belongs to the future.

II

BLUE PRINTS

Her jet black hair was tied in a loose knot at the crown, falling in two sweeps to frame her wonderfully ornamented and mutilated face. Her eyes had irises electronically modified to match her emotional field, so that not only sensitives able to perceive her aura but all might see the colour of her feelings, now the palest azure shot through with flecks of rose. A crescent of nutrient graft swept across her face, with its points touching the corner of her eyes and its base passing over her chin and lower lip. Within the crescent the violet and olive green of the oleander hawkmoth's wing formed and reformed, as mobile as the flux itself, celebrating alike the skill of the surgeon and the loveliness of its bearer. Her only clothing was a simple shift of creamy raw silk, fastened at the waist with a cord. Flashes of light from beneath it indicated a pubic strobe, cued into the colouration of her irises and responsive to the flickering resistances of her body-electric. Long brown legs, bare feet touched at the nails with the iridescent blue of morpho butterflies, hands of great sensitivity and strength, the third finger of the left missing save for a ghostly residue invisible but for the shadow it cast, full breasts with their exposed nipples tattooed with scarlet star-maps, one of the northern hemisphere, one of the southern. When she smiled, she revealed a set of perfect teeth, of which the upper left canine had been micro-programmed to show movies, currently Hiroshima, Mon Amour. On each of her upper arms she wore five tight bracelets, of the finest gold filigree, squeezing the flesh into a series of curved ridges.

Spellbound, unable to speak, Mesmer could only lie back on the cushions of the gondola, while April and May plied its great oar and Very maintained a running commentary on the river frontage gliding slowly past. Where they were going mattered not a jot to him, as long as June was going too. To have summoned the words to describe her unnatural beauty would have taken more energy than he could have mustered. He was solely a witness, and happy to be such.

*

The ravished corpus of this June makes me wonder how soon the weather will break. The forecasters expect a thundery July, and I am not one to challenge their expertise. Best then I render the next case fact before the storm is upon us. I only wish I could place my finger on who or what it is his near-naked flame reminds me of, but I cannot, and shall have therefore to let Mesmer have his say.

(5) Every midday, after work, Mesmer took the train into Manchester Piccadilly, whence a short walk to the Central Library, under whose domed roof he conducted much of the research for his Blue Prints, as he insists they be called. He would order a microfilmed batch of past newspapers, which he perused in the dim light of the machine he came to think of as his, occasionally making entries in the clothbound notebook he'd acquired for the purpose. In three months he'd worked his way through ten years of news and had enough material for the first Blue Print. Thereafter he rarely left his room in the Partridge house except to work in the previously mentioned bodyshop. That the results of his solitary labours have survived to take up space in my desk merciful thanks must go to Vicky, the elder of Mesmer's two sisters, who persuaded him, before his final breakdown, to hand them to her for safe custody. Without these documents there would be much of his illness that

would be incomprehensible. They are, accordingly, to be presented in their entirety, both as symptom and cause of his accelerated decline.

Blue Print Number One

SOLITARY CONFINEMENT
SPRAWLING SUBURBS
MINDLESS REPETITIVE LABOUR
URBAN MOTORWAYS
CONTEMPT FOR KNOWLEDGE
THE DOLE
COMPULSORY OVERTIME
FORCED RETIREMENT
PERMANENT ARMS ECONOMY
CHILEAN JUNTA
RAPE
OVERCROWDED CLASSROOMS
GUTTER PRESS
MUTILATION ON THE ROADS
RACISM
CUT PRICE HOUSING
SPEEDED-UP PRODUCTION LINES
ASBESTOSIS
SUS LAWS
PRISONS
DECLINING INDUSTRIAL BASE
INTERNATIONAL MONEY MARKET
PROPERTY SPECULATION
WHALE SLAUGHTER
DESTRUCTION OF AMAZONIAN RAIN FOREST
UNWANTED BABIES
SONIC BOOMS
CORPORAL PUNISHMENT
HYPOTHERMIA

DOUBLETHINK
ANOREXIA
ORBITING WEAPONS
REDUNDANCY
COMPETITIVE EDUCATION
BUREAUCRATIC IMPERMEABILITY
JUNK FOOD
CIA DESTABILIZATIONS
ERSATZ BEER
LOCKOUTS
MANIPULATIVE ADVERTISING
SECTARIAN STRIFE
TORTURE
ALCOHOLISM
INVASION OF PRIVACY
OBSCURANTISM
THE BERLIN WALL
PLANNED OBSOLESCENCE
CLOSED BORDERS
SECRET POLICE
DEMAGOGY
NON-CONSULTATIVE PLANNING
ANTI-SEMITISM
GHETTOES
MACHISMO
PURDAH
INTELLECTUAL DISHONESTY

MARY PICKFORD, an entry I had trouble squaring with the tenor of the preceding until a question put on his first and exploratory consultation accounted for if not exactly justified its inclusion. I wanted, he explained, to list everyone I've heard of whose initials were mine and who wasn't me. I nodded, having heard stranger desires most hours of my waking life, and said nothing. Like, for example, he went on

       MICHAEL PARKINSON

       MARCO POLO

       MAX PLANCK

Or, I added, entering into the spirit of the thing,

       MARCEL PROUST

Never thought of him, said Mesmer glumly, and I realised I had broken the cardinal rule just five minutes into the session.

       MALFUNCTIONING LIFTS

       THE VOCABULARY OF WAR

       FAMINE

       ALIENATION

       FEAR OF AUTHORITY

       DUSTBOWLS

       BOARDS OF DIRECTORS

       DIOXIN

       MERCENARIES

       CLOCKING IN

       INADEQUATE PENSIONS

       FAMILY LIFE, at which juncture I lifted a lazy eyelid to study my supplicant, recognising homage to Laing & Co, a firm which despite their irritating flirtations with philosophy I find myself allied with against the massed ranks of prescribers and electrocutionists.

       DAMP WALLS

       RELIGIOUS INTOLERANCE

       THE NATIONAL FRONT

       AGORAPHOBIA

       LITTER

       MILITARY ACADEMIES

       ONE CROP ECONOMIES

       INFLATION

       EXCREMENTAL BEACHES

DANGEROUS MACHINERY
NON-SELECTIVE INSECTICIDES
SPECIAL BRANCH
MERCURY POISONING
MINISTERIAL LIES
SILICOSIS
MAFIA CONTROL OF GAMBLING
LATIN AMERICAN OLIGARCHS
GULAG
MISUSE OF PSYCHIATRY, at which point I wondered whether I could not stretch further the elastic of my timetable and take him on. If I couldn't provide him with a counter-example to this last then I was not worth the salt so liberally distributed by Providence on my so-called tail.

SHANTY TOWNS
WHITE SUPREMACISM
POLICE BRUTALITY
COVER-UPS
EVANGELISM
BROWBEATING
TIME AND MOTION STUDIES
PUBLIC SCHOOLS
PRIVATE MEDICINE
U.S. BASES
PERSECUTION OF SEXUAL MINORITIES
EDUCATIONAL SADISM
SLAVERY
WIFE BEATING
PLAGUES OF LOCUSTS
PHALLOCRACY
LACK OF COMPENSATION FOR VICTIMS OF VIOLENCE
PROHIBITION OF MARIJUANA
DUTCH ELM DISEASE

SELF-HELP IDEOLOGIES
DRUG OVERDOSES
TORREY CANYON DISASTER
PHILISTINISM
EMOTIONAL BLACKMAIL
CIGARETTE ADVERTISING
MUSAK
UNEMPLOYMENT OFFICES
BUSTARD HUNTING BY OIL SHEIKS WITH AUTOMATIC
RIFLES AND RADIO COMMUNICATION, sic
DETENTION CENTRES FOR NON-WHITE IMMIGRANTS
CENSORSHIP
LITTLE ENGLANDISM
SECURICOR
OZONE DESTRUCTION
ILLITERACY
IGNORANCE OF CONTRACEPTION
POLICE CHIEFS
COMPULSIVE EATING
CARIES
ISLAMIC FUNDAMENTALISM
DEPRESSION
ORGASMIC IMPOTENCE, a complaint to endear him to
Beanbag, should he ever get to hear of it.
THE GOOSESTEP, and this.
SINGLE SEX EDUCATION
ABANDONMENT OF THE OLD
UNEMPLOYABILITY OF EX-CONVICTS
EUPHEMISM
STEALING FROM PUBLIC LIBRARIES
VANISHING FISH SPECIES
THE ART MARKET
TRAPPED MARRIAGE PARTNERS

TYRANNY OF FASHION

PRESS BARONS

UNWANTED UNIFORMITY

DIESEL FUMES

DEFEATISM

URBAN DECAY

RICKETS

COMMERCIAL VANDALISM

BERUFSVERBOT

OVERFISHING

CHILD PROSTITUTION

INTERROGATION TECHNIQUES

PAVEMENT DWELLERS

VITAMIN DEFICIENCIES

CHEAP BLACK LABOUR

ARBITRARY STANDARDISATION

NEO-NAZISM

THE PENTAGON

DESTRUCTION OF HABITAT

PROHIBITION OF BIRTH CONTROL

RADIATION HAZARDS

ESTATE AGENTS

THE CHICAGO SCHOOL

COMPULSORY SPORT

ALL MALE POLITBUREAUX

REPATRIATION

GLORIFICATION OF VIOLENCE

FIG LEAF MORALITY

AMBUSH

CRUCIFY

FLUMMOX What's all this? I asked, thoroughly flummoxed by the radical change in the complaint. Verbs, he explained, got a thing for verbs, and these seemed, well, sort of to sum up what people do to each other. It turned out he had taken nine such, randomly but selectively, from the Random House Dictionary given him on his entering University by his Auntie Mimosa. On your father's side, unmarried? I interrupted. Yes, how did you . . . ? In that case, I said triumphantly, you've missed another M.P. She should go in after Proust. Shit, he said, ungraciously.

GRIEVE

MUZZLE

NAUSEATE

OUTSTARE

VILLIFY

ZERO IN ON.

Such an excess of exegetical zeal as I have shown today, eroding Mrs Minceberger's hour, thus given her ammunition to support her contention that I Simply Don't Care, has left me tired and a little shaky. There are times I envy his delusions. How agreeable it would be to be floating down a river, facing one's beloved, towards a destination unknown, rather than limbering up in the thirty seconds remaining before the redoubtable Mrs M charges through my doubled door.

*

By my watch he is fifteen minutes late and therefore unlikely to show up, which may be interpreted either as evidence of a resistance he is loath to have me inspect, or as no more than the effect of one of a myriad possible insignificant causes of delay, like the derailment of the Stockport express. I am not one who insists there are no accidents. Nor am I one to deny Sonia the afternoon off when it is a matter of life and death struggle to secure the best of the summer sales. Since our weekend I have been the model employer, fair, just, ready to listen to any grievance, ready to grant any wish consonant with a lenient understanding of the terms of her contract, while she has been meticulous, deferential and has avoided eye contact by a lash's breadth. The game we play, she and I, if game it is, not having found it listed between Loo and Nap in the rulebook, is one she plays with skill and for stakes that appear to have no upper limit.

The coincidence of her absence and his this windy Tuesday exemplifies her approach. Suppose she has arranged to meet him in the basement of John Lewis, between the hat stand and the hot dog counter, in order to arouse my jealousy. That she has succeeded in doing the latter without my knowing whether she has done the former only goes to prove the lack of necessity for her to go to such lengths. She is not stupid, therefore she is innocent. Similarly, knowing that I am neither stupid nor innocent, she would be stupid to arrange such a meeting at all giving the possibility of my doing a little elementary paranoid arithmetic. Again, since she is not, once more innocence. Further, given the potential unconnectedness of social events, she could be merely ignorant, hence yet again innocent. Finally, having presented me with proof positive in triplicate of her innocence, she is in a position to proceed with her nefarious appointment undisturbed. Do I call her bluff? Not with two small pairs I don't, raise or fold, and fold it'll be.

The sun has just emerged from behind a cloud. I give it fifteen seconds before it gets its comeuppance from that nimble nimbus to the west. I think perhaps I am a trifle bored. If it's Mesmer I'm missing then I should do justice to his case by making the most of mine.

My choice of profession was a product of necessity and accident, both in large doses. My father's wish was for me to succeed him in his monomania, mine to become a brain surgeon. Make money, was his sole advice during our twenty five years of acquaintance. That I have done so, a measure of his power even from the grave he's occupied since an undiagnosed disease carried him off to join the wife he'd sent there eighteen months after she landed me on this pestilential sphere.

The underlying motive in pursuing medicine was to acquire the skill to perform a long overdue lobotomy on my sire, with a single decisive stroke of the scalpel handed to me by one who bears more than a passing resemblance to my current beloved. Son, he'd have subsequently mumbled from his vegetable patch, do what you like in life, only keep my leaves clear of greenfly, my flowerhead free from blight. Oui, papa, I'd have concurred, giving him a hefty swipe from the watering can in passing.

The brilliant success I achieved in my examinations owed much to these hopes, thwarted though they were, that night of celebration, through my meeting a remarkable stranger whose whispered revelations careened on into the small hours, while all about my co-jollifiers fell victim to the successive avatars of the grape. But this makes the scalpel seem like a meat cleaver, I exhaled. Like a bloody bludgeon, he agreed. Neither of us was exactly sober, but neither so drunk that he could not relate and I not follow.

He told me a story whose beginning concerned the curiosity I know so well, whose middle was a tangle of threads knotted together to form a distinct though lumpy string, and whose ending, happily, was happy. As footnotes, as it were, to his tale, he spoke of the movement known as psychoanalysis, of its infancy in the neurological clinics of France and Germany, of its childhood mocked and scorned, of its acquisition of self-reliance in the monumental discovery that little Helga hadn't been the victim of Uncle Ludwig's uncontrollable urges but of her far more shocking own, of an adolescence rich in the stuff of language and dream, of a young adulthood marked out by the great metapsychological papers written while their author and all Vienna starved, of the crises, the splits, the dissensions, the defections so characteristic of growth, all this and more. Fascinated, I listened, and listening, rewrote my future history. No longer would I become a medical mister, terrorising the junior doctors and flattering fluttering matron, instead I would pace out the path taken by the master, extend it even, win new friends, make new enemies. How do I begin? I asked my informant. You must find yourself an analyst, one who has been trained by one who has been trained by one who has been trained by Freud himself. You? I said. Not I, he replied, and his eyes glittered with a terrible irony amid the upturned chairs and dormant bodies. Who are you? I whispered. He laughed and began to pull on his gloves. Tell me, I insisted. If you wish, he said, making for the door. You will find my case history among the five that all analysts young and old must return to, time and again, for it is they that first established the desideratum of cure. And your name? I am known, he replied, turning in the doorway, by my affliction. Yes? I cried, stumbling towards him over the obstacle course of my drunken companions, What? Through the crack of the closing door he smiled with the weight of infamy resting on his elegantly clad back. Rat Man, he said. But Rat Man, I said, let us meet again, anywhere, anywhen, you name the venue, and I shall sign the bill. Once more he laughed, with what I now know to have been a skeletal ring, and said, My visitations are not in my hands. But whose? I said. I cannot say, he said, only this, that I died seven years ago in the Great War. Even as I rushed to the door he pulled shut behind him I knew I'd find nothing behind it. Since then I have spent many a night poring over his case, seeking the key to his return, knowing that it must be there somewhere, without having so far found it.

*

One missed appointment signifies little, but three, successively, without so much as a phone call, or a note, to proffer an excuse, can only be read as evidence by one, such as I, trained in the most rigorous of schools, where a single minute's tardiness, or a second's hesitation, called for an explanation, that there is something, or somewhere, to hide. But seek I shall not, and if my breathing has become a trifle irregular, I assign the aetiology to the less than satisfactory omelette it was my lot to consume for lunch. The analysis continues, until such time as my bills are unpaid, whether he's here or not. An empty couch causes me no more distress than the cavity occasioned by the pulling of a painful tooth, a welcome relief is the consensus on that, and if the tongue strays to the site, statistics not psychology is the discipline to tap. It, the couch, would make a welcome change from the hardbacked chair behind it, however well-padded its seat in homage to my imperious haemorrhoids, but I resist the lure of its brocaded rosewood, whereon I might lay my head, to speak, perchance to dream. Ha! Literature! The one issue of substance I have taken with our founder, this insistence on the novelettish pretext. Science is all, and nuts to your Danish princes.

As evidence of this stance I shall without ado submit the next fact of the case.

(6) Once again availing himself of Auntie Mimosa's dictionary, Mesmer constructed this the second of his Blue Prints, a document calling for little in the way of exegesis, except to point out that the initial letters of the first fifteen entries spell out his name. Uncanny how the unconscious writes its subject.

Blue Print Number Two

MADDENED BY A HISTORY PROMISING SO MUCH
    YIELDING SO LITTLE,
    NO GAIN WITHOUT LOSS,
    CONTRADICTIONS EVER DEEPENING,
    HORIZONS OF HOPE RECEDING,
    WAR FAMINE ECO-COLLAPSE FASCISM APPROACHING,
    POWERLESS TO DO ANYTHING.

ESTRANGED BY THE MACHINERY OF POWER,
    DIM BUREAUCRACIES GENERATING ORDERS FROM WITHIN,
    BANKS,
    DUMB GENERALS WITH ITCHY FINGERS,
    IBM,
    OVERLAPPING INTERLOCKING CIRCLES OF CIA KGB MI5 AND OTHERS UNNAMED SPAWNING SPY LOGIC,
    TRIPLY DAMNED DICTATORS,
    HORRIBLE OLIGARCHS,
    AND SELF-SEEKING REPRESENTATIVES OF THE PEOPLE.

STUPEFIED BY THE BARE-FACED LIES HALF-TRUTHS

OMISSIONS EVASIONS SPEWED FORTH BY PRESIDENTS,
ADVERTISERS,
STATE BROADCASTING CORPORATIONS,
PRESS BARONS,
MONSTROUS JUDGES,
POLICE,
THROUGH NEWSPEAK ADVERTESE OFFICIALESE LEGALESE AND
ALL LANGUAGES WHERE THE LISTENER CAN'T SPEAK BACK.

MANGLED BY THE ARMAMENTS INDUSTRY,
ENOUGH NUCLEAR WEAPONRY FOR A FIFTY TON TNT
EQUIVALENT FOR EVERYONE OF US,
COMING IN ROCKETS PLANES MIRVS SUBMARINES,
AND NAPALM WHICH STICKS AS IT BURNS AS IT FRIES,
ARMALITE RIFLES WHOSE BULLETS KILL THROUGH THE
SHOCKWAVE,
BOMBS CONTAINING TEN THOUSAND PLASTIC NEEDLES
INVISIBLE TO X-RAYS,
NERVE GAS,
ANTHRAX,
AND UNSENSED RADIATION.

ENERVATED BY SITTING IN THIS ROOM DOING NOTHING,
WATCHING TELEVISION,
LISTENING TO MY FATHER BULLY MY MOTHER DOWNSTAIRS,
MASTURBATING THREE TIMES A DAY,
WISHING I KNEW WHAT I'LL NEVER KNOW,
THINKING OF GIRLS,
WISHING I WAS A PLANT,
READING THE DICTIONARY,
WONDERING WHAT AUNT MIMOSA FEELS NOW SHE'S DYING,
WORRYING WHETHER THIS LUMP IS CANCER,
SLEEPING TOO MUCH.

REPROACHED BY THIS LAST ENTRY WHEN I COULD BE STARVING,
    IMPRISONED,
    HAVING MY FINGER NAILS PULLED OUT,
    WORKING IN A COPPER MINE TWELVE HOURS A DAY,
    TERMINALLY ILL,
    MOURNING MY WIFE AND FOUR CHILDREN,
    ABOUT TO BE SHOT,
    BLIND,
    OR LEGLESS.

PERPLEXED BY THE SILENCE ON NORTHERN IRELAND
    WHERE A WAR IS GOING ON IF 600 DEAD SOLDIERS AND 1500
    DEAD CIVILIANS MEANS ANYTHING,
    AND WESTMINSTER BBC PRESS UNIONS WON'T OR CAN'T SAY
    WHAT THEY THINK, MAYBE BECAUSE IT'S UNTHINKABLE,
    A POLITICAL SOLUTION TO SECTARIAN STRIFE,
    PRODS VS TAIGS.

ANGUISHED BY THE FATE OF THE INDIGENOUS PEOPLES,
    TASMANIANS HUNTED DOWN FOR SPORT,
    AUSTRALIANS IN RESERVATIONS UNABLE TO WALK ACROSS
    THEIR LAND,
    THE SIOUX NATION SICK AND ALCOHOLIC,
    POLYNESIA RAVAGED BY SYPHILIS AND TOURISM,
    BUSHMEN,
    ESQUIMAUX,
    THE TRIBES OF THE AMAZON DYING OUT IN PROSTITUTION
    AND SLAVERY.

REVOLTED BY THE HYPOCRISIES OF THOSE IN POWER,
    ATTENDING BANQUETS,
    HANDING OUT TO CHARITIES,
    WRITING MEMOIRS,

MAKING SPEECHES,
WHILE THOSE IN THEIR POWER DRAW THE DOLE,
GO HUNGRY,
ROT IN PRISON,
DIE FROM THEIR INJURIES.

TROUBLED BY THE COLLAPSING NATURAL ORDER WITH ITS
OZONE LAYER THINNING,
CO2 INCREASING,
OCEANS DYING,
RAINFOREST VANISHING,
GRASSLANDS ERODING,
ANIMALS BECOMING EXTINCT.

RIVEN BY CONTRADICTIONS,
LIKE FAMINES CO-EXISTING WITH FARMERS BEING PAID NOT
TO GROW FOOD,
LIKE NOT BEING ABLE TO AFFORD NURSERY SCHOOLS WHILE
LUXURY HOTELS ARE BEING BUILT,
LIKE HOMELESS FAMILIES OUTSIDE EMPTY OFFICE BLOCKS,
LIKE PUTTING PEOPLE OUT OF WORK TO ENRICH THE
ECONOMY.

INFURIATED BY REGIMES CALLING THEMSELVES
SOCIALIST WHICH COURT AMERICA, WHICH SEND ARMS TO
CORRUPT OLIGARCHIES,
WHICH SUPPRESS POPULAR UPRISINGS,
WHICH DENOUNCE OTHER REGIMES CALLING THEMSELVES
SOCIALIST,
WHICH INVARIABLY DENOUNCE TROTSKY,
WHICH HARBOUR GENOCIDES,
WHICH CONDONE RACISM,
WHICH SUPPRESS MODERNISM,

WHICH DENY POLITICAL POWER TO THEIR OWN MASSES,
WHICH MAKE SOCIALISM SO MUCH HARDER TO ACHIEVE
ANYWHERE.

DERANGED BY THE PRICE OF EVERYTHING,
 £20 FOR A SOCIAL SECURITY CLAIMANT,
 £20,000 FOR A PICASSO SKETCH,
 £200,000,000 FOR A YEAR'S WORTH OF DOG FOOD,
 £200,000,000,000 FOR A YEAR'S WORTH OF ARMAMENTS,
 WHILE A HUMAN LIFE IS PRICELESS, TELL THAT TO THE
 CAMBODIANS,
 OR THE INHABITANTS OF THE FALLS ROAD,
 OR THE SOWETO BANTU.

GELDED BY THE GULF BETWEEN KNOWING AND DOING,
 BETWEEN INTERPRETING AND CHANGING,
 BETWEEN WANTING AND GETTING,
 BETWEEN MADNESS AND HEALTH,
 BETWEEN WHAT IS AND WHAT IS NOT.

EXCORIATED BY THE CRUELTY THAT CAN FLOG A MAN
 SO HE SCREAMS ON THE FIRST STROKE,
 FAINTS ON THE TENTH,
 IS REVIVED BEFORE THE ELEVENTH WHICH GETS THROUGH TO
 BONE,
 IS RENDERED IMPOTENT BY THE TWENTYFIFTH,
 IS DEAD BY THE EIGHTIETH,
 WHICH DOESN'T PREVENT THE FINAL TWENTY BLOWS TO THE
 CORPSE.

OR DO I STAY SANE BY GIVING NO MORE THAN A ONE-EYED MONKEY'S
FUCK IN A SNOWSTORM?

*

I have had time to think, in the days intervening between the last non-session and this latest, about his half-sighted simian copulation, a phrase whose original bleakness distills the essence of our condition, tentatively assumed to be human. Certainly, what he presumes to give is not much, but it is not nothing.

Such thoughts take me back half a century to a walking holiday in the Black Forest, where one afternoon my path converged with that of another solitary hiker, and did not diverge again till dusk. As we walked, we talked, necessarily in Latin and occasionally in Greek, for my German has never surmounted the most basic commands. He related a fable concerning the origins of man, to the effect that whatever the claims of Jove on his spirit and of the Earth on his body come death, it was Care who first shaped him, and therefore possesses him as long as he lives. Consider, the philosopher said, the double meaning of care, on the one hand burden, on the other devotion, phenomena deriving from a primordial unity, our being in a world not of our own choosing. To imagine, he continued, that we can, as now, be carefree for more than a fleeting hour or two is both to court and deny death, the one because only death ends care, the other because it is death that founds it. How exactly you put it, I said, the one thing for which there's no cure. Ah, he said, you are a physician. Of a kind, I said, I cure by doing nothing, saying nothing, so that they can say what they like, in order to do what they could not. A caring profession indeed, he laughed, and I laughed too, for in the Latin we spoke there was but one word for care and cure.

Our candid Arcadian discourse fortifies me now as I contemplate the depths of Mesmer's despair, as I seek to cure him of the care that has proved too much for him. Only in his coda, with its minimal quantum necessary for existence, and consistent with sanity, do I find that to lend credence to my hopes.

More mundanely, and a propos of his continued absence, I have taken the unprecedented step of putting through a phone call to the Partridge residence to enquire in the most general terms imaginable whether my patient was indisposed. So far as I know, said a woman's voice I had no difficulty in attributing to Mesmer's mother, he's been down to see you like he's supposed to, hasn't he been? the so and so, and it's costing Mr Partridge a pretty penny, I shouldn't say that should I? not to you leastways, where do you think he's going? what's he getting up to? My dear Mrs Partridge, I managed to get in, pray don't concern yourself, such absences are all part of the process of getting well, and please, under no circumstances should you let him know either that I have been in touch with you or that you know he's been playing truant, nor if I may be so presumptive should you relay this quite unimportant fact to your good husband, just a little something between yourself and me, all right?

As I replaced the receiver, I vowed I would never again break my rule of non-interference. Should news of this leak down the street, I thought, and chose not to think further, so dire were the imaginable consequences, what with a dozen rivals waiting to step into my alligator-skin shoes.

More mundanely still, Mesmer's absences have coincided with a thaw between Sonia and myself, after our brief cold spell, with certain determinate results, or nearly so. Were it not for the empty couch on Tuesday and Thursday, with an attendant squiggle of suspicion I cannot entirely lay to rest, these last three weeks would rank among the most cheerful of recent years. Only yesterday, as she massaged my back after a particularly enervating session with Mrs Spein-Chiller, she told me she couldn't make up her mind about me, one way or the other, though she certainly felt something. As did I dare to think did I, a tremor of movement where no movement except that promoted by extraneous forces had occurred for decades. You must say, Sonia, whatever you feel, no more, no less. So vulnerable, she said, pressing her thumbs into the tender reaches of my kidneys and causing me pain such that I would have begged her to stop had I not simultaneously experienced, this time without doubt, a surge of blood into the long-empty vessel of my once-virile member. So thoughtful, she said, with her knuckles roller-coasting along the switchback of my vertebrae. Do you think I might have the afternoon off? When? I moaned. Tomorrow, she said. Tomorrow, with my charge wandering loose around this shabby greedy metropolis and her likewise, meeting planned or unplanned, hinting their interest in a reciprocal ear, scenting the thickening atmosphere of libidinal response, sating their doubled lust multiply on the concave bed of a flea-ridden hotel in Somers Town or some such station-bordered alcoholic's revenge of a sub-suburb. Yes, yes, but Sonia, I implored, feel this. Progress, she said. Revolution, I corrected her. The next patient's due in, we really don't have time. Forget the next patient, this hasn't happened since Suez, over on the couch, quick. But not quick enough, for by the time we'd completed the transit and made the necessary adjustments to dress, the great moment had passed. Don't worry, she said, I love you all the same. Fuck love, I wailed as she made her way to the door to let in the next sufferer, it's the other I want.

Only today has the import of what she said sunk in. To be loved, tensely passive, is not such a poor consolation for what I had in mind as yesterday's man would have had it. Yerse, my sentence is not the unambiguous affair it first seemed.

And what is this? Footsteps in the hall? A patter on the parquet? A hand on the outer door, followed by another on the inner?

Come in, come in, lie yourself down, make yourself comfortable, and tell me where you've been.

*

The rasp of gravel on the bottom of the gondola was the first sound from the outside world he'd noticed since his enchantment had begun. It was evident they'd arrived at a destination, for the two girls leapt on to the bank in a flurry of nautical expressions.

'Allow me, dear lady,' said Very, with courtesy, offering a steadying hand to June, as the gondola rocked from side to side.

'Catch,' called out May, throwing a rope towards Mesmer. He lunged for it, but in doing so lost his balance, and would have fallen in the water, had he not flailed his arms wildly, causing the free end of the rope to whip across the boat to where Very was in the process of handing June ashore. The rope tangled itself in the leather thong around Very's neck from which hung the dragon's tooth, somehow hooking it over his head, and flicking it through the air. The tooth shone as it arced towards the still waters of the Trent.

'Me dragon's tooth,' cried Very. 'Save it, sprout, if you can.'

Galvanised by the old timer's cry, Mesmer dropped the rope and made a grab for the tooth just before it fell into the river. As his fingers closed around it, a swirl of water revealed a sizeable fish just where it would have gone in.

Simultaneously with the tooth's curious warmth once more making itself felt between his fingers, Mesmer's deep enchantment lightened and elaborated itself across a whole spectrum of charms, one for each organ, sense, mood and body, so he could participate fully with her every aural tint, without ever being unwelcome.

'Saved it. Well done, sprout. Worthy of the circus itself.'

But Very's exultation was premature, because just then the fish beneath the tooth turned on its side to expose the word EXPAND. What with the shock of this new and unexpected instruction, and the peculiar shape of the tooth, which made it difficult to hold on to at the best of times, Mesmer must have squeezed too hard. The next thing he knew it shot from his grasp and flew in a second trajectory back across the gondola.

With surprising agility and a great shout of 'Avast' Very leapt into the air as it flew over his head.

'Well caught!' applauded April and May.

And indeed it was, except that the leap he'd made had taken the trapezist clear of the boat, to fall backwards with an enormous splash into the river behind him. Whereupon Mesmer's allcock began to transmit uncalled for the most amazing succession of noises, with words, grunts, cries and hoots of laughter all mixed up together. Appalled by its unprecedented behaviour, Mesmer tried to silence it with thought, then with verbal command, lastly with the little-used manual, but to no avail. He was on the point of banging it against the prow of the gondola, in order that Very, now being hauled from the river by six willing hands, should not hear its extraordinary broadcast, when he felt a restraining hand on his shoulder.

Turning, he found himself facing a tall strong blonde woman, perhaps twice his age, regarding him with an expression of friendly amusement.

'Let me try,' she said. With a single pass of her hand she silenced his still chuckling allcock.

Mesmer could only stand there and blink his thanks. 'Welcome to Village, where we live,' the woman continued.

'It's New Stoke's most peaceful fifth, and will suit your needs at this time.'

'O woman,' said Mesmer, inclining his head towards her in gratitude and respect, 'how right your intuition is. I'm but twenty and from Stock Port, a peaceful commune devoted to horses, admin and yarning, and I'm not sure I can cope with all that's happening to me. All these significant fish and pentacular accidents have shaken my resolve, and fond though I am of the old timer who's been at my elbow this day and a half, I've discovered and had confirmed these past instants through the agency of the dragon's tooth he wears around his neck that he's not what he thinks he is, a harmless highflier from Wick and onetime architect of the Russian Revo, but the bearer of a temporal succubus of unknown intentions, to put it mildly.'

All this he blurted out in a rush, out of Very's earshot, while the old man was briskly drying himself off with his beard, and laughing off his ducking with characteristic good humour.

'Perhaps I should return to Stock Port and confess I'm not ready for the boundless exigencies of Journeying, taking up admin like Old Jack before me. Even my allcock seems to have become affected, picking up flux knows what.'

'Calm yourself. There's nothing wrong with your allcock. It's encountered something from the past, still lingering in some corner of the flux as a resonance. Traces abound hereabouts, and your high flier's a likely enough host. Besides, most entities are harmless enough, if they're treated kindly. May I see your allcock for a moment?'

Mesmer was happy to pass it to one who evidently knew so much about the flux.

The woman inspected it carefully before handing it back. 'I'd recognise Mandy Rocket's work anywhere. Always leaves room for the unexpected, Mandy does. How is she?'

Pleased she knew his electronicist friend, Mesmer told her about the fun they'd had working on it together. By the time he'd got on to the selection of movies he'd quite forgotten his earlier agitation.

As they conversed they made their way through oak groves away from the river, following in the track of Very's damp footsteps. He had rushed on ahead to keep warm, encouraged by April and May who'd challenged him to a race. Behind them June was making fast the gondola, as Mesmer could see from the flicker of her pubic strobe in the gathering dusk. The sight of her was all he needed once more to set his heart beating fast.

'Talking of movies,' he said, thinking of the filmic tooth in her upper jaw, 'I have also become utterly entranced since arriving here in New Stoke. With she who is back there. Her every charm takes me by surprise, and leaves me helpless. I can think of no remedy, and wouldn't want to. Are you close to her yourself?'

The woman passed an arm around Mesmer's shoulders and said, 'As close as can be. My name's Julie.'

Mesmer could feel the warmth from her body as her hip made contact with his own. Just then June caught them up and fell in alongside Mesmer on his other flank. No doubt about it, he thought, with not a trace of his earlier anxiety, and as the three of them walked along arm in arm, the flux had a way of throwing up the nicest things one could imagine.

*

His growing collection of females forces me to redress the balance by displaying mine, of which the earliest and rarest specimens, purchased at considerable cost, have been wretchedly mislaid. I begin then with my first wife, towards whom the figures of love and lust were perfectly aligned. When, that day in St Marylebone, I placed the wedding ring on her left hand, and she on mine to match the signet bearing the family crest of ibis atop a pyramid, misconceived throughout my childhood as a vulture astride a dungheap, I imagined happiness could only be ours. I was an age my father scoffed at as too irretrievably childish to be married and adjusted my funds accordingly, she twenty two and to my horror, non intacta. How did this happen? I wanted to know as the train tore through the Flanders night, towards Cap Ferrat and sunshine. On horseback, she claimed until my persistent questioning forced her to come up with a more likely story of which the hero was a subaltern in the same regiment as my favourite Canadian uncle lying not so far to the east, according to my calculations that marriage night, below the scarp of Vimy Ridge. Were there others? I asked. A defiant nod from the head I so adored, or had done until twenty minutes previously. How many? Fingers raised, five on one hand, then, as an afterthought, two on the other, the last of which bore the dully glowing band of gold bestowed in love that very day. Whore! I screamed in my tempestuous innocence, and struck her. She fought back, displaying a knowledge of the male anatomy in so doing that confirmed all I had just discovered about her history. But my rage gave me the edge, strong though she was, and within five minutes I had her pinned down on our couchette, with one forearm pressing against her windpipe, and the other inserted between her thighs, forcing them apart. Now! I panted into her ear, and thrust my standing organ into her, to spill myself immediately. You bastard! she hissed, and came herself. Thus matched, we called a truce, one I am still convinced might have become extended and honourable had she not presented me with a healthy seven and a half pound boychild six months later. The divorce was a quiet one, and my wife, whose name I forget, and my son, whose name I never knew, passed from my ken.

A pitiful tale, and one I'd have no compunction in excluding from the annals had I not taken the vow, some years after these wretched events, following the decision to practise the practice founded in Vienna, to hold nothing back, not even that which I'd rather had gone the way of her name and of my legal son's, into oblivion. It amuses me to speculate, when idle, whether among the many who have crossed my threshold seeking alleviation of some nameless pain there has not been my son and onetime heir. Would I have seen her features in his? Would I have seen, no, how easy it is to forget, his brow would have been angled according to the genetic contribution of any one of seven prospective fathers, but never mine, never mind. If he has sat there, I point, seeking to find the words to fill the lack engendered by the absence in his life of the one whom he addresses, the symbolic da da, I trust I had the grace not to sabotage his return to health and happiness, though I doubt it. Of one thing I can be sure, lest interpreters of the interpretation take it upon themselves to adduce some abortion of a father-son dialectic in respect of current casehood, Mesmer's genial genealogy equips him not at all for that dubious position, he's Partridge from the egg to the entrée, and for those who insist on proof, to the pudding too.

*

'Œufs en cocotte!' cried May from the kitchen.

'Et perdreau sauvage!' came April's higher pitched squeal of delight a moment later. 'Oh momma, you must have known we'd be having company.' Putting her head around the door she explained to Mesmer, 'We only kill to eat when there's something special on.'

Pleased he should be part of something out of the ordinary, Mesmer sat down next to Very at the oaken table opposite June and Julie. April and May, who brought in the food and served it, sat at either end.

It was a real family meal, erotically suffused and full of tales. June recounted how she and Julie had first met at Downtown Stoke's famous night spot, the Flaming Flamingo, when she'd stopped off en route from

Shang Hi to Greenland. Apart from the odd week back in China at the old commune, she'd stayed ever since. Together, they'd come to be known as the youknowduo, adding further to the Flaming Flamingo's reputation.

'Pure energy,' said Julie, as she passed the salad.

'We couldn't put a foot wrong,' agreed June.

As their friendship had crossed the many stations of attraction, deeper into the caring-sharing, they'd decided to commit themselves to a cloning-zoning. The cross-fertilization had been spaced so that eleven months lay between the two, with Julie giving birth to May one spring, and June to April the following.

Mesmer found it hard to imagine a happier family could exist as he looked from face to face around the table, with mothers and daughters echoing each others genes and style in a wholly delightful way. Struck by a sudden thought, he turned to Very and said, 'How did you get here? If you don't mind my asking.'

'Ask away,' the highflier replied, lifting his face clear of a large slice of peach pie. 'It was Candle all the way. A virgin birth. Not even Angus Bar-Higgins could persuade her to share her genes, though many were the time they took pleasure together when his lions were asleep. She said she wanted one to follow her on the high wire, and who else could she trust not to implant a sense of vertigo? From the beginning I was there at her breast, high above the ring, with never a fear of falling. Hence me nature, hence me spirit. And you, dear lad?'

'As unremarkable as you could find. Nothing's out of the ordinary in Stock Port. My breast-mother asked a dozen of her favourites over one night, they had a party, and I was the result. Old Jack was one of them, and somehow I've always thought of him as more than a friend. Perhaps Mum knows more than she's let on, because it's Jack she's settled for in a caring-sharing these last five years.'

More family talk carried them through the rest of the evening, for there were always forgotten details to be uncovered, which jogged another memory, or gave rise to a good joke. At last Very yawned and said, 'At my age sleep is as important as life. Have I said I am a hundred and twenty one? Therefore, whatever my condition, it behoves me to bed, booked in the west wing of stately New Stoke House. Dear ladies, do you perchance have a bike handy with which to wobble my way from here to Park, Bert having taken it into his head to refuse to budge from a meadow where he's inexplicably surrounded by sheep?'

'There's a lovely green racer you could take,' said April, forgetful of the quantity of armagnac Very had consumed during the evening. 'You can go incredibly fast on it.'

With the tact of her eleven months seniority, May said, 'Or a nice upright.'

Very, it seemed, would prefer the upright.

'Mommas,' said April, 'can we go with him? Just in case he wobbles into the river.'

'And two duckings in one day might upset his balance for good,' said May.

'And if we're going that far,' said April, 'can we stay the night? You've always said there's nothing better for old minds than to have young ones tripping them up.' For emphasis, she repeated this last in her beautifully accented High French. 'Rien de plus salutaire pour le vieil esprit que de se voir désarçonné par le jeune.'

'*Please* can we join the gerries for the night. We promise to return tomorrow.'

June and Julie conferred briefly as mothers will, before agreeing on condition they respected the bodies-actual of the older residents. At a hundred and fifty you didn't necessarily want two little girls frolicking on your bed at six in the morning. Not like the last time when Fernando McMao, New Stoke's oldest and some said greatest living poet, had to have heart massage to get it ticking again.

'So watch it, kiddos,' warned June.

'It's not me heart as worries me,' said Very, as he mopped up some spilt brandy with his beard. 'It's one thing to have led a revo, quite another to keep up with a pair of winkies. Still, you're only a hundred and twenty one once, as Candle said before she snuffed it.'

Minutes later April and May were ready, on the path outside the cottage, with the gaslights of the Village green behind them, and a bicycle between them, clutching a comic and a toothbrush apiece.

Unsteadily at first but with increasing speed the trio set off across the green, Very with his beard tied in a bow to keep it out of the spokes, April and May jogging along beside him.

Mesmer, June and Julie stood in the doorway of the cottage watching them disappear into the grove of oaks beyond the green, from where they heard a faint cry.

'Never used a net, never ever.'

'Come back in with us,' murmured June to Mesmer, taking his hand in hers. As she gripped him he could feel the absence of her third finger, both shocking and exciting. On her face the oleander hawk graft swirled its never-repeated pattern, slightly luminous against the dark behind her, her irises glowed with the tawny light of desire, and her pubic strobe took up the colouration with a fast insistent pulse.

'Just the three of us,' said Julie, closing the door behind them. Turning to June she caressed her neck so as to make her lovely eyes glow cherry red. Then reaching up she pulled clear the platinum pin holding June's jet black hair in place, so it fell in a cascade down around her shoulders. At the same time the film that had been showing whenever she spoke came to an end. It had been Letter from an Unknown Woman. 'Shall we take our friend to bed with us?'

'Let's,' said June, pulling Mesmer a little closer, to make once more a triangle, except this time one whose reality was unquestionable.

*

Quite so. And as for questions, not one has so much as crossed my mind. Nevertheless, I can state these scenarios à trois never pan out exactly as one would hope, but wild asses couldn't drag this untimely advice from my lips. Let the boy find out for himself whenever he acquires the wealth or cunning to carry off such coups that the details cause the problem, never exactly spot on, like dividing any given angle into equal thirds, a practical impossibility. What interests me about this latest instalment is the emphasis upon the elementary structures of kinship, evidently so much looser in their syntax than those of the classics.

My own efforts to found a dynasty foundered on the reef of my second marriage. This next to adopt the name of Reed was selected strictly with an eye to my heir, none of the passions of the lower depths to be lavished on her. Our two houses met, conferred, bargained and exchanged contracts specifying everything our solicitors could imagine, from the school he would attend to the terms of his inheritance. If second, third, fourth, ad infinitum sons should appear, or any daughters, there were formulae to cover them. In short it was as watertight a scheme as any concerned with posterity could wish for, down to the physique of my espoused, which all judged so well-designed for her appointed task in life as to conclude God himself held a small portfolio of our joint stock. Unfortunately, her attributes did not prevent her from being barren. Tests showed our years of matrimonial toil to have been wasted. In fairness, and according to the terms of our contract, I allowed a technician to mathematicise my own fertility, following on from a humiliating quarter of an hour in a draped ante-room. I was pleased to report to my attendant wife that the count was agreeably high, and that I could not therefore co-shoulder the responsibility. Mildred, I boomed, or did not, for her name is not Mildred at all, another of those contingency clauses our solicitors saw fit to include, and besides, she is alive and not unwell somewhere in Buckinghamshire. Mildred, lesser men than I would forgive you for what is in no way under your control, would take you to their breast and let you assuage the tears that I see have already begun to flow. She approached me, mascara-streaked, ready to press her mammaries against me, as so often and so fruitlessly in the past, until I recommenced the speech she had understood to be at an end. But lesser men, I went on, would fail to appreciate the inner necessity of the bourgeois spirit, before which all considerations of compassion must yield. I am sure you appreciate that and would not want it otherwise. The divorce papers will be served in the morning. I wish you well in the remaining forty or fifty years statistics expects will be your lot. Adieu.

My hypothetical heir, instrumental in booting poor Mildred down the stair, soon became distasteful to me, and henceforth I directed my mistresses to ensure there would be no unwanted Reeds littering the vestibule. My only concession to my earlier wish, one I now realise died along with my papa, was to speculate what I, through them, might have brought into the world. Among my favourites were, first, a great soprano destined by paternal encouragement and maternal endowment for La Scala from an early age, second, a male, improvident, feckless, profligate and broke at thirty, who begs forgiveness and cash, both freely given on condition he renounces the good life and enters a curing profession, ideally at a leprosy clinic in a Calcutta slum, third, and last, lest a list worthy of Mesmer himself, an outstanding athlete, modest, beloved of women, winner of the Decathlon in the 1984 Olympics, Lysander Reed by name.

Enough now of my past. His future is bursting to have a say, and our collective present, his, mine and darling Sonia's, has not been without its share of intrigue. All this must wait while I attend to Mrs Skywide and her poodle, a beast whose ills are so various and baroque there is scarcely time left for her own petty problems. Be so kind, Sonia, if you would, as to show her in. I stifle a yawn and prepare myself for the continuation of the story of the evil vet.

*

It was Julie who made the suggestion, when she brought them croissants and coffee in bed, with the sun already high in the sky, and the sounds of morning beyond the chintz curtains of the room.

'I'll be going to the under-city today,' she said to Mesmer. 'Would you like to come along?'

Mesmer had needed no second bidding to follow every idea these last ten hours, from when they'd taken him up the winding staircase to their room and throughout the extravagances of a night such as he'd never known, not even with his sisters Lois and Marushka. So he was not going to say no to this latest, sleepy as he was, and despite the feeling that to be alone with June would yield fresh delights.

'Yes, indeed. But what is the under-city?'

'Hasn't she told you?' said June, propped up against a stack of silk cushions, sipping her coffee. 'She's on the shit-commit.'

'If she's told me that,' said Mesmer, 'it's slipped my memory.'

In truth, so much had been murmured throughout the night, he'd have had trouble saying exactly what he had been told. 'But do explain.'

The star-maps on June's nipples were palest pink this morning. A movie was playing once again on her filmic tooth, and her nutrient graft swirled lazily.

'The shit-commit,' said June, 'is responsible for making sure everything's working in the disposal of the city's effluent.'

Even in 2411 there were unenviable tasks, needs of the body-social requiring human intervention to satisfy them. It was considered to be an honour to be asked to help discharge such unpleasant necessities, for the good of all. Garbage collection, cleaning the streets and sewerage maintenance were jobs no-one really wanted to do, however mechanised and sanitised they'd become. In the course of your life, you could be expected to be called upon to perform such a task, especially when your standing in the community was highest. This last fact, June explained, together with her advanced mathematics, including the all-important separation equations, had recently resulted in Julie being elected the fifth member of the prestigious shit-commit.

'Take your time,' said Julie, 'there's no rush, not here in New Stoke. Have another croissant before we go.'

Two hours later Mesmer and Julie left the thatched cottage next to the Old Oak on Village green, wandered down to the river, hopped on to a passing gondola which took them as far as Downtown, along the crowded boulevards of which they strolled, stopping to exchange greetings and embraces, towards the penta-centre, point of entry to the under-city.

The great open concourse of the penta-centre must have been three hundred yards across, and was featureless but for the expanse of the prosaic-mosaic beneath their feet, depicting in detail the history of New Stoke, from its founding to the present. Each year the tableau would be altered in a few respects, to bring it up to date.

It was here too, in the penta-centre, that the collectivity would gather in order to enter into the political debates and decisions of the day, via the noble-global. It was a moving sight, Julie said, when all of New Stoke, from the youngest to the oldest, were gathered here to thrash out some major issue, effecting not only themselves, but all those who lived in the region, even indirectly the whole world.

As it was now approaching siesta time, only a few small groups were present, politicking away among themselves or with others unseen from other regions through the resonating kiosks of the noble-global built into the prosaic-mosaic beneath their feet.

'There's something I find rather odd,' said Mesmer, 'and that's why you've got the point of entry to the under-city at the penta-centre.'

'The dead penta-centre,' said Julie.

'Even odder. I'd have thought you'd have a great fountain, or a noble tree, or even the commemorative statue of the potter and the go-go dancers, rather than a mere passageway to the lower depths.'

'There are things it is easier to demonstrate than explain. For the moment accept that the design of New Stoke incorporated certain truths, of which the simplest is that for every mouth there's an anus, and the strangest you will encounter shortly.'

Interest in what Julie was telling him prevented Mesmer noticing the solitary figure standing in the penta-centre until they were almost upon him. Only the sound of a familiar voice made Mesmer take his eyes away from Julie's delicately concernful face, devoid as it was of all decoration.

'Good morrow, sprout. If coincidence it is, then the flux be praised. Here I am, where you are heading.'

'Very!' exclaimed Mesmer. 'Whatever are you doing here, so relatively early in the day?'

The high flier chortled happily at Mesmer's surprise, made a low bow towards Julie, so that his beard brushed the prosaic-mosaic, and said, 'Where me dragon's tooth points, there go I. Walked too, when I'd have ridden given half a chance. But the winkies went off early on the bike and Bert, leaving only me feet. So here I am, wondering what's next.'

*

As do I, as do I, though no first head of a Council of People's Commissars can I claim to be. The drift towards New Stoke's back passageway I do not find encouraging, carrying with it the imputation of impending buggery, that oft theorised but rarely practised figure of my youth, squeezed in between the squash court and Primary Eating, ah me, such was my prep school. If he imagines he can restore my potency by proffering himself in this altogether unseemly way, he reckons not with the ox-bow lakes the river course of my sexuality has deposited in its fourscore years of flow, now cessant in the stagnancy of its present swamp. Alternatively, the descent may be an escape route from an unmanageable ménage, if the wenches he's taken on are more than even his enthusiastic libido can satisfy, eyes ever being bigger than stomachs. Or perhaps merely the density of textual events has reached the point where matter can no longer take care of itself, resulting in what my friends in Cal Tech refer to as a black hole. They said, out there on their sundrenched campus, with the Pacific pounding not a stone's throw to the west, that I displayed an aptitude for their arcane discourse as would put me in the running for a Nobel prize in physics, were I not so evidently lined up for one for peace. Like Mesmer, therefore, I shall avail myself of this black hole between hours, these ten minutes of hyperpressure, to bring the case up to date with a new fact, redeeming my promise of a thoroughgoing aetiology, so rare in these days of shoddy workmanship.

(7) With the assistance of the Partridge encyclopaedia whose twenty four volumes present a united front against the twenty four inch screen

opposite, Mesmer knocked together this the last of his Blue Prints, which he still insists makes the most of his case.

Blue Print Number Three

FROM CASE TO KNOWLEDGE,
FROM KNOWLEDGE TO CASE,
FROM KNOWLEDGE TO KNOWLEDGE,
FROM CASE TO CASE.

FROM SICKNESS TO HERBARISM
FROM THE WILES OF ANIMALS TO ENTRAPMENT
FROM FIRE TO COOKERY
FROM THE STRENGTH OF THE CAMEL TO TRANS-SAHARAN TRADE
FROM POWDERED RHINOCEROS HORN TO POTENCY IN OLD AGE, yerse, I wonder
FROM THE PHASES OF THE MOON TO THE TREATMENT OF LUNACY
FROM THE MAGIC OF MUSHROOMS TO ECSTASY
FROM SALT TO THE PRESERVATION OF MEAT
FROM GROOMING TO WOAD
FROM WILD GRASSES TO FIELDS OF WHEAT
FROM 3-4-5 TRIANGLES TO PERMANENT DWELLINGS
FROM PLOUGHSHARES TO THE SMELTING OF IRON
FROM THE POLESTAR TO NAVIGATION
FROM PROPHECY TO THE MOVEMENT OF THE PLANETS
FROM WRITING TO PAPYRUS
FROM WHAT PLEASES THE GODS TO PROSPERITY
FROM THE TRUE NATURE OF MEN TO LEGISLATION
FROM WHEELS TO THE GEOMETRY OF THE CIRCLE
FROM SARTORIAL PREFERENCES TO THE PRODUCTION OF SILKWORMS
FROM FLOODPLAINS TO THE PYRAMIDS

FROM THE MALLEABILITY OF LEAD TO PIPED WATER

FROM ARCADIA TO THE POLIS

FROM DRIED HIDE TO THE TESTUDO

FROM TRAPEZIA TO RHOMBI

FROM MERCANTILE PROFITS TO SLAVE GALLEYS

FROM SOPHISM TO CYNICISM

FROM THE GREAT WALL TO THE MANDARIN ELITE

FROM DORIC COLUMNS TO THE ROMAN SENATE

FROM THE TAMING OF HORSES TO GENGHIS KHAN

FROM EMPIRE TO CRUCIFIXION

FROM ZERO TO ABACUS

FROM THE ORACLE TO PARRICIDE

FROM MARITIME TRADE TO THE PUNIC WARS

FROM ORATORY TO DEMAGOGY

FROM ANATOLIAN NIGHTS TO THE CONSTELLATIONS

FROM ALEUROMANCY TO WHEATEN CAKES

FROM BAKED CLAY TO THE STORAGE OF OLIVE OIL

FROM INDIGESTION TO THE SPICE TRADE, or vice versa, on the basis of the goulash I had for lunch.

FROM THE EXTENSION OF THE IMPERIAL FRONTIERS

TO METROPOLITAN DECLINE. Goulash, I repeat.

FROM THE UNIVERSITY AT ALEXANDRIA TO THE ALHAMBRA

FROM GERMANIC MIGRATIONS TO EASTERN ORTHODOXY

FROM REGAL ADULTERY TO THE HOLY GRAIL

FROM TIN TO SEA COAL

FROM THE DIET OF WORMS TO FISH ON FRIDAY

FROM PTOLEMY TO THE INQUISITION

FROM RATTUS RATTUS TO THE HUNDRED YEARS WAR

FROM ALCHEMY TO GUTENBERG

FROM THE FLYING BUTTRESS TO STATICS

FROM THE POINTS OF THE COMPASS TO THE CLASSIFICATION OF TEMPERAMENT

FROM THE THEORY OF SIGNATURES TO THE NAMING OF FLOWERS

FROM THE INFERNO TO HELIOCENTRIC ASTRONOMY

FROM THE DISCOVERY OF AMERICA TO GRATIN DAUPHINOIS, an altogether more palatable creation than the peppery concoction still fighting its way through my system. His emphasis throughout upon the demands of the stomach is undoubtedly a sign of hope. No-one who is that hungry can be utterly crackers.

FROM THE LAW OF FALLING BODIES TO THE PENDULUM CLOCK

FROM THE ACCUMULATION OF CAPITAL TO THE SUBJUGATION OF THE INCAS

FROM THE REFORMATION TO PARADISE LOST

FROM CRANACH TO HOLBEIN

FROM METAPHORIC CLOSURE TO THE PROTESTANT CONSCIENCE

FROM MILLENARIANISM TO CALVINISM

FROM GUILD GLASS MANUFACTURE TO THE OVERTHROW OF THE PHLOGISTON THEORY

FROM EXPOSED NIPPLES TO COVERED ANKLES

FROM THE ACT OF ENCLOSURE TO CAPABILITY BROWN

FROM TOLEDO STEEL TO BESSEMER CONVERTERS

FROM THE BOOK OF REVELATION TO THE ENGLISH REVOLUTION

FROM THE DECLINE OF THE HARPSICHORD TO ROMANTICISM

FROM THE DEBASEMENT OF THE COINAGE TO THE DEPOPULATION OF THE HIGHLANDS

FROM STEAM TO SENSE AND SENSIBILITY

FROM RURAL POVERTY TO URBAN POVERTY

FROM FREE TRADE TO THE SPREAD OF SYPHILIS

FROM PALLADIAN ARCHITECTURE TO LAKELAND SCENERY

FROM THE CONDITION OF THE WORKING CLASS TO ASSOCIATION FOOTBALL

FROM PRAGMATISM TO VICTORY IN THE AMERICAN WAR OF INDEPENDENCE

FROM DEMOCRITUS TO DALTON

FROM FROGS' LEGS TO THE BELL TELEPHONE CORPORATION

FROM QUATTROCENTO PERSPECTIVE TO THE HUNDRED AND EIGHTY DEGREE RULE IN CINEMA

FROM GALAPAGOS FINCHES TO SOCIAL DARWINISM

FROM THE SECOND VOLUME OF CAPITAL TO THE FIRST WORLD WAR

FROM NAPOLEON'S RUSSIAN CAMPAIGN TO LENIN'S COMMENTS ON TOLSTOY, an entry I tried to make yield meaning in the wider context of 2411 before concluding it was another of those damnable accidents that make paranoia so unreliable.

FROM PROPERTY RIGHTS TO PATENT LEATHER

FROM MICHELSON AND MORLEY TO THE ORBIT OF MERCURY

FROM THE DEFEAT OF 1848 TO THE DEFEAT OF 1926

FROM WARTIME SURGERY TO THE FACE OF MARILYN MONROE

FROM ASHANTI SLAVERS TO CHARLIE PARKER

FROM SARAJEVO TO MUNICH

FROM PRINCIPIA MATHEMATICA TO PARLIAMENT SQUARE

FROM OPTICS TO SATELLITE SURVEILLANCE

FROM POINTILLISM TO MINIMALISM

FROM HEATED WIRES TO IBM

FROM THE JAMES I BIBLE TO JOURNALESE

FROM THE OXFORD UNION TO THIRD DEGREE

FROM CYCLAD FORESTS TO MERTHYR MINERS

FROM ANILINE DYES TO PLASTIC BAGS

FROM THE MAGIC LANTERN TO UGETSU MONOGATARI

FROM FATHER BROWN TO KOJAK

FROM THE MODEL ARMY TO SOUTH ARMAGH

FROM MACADAM TO THE NEW JERSEY TURNPIKE

FROM PAVLOV TO THE KENNEL CLUB

FROM THE PAVEMENTS OF BOMBAY TO NEO-MALTHUSIANISM

FROM THE FALLING PRICE OF ELECTRONICS TO THE RISING PRICE OF BUTTER

FROM EGYPT TO BUCHENWALD

FROM SOPWITH CAMELS TO B-52S

FROM AQUINAS TO THE FOUR QUARTETS

FROM NATURAL SELECTION TO TARAMASALATA

FROM THE MODEL T TO BRAND X

FROM GUNPOWDER TO PEENEMUNDE

FROM THE EAST INDIA COMPANY TO GRUNWICK

FROM CLARA BOW TO BO DEREK

FROM AL CAPONE TO THE MAN FROM THE PRUDENTIAL

FROM PAGE THREE OF THE SUN TO THE FESTIVAL OF LIGHT

FROM THE STRUCTURE OF CELLULOSE TO THE FINANCIAL TIMES

FROM POLLEN ALLERGY TO THE PROFITS OF ROCHE

FROM TURKISH FIELDS TO NEEDLE PARK

FROM DIEN BIEN PHU TO WATERGATE

FROM MARATHON TO THE PARAPLEGICS OLYMPICS

FROM THE KINDER TRESPASS TO THE ACCESS TO MOUNTAINS ACT 1939

FROM THE MANCHESTER ANCOATS AND SALFORD WORKING MEN'S COLLEGE TO THE UNIVERSITY OF CALIFORNIA

FROM DUTCH FORMAL GARDENING TO HYDROPONICS

FROM THE PANAMA CANAL TO THE GULAG ARCHIPELAGO

FROM THE PROPHET ISAIAH TO CECIL B. DEMILLE

FROM OCCAM'S RAZOR TO PHILISHAVE

FROM CRAZY HORSE TO THE WEATHERMEN

FROM HERRING MIGRATION TO THE ICELAND FISHING DISPUTE

FROM ATHLETE'S FOOT TO MORE PROFITS FOR ROCHE

FROM TAMMY WYNETTE TO THE WHITE HOUSE

FROM ARGUMENT AD HOMINEM TO ELECTRIC CATTLE PRODS

FROM INVESTMENT DECISIONS IN OMAHA TO DENTAL DECAY IN OMSK

FROM A MILLION DEAD VIETNAMESE TO TEN MILLION DOLLARS IN FIRST NATIONAL CITY BANK

FROM BOB JONES UNIVERSITY TO PIE IN THE SKY

FROM THE CONCEPT OF GENIUS TO THE EXHIBITION OF DOGSHIT IN ART GALLERIES

FROM COPULATING DRAGONFLIES TO JOINT BBC TIMELIFE PRODUCTIONS

FROM KEYNSIAN ECONOMICS TO SIR KEITH JOSEPH

FROM BISLEY TO RUSSIAN ROULETTE

FROM HUGH MACDIARMID TO CLYDESIDE UNEMPLOYMENT

FROM THE CORRIDORS OF POWER TO THE LEICESTER SQUARE GENTS

FROM THE MASTER OF BALLANTRAE TO A CELTIC RANGERS FINAL

FROM SANDHURST TO THE INTERROGATION OF IRA SUSPECTS

FROM MOTHERCARE TO BABY BATTERING

FROM SHOVE HALFPENNY TO JEUX SANS FRONTIERES

FROM THE CAVES AT ALTIMIRA TO PAINTING BY NUMBERS

FROM THE BOW AND ARROW TO THE NEUTRON BOMB

FROM PARK AVENUE TO PARCHMENT FARM

FROM THE PERFECT COCKTAIL TO THE ASSASSINATION OF TROTSKY

FROM SOFTWARE TO HARD SELL

FROM THE NATIONAL QUESTION TO THE INVASION OF CZECHOSLOVAKIA

FROM HIGHWAY 61 REVISITED TO SLOW TRAIN COMING

FROM HYPE TO HYPODERMIC

FROM THE PETROGRAD SOVIET TO THE BRITISH ROAD TO SOCIALISM

FROM ORGASM TO THE RESOLUTION OF PLOT

FROM SELF REFERENCE TO AUTO DA FE

FROM BIRTH TO DEATH

FROM THE PLEASURE OF FREE FALL TO THE FEAR OF ITS ENDING

FROM THE BREAST OF THE MOTHER TO THE NAME OF THE FATHER

FROM THE POSSIBILITY OF CONTINUING IN THIS VEIN TO THE LIKELIHOOD OF FINDING ANOTHER
FROM BLUE PRINTS THEREFORE TO GREY DAGGER.

All of which seemed straightforward enough to save the ultimate. This grey dagger, I said after reading through the sheaf of grubby papers, something perhaps to plunge between the shoulder blades of the father class? A quid pro quo for good old Trotsky to whom, I note, you pay your respects somewhere in the thick of this thick wad? No, no, he said, nothing like that, the night flier. Further he refused to be drawn, though by now I had my own ideas on the subject, conversant as I am with the common names of British lepidoptera. What a moth might be doing in his history, fluttering its way towards the light, candle or otherwise, I could not then imagine. Explication will be forthcoming in its proper place, when the next pair of case facts are inserted in the text.

*

Under-Stoke had been undeniably interesting, Mesmer thought as once more they emerged into the penta-centre, and he could see why the shit-commit was accorded such respect. Even the fascinating topology Julie had elaborated as they'd sped along miles of conduits hadn't been entirely able to take his mind off the pervasive stench. Now at least he understood that the city was constructed in the form of a torus, as well as a pentacle.

Julie explained further, 'Through its ring passes the effluent of the city, being converted in the process to the sparkling fresh water of our lakes and fountains, teeming, as you know, with fish.'

'Significant,' said Very, abruptly.

'I beg your pardon,' said Mesmer, giving a helping hand to the old trapezist as he climbed the last rungs of the ladder leading up from the under-city.

'Significant fish. When I fell into the river last night.'

'Afternoon, you mean,' Mesmer corrected.

'Night, sprout. In off the bike, for all the winkies could do to stop me. Luckily I dry easily.'

Mesmer could only marvel at Very's resilience and cheerful demeanour. Many old folk would not have taken kindly to a second soaking. 'But what of these fish?'

'A whole line of them, swimming past, each with a word emblazoned on its side, making sense.'

'What did they say?' said Mesmer, seized by a sudden curiosity.

'They spoke of you, dear lad.'

'Yes?'

'And Candle.'

'Yes?'

'That you could be instrumental in restoring her flicker.'

'Gosh,' said Mesmer, 'but how?'

'They didn't say,' said Very, with the nearest Mesmer had yet heard to sadness in his voice.

*

Only a millenium of breeding prevents me from terminating the hour after twenty minutes. An analyst's lot is not a happy one. Yet whose is?

*

'I think,' said Julie, 'you might like to visit the moister-oyster. It's no great distance from where we stand, a little way to the North, at the junction of Park and Town.'

*

Approached no doubt via a grotto of quite beguiling aspect, flanked by portals thickly foliated in exotic succulents, its coruscated nacreous lambency, et cetera. I yawn in sympathy, and consult the watch God in His wisdom has seen fit to encircle my wrist, nothing like the banal to slow time to a crawl, that and pain, I suppose. Still, I should not begrudge him his pleasures, well-earned as they are in the protestant manner with a day's work behind him, though give me Bach anytime in preference to these well-trodden geological and architectural metaphors. Three minutes. Time enough for albumen to set, and them to make the transit.

*

They were inside a large cavern, of symmetrical design, comprising a gently upward curving dish for the floor and its mirror image for the roof, with the one meeting the other at a circumference, one point on which they had entered. Four other doors could be seen, equally spaced around the dividing line between floor and roof. The incline of the floor, as it fell gradually away from them, was corrugated by a number of smooth ridges, like a sandy beach with the tide out, though larger by far. These were just the right size to form seats, in concentric circles, tier upon tier of them, facing towards the centre of the bowl. The roof too was similarly ridged. More than anything else, what put Mesmer in mind of the inside of a giant bivalve's shell was the material out of which it was made, like nothing so much as mother-of-pearl, translucent and silvery pink.

Suspended with no visible support halfway between the roof and the floor, was a gelatinous flattened spheroid some twenty feet in diameter, continually modifying its shape, around which slowly orbited five creamy-white globes, each a foot across. That, Mesmer supposed, was the moister-oyster, with its own fiveplay of pearls.

'Come with me,' said Julie, and stepped forward from the rim of the bowl. Surprisingly, her foot didn't make contact with the floor sloping away in front of them, but came to rest above, on the same horizontal plane with her back foot. As she walked away from Mesmer and Very, apparently on air, she turned and beckoned them to follow her.

'But how, dear lady?' said Very, chewing a tip of his beard. 'Along a wire, yes, I can walk with the best of them, but here there is nothing.'

'Just walk behind me,' Julie said. 'There's a perfectly solid bridge, with handrails to stop you stepping into space. We made it clear so the views of the moister-oyster wouldn't be obstructed. They developed this ultra-glass in New Stoke nearly fifty years ago for the aesthetes who wanted their goblets to be invisible. Refractive index the same as air.'

'Hold on to me beard then, sprout,' said Very, 'in case you tumble. And you go first, being younger than I.'

So Mesmer stepped out, holding Very's beard as requested, in Julie's footsteps. When at last Julie came to a halt they were sixty feet above the floor below.

'If only Candle were here,' Very muttered, half to himself, looking down. Then, to Julie, and pointing straight ahead, 'Tell us what it is.'

In front of them, not a dozen paces away, the moister-oyster pulsed and writhed. Its attendant pearls wove a complex pattern around it, passing so close at times as to graze the surface, at others flying outwards on orbits that took them behind the watching trio.

'It's a universal index,' said Julie.

Immediately the moister-oyster quivered and emitted a series of gurgles, and its pearls shone with increasing luminosity.

'No further,' she warned Very, who'd taken another step forward. 'It's very sensitive.'

'As I, madam. As I,' rejoined Very, straightaway re-tracing the step he'd taken.

'Nothing can happen, anywhere in the world,' Julie continued, 'without it responding. It's open to every register. Bodies-social, bodies-symbolic, bodies-electric, bodies-actual, it's tuned into them all.'

'And it's right here in New Stoke,' Mesmer breathed. He'd heard of such things, but had never imagined one to be so close, just a day's ride away from Stock Port, and three days into his Journey.

'Its placement is all important. Here, we've discovered is best of all, a little away from the penta-centre, and beneath the surface of the city. Dead centre, it could not receive at all, and out towards the periphery its powers diminished proportionately. Its topological status is distinguished from the rest of New Stoke, including the under-city. It is inside the torus, as are we at this moment.'

Very, whose maths were by his own admission weak, was paying scant heed to what Julie was saying, instead was sniffing the air.

'Babies, sea-shores, mountain tops, and the heavenly aroma of Candle's breath when she'd been exerting herself,' he concluded, giving his nose a congratulatory wipe with the back of his hand.

Apart from this last, of which he couldn't speak, Mesmer could only agree with Very's diagnosis.

While they'd been talking the moister-oyster had deepened its hue towards a deep carmine, and its motion had become more labile, so that one moment it had all the delicate complexity of a snowflake, the next the endless spiral of a helix, now a protoplasmic formlessness. Its orbiting pearls had increased their velocity and range, flying in great curves almost to the boundaries of the surrounding chamber.

'It seems,' said Mesmer, 'to be responding to something.' Julie smiled, and favoured him with a long and tender look. 'It's because there's a Journeyer so close at hand.'

'Me?' said Mesmer, taken aback.

'It wants you to approach,' said Julie.

In front of him the translucent body towered up, while the composite aroma from it was like a physical force. He wasn't sure whether he felt joy or apprehension. Slowly he walked towards it, along the ultra-glass bridge, until he stood within touching distance of its surface, now almost still but for a continuous tremor, and spherical in shape. Around it the pearls whirled so fast as to leave only the mark of their passage, like the wake of an ocean-going schooner under way, a tracery of bands binding him into the space of the moister-oyster.

'Go on, sprout,' he heard Very say, as from a great distance. 'One last step.'

And Julie, 'It can do you no harm. It is utterly benevolent.'

Then, incredibly, it was all around him, supporting him, warm and slippery, the most delightful and uncanny of sensations. Somehow he could still breathe, though the substance of it had entered his nose and mouth, had descended into his lungs, had filled his every orifice and pore. Nor was his vision impaired either, for he could still see Julie and Very, but distortedly, as if they belonged to another element. Inside the sphere he could see hundreds of brilliantly coloured motes, like the tropical fish in the lagoons off the coral reefs of Angle Sea. As he peered closer he saw that they were indeed the tiniest of fish, each one different from all others.

With a feeling of calmness such as he'd not known before, not even at the breast of his dear breast-mother, he waited for whatever it was the moister-oyster wanted from him.

One fish, a tiny streak of red, was dancing before his eyes. A moment later it swum into his left nostril. He could feel the squiggle of its passage through his nose, back into his throat, into his windpipe, down the bronchi into the recesses of his right lung, giving him a tickling sensation between his third and fourth ribs. Once more it was on the move, upwards now, up into his throat, down again to his stomach, a fluttering moth of a fish, passing into the coils of his intestines, round and about, to emerge suddenly from his anus. Two loops it made around his surprised body, before plunging inwards once again through his urethra, down to his right testicle, up into his bladder, and out again through his penis. Twice more it swum around his body, this time about a vertical axis, passing from his abdomen up in front of his face, over his head, down behind his back and between his legs. Finally it stopped suddenly six inches in front of his face and floated there motionless.

Mesmer noticed that the brilliant red integument had apparently suffered some slight damage from its travels, a series of scratches along its tiny flank. He'd been staring at it for some few seconds before it occurred to him the scratches were in fact letters.

Concentrating his vision to the scale of the minute script, he mouthed each letter in turn.

R, E, A, D, he read, READ.

He became aware of a shaking all around and inside him, a series of convulsions that stopped momentarily, only to be renewed with increased vigour. The rhythm and interludes reminded him of something, though at first he couldn't say exactly what. Only when he felt his own lips draw back from his teeth, and his mouth open wide, with his head thrown back, did he realise that the moister-oyster was caught up in the throes of evidently uncontrollable laughter.

III

GREY DAGGER

Without preamble, a fact of the case.
(8) Having delivered himself of his Blue Prints, Mesmer cast around for the next stage of his project, increasingly perceived in terms of necessity, though to or for what he was not yet able to say. Pleading indisposition, he rarely left his room in the Partridge home, and would sit for hours cross-legged on his bed staring at the space on his wall between a poster of Karl Marx and a Pacific idyll by Gauguin titled Day of the God. At last he sensed a way forward, and at night, in order to avoid notice, ventured forth into the gardens of suburban Stockport to hunt pebbles of a precise size and roundness. Within a week he had procured a dozen, indistinguishable but for variations in colour, which he swallowed one evening with the aid of several pints of Boddington's bitter, a beer that he had found acted upon him as a laxative. For three days following he examined his faeces, until he had recovered all twelve. These, carefully washed, he lined up on his window sill and proceeded to hurl at passersby in the reverse order of their emergence from his bowel. The penultimate, named Red Snapper on account of an ochrous tinge to it, he was pleased to see picked up by the anonymous pedestrian it had struck and put in her coat pocket, for luck, he felt sure. The last he named Grey Dagger, wrapped in cotton wool, and hid away in his chest of drawers until he should be ready to make use of it in the next stage of his enterprise.

*

During the four and a half months following his incorporation into the moister-oyster Mesmer remained in New Stoke, as much a member of that city's sifting-shifting as any other. He saw little of Very during this period, for the old man was involved in setting up a school to teach the art of the circus, a project that found instant popularity among the youth of the town.

Many were the tales Mesmer might have told of that fine summer. He could have told, for example, of April and May's excursion to central Asia to watch Tash Kent play P. King in the semi-finals of the World Cup and how they'd returned via Pan Tan Zania with solidos of wild life all mixed up with those of the six brilliant goals of the match. Told too of the theatricals he played in through the ducts of the under-city, along with a co-cast of five hundred, in celebration of the kamikaze shit-cultists of the late twentieth century, whose awful power to strike back through the wastepipes of Whitehall had demoralised a whole generation of top civil servants. Or of his nights in the New Stoke banlieu, with only his allcock for company, getting amazing shots of owls and listening to the song of the nightingale. He could have told of Doris M'Tali, chef at the Cheery Wryneck, with whom he struck up a friendship based on a shared taste for exotic confectionery, and who'd been as good as her promise when she left for the salmon project in South Greenland to beam him in the latest each evening around nine should he wish to tune in on his allcock. Or of the two oldsters, off on their Pyrenean trip, who projected him a solido each week of the highlights of their trekking. Then, too, there was much to relate about his involvement with the sifting-shifting, variously plying a gondola up and down the Trent after April and May had shown him how to handle the great oar, learning from Julie the maths of separation equations and her celebrated negentropic series, and helping tend the moister-oyster with the children of the city. He might have told of the mental mathematics he'd enjoyed with April and May, beside which his first encounter with them in the pub overlooking the Trent had contained only the most elementary geometry.

But of all the stories he'd have liked to tell, none would have been so richly textured, so finely crafted, so narratively moving or so endlessly resourceful as that of his and June's romance. From the instant of his entering her spell, through all the elaboration of her charms, he'd found with her deeper enchantment even than Elmsfootloose had prepared him to expect on his Journey. At night, beneath the eaves of the Cheery Wryneck, when she came to visit him from her house on the Village green, they'd enjoy magic like he'd never known. He came to read the colouration of her electronic irises, from the deep cobalt of her rare fury to the rose-flecked azure of her most extreme innocence, and to respond to the rhythms of her pubic strobe, at times so complex as to outplay the most supple-wristed of drummers. How he loved to lie with her, sensing the ever-changing swirl of her nutrient graft by his adjacent cheek, bound together in the field of their bodies-electric, glimpsing odd scenes from movies on her filmic tooth.

Or, sometimes, he'd visit her and Julie in their thatched cottage, to enjoy the excellence of their cooking and afterwards to go upstairs with them to their marvellous five-sided bed, there to experience once more the inexhaustible repertoire of the youknow-duo.

But the summer of 2411 was drawing to a close, with still autumn, winter and spring before the year was up, and intuitively he knew his Journey would not end in New Stoke, happy though he'd be otherwise to spend the rest of his life there. One evening in mid-September, with the first nip of autumn in the air, he was sitting with June and Julie in front of the fire blazing in the hearth, when he announced that on the morrow he must Journey on.

*

Outside the leaves have started falling, induced by gales of exceptional ferocity this equinox. Inside the fire flickers in the grate, inviting adverbs like cheerfully or brightly, which I decline. The sensitivity I display in listening to his tale, emoting just enough to thicken the air around the couch with an aura of receptivity and not so much as to intrude upon the more exquisite details of the telling, finds a corresponding reticence to impose upon the attentions of the student the affairs of my heart. Only the requirements of the case make me yield up what good taste and a knowledge of the use such titbits get put to would keep under wraps. The rattling of my syntagmatic chains doesn't only keep me awake at night I might add, ah thank you Sonia, a mid-evening tisane may be just what is needed to loosen the bowel of my prose, and would you be so kind as to remove this ashtray in which two cigar butts are preparing to copulate.

Twice married, I, Reed, have again contracted to enter the state of holy matrimony. Not only Mesmer, but I, have been busy these weeks, as his time has caught up with mine. Sonia has consented to become my bride.

Sonia, I said, perfect happiness would be mine if you would consent to become my bride. Gulliver, she purred, revealing in her sweetly scented exhalation the label I acquired at an early age and that has travelled with me ever since, you are a liar. Not I, madam, I replied with formality, as the occasion demanded, I am quite serious. Serious, she said, but truthful? Both, I said definitively. In that case, she said after a minute in which my held breath threatened to tear wide the tattered and multiply-patched fabric of my lungs, I will.

Perfect happiness, complete without a verb.

I said, I have drawn this up with the aid of Smallpiece and Cohen, there should be nothing missing. She placed the carefully worded document next to her glass without looking at it. And there's this, I continued, and removed from my pocket the ring with the single stone, a white diamond with a curl of yellow in its depth, a flaw I judged would signify all that might mar the perfection of our union. She placed it on her finger. In the gloom of the restaurant it condensed what little light there was and beamed it forth like a beacon into my love-struck gaze. Lovely, she said. Another bottle? I suggested. Why not? she said, and drained her glass. I indicated the heavy sheaf in front of her. Not for me, my dear, to intrude upon that which chance in its mysterious way has deemed possible, the coming together of two souls, the one saved from the pit only by the wealth of an experience sufficient to pay off the narrative demands of Old Nick himself, the other so finely wrought in so delicate a . . . Gulliver, she interrupted. Yes? I replied. Your sleeve is in the butter, and weren't you going to say something about this? This being the contract, there beside her glass, now being filled by the flunkey in blue, how I detest these contemporary departures from black in the dining room. Catching hold of the document while indicating to the waiter he should do something about the smear of grease violating my cuff, this something promptly executed with a hot towel and wedge of lemon a miracle materialised in his hand, I said, Exactly. The terms of our marriage. All these clauses are to protect you, and to allow me merely to sniff the spoor of your passing. Like what? she said. Like, I said, you shall have your own room to remain sacrosanct at all times, across the corridor from our marital suite, wherein no more than once a week shall you be required to avail yourself for your husband to do with you what he will, and can. Go on, she said, chewing reflectively upon a morsel of bread. Your allowance will be, and I named a figure suitably indexed for inflation. What else? she murmured. On the subject of any extra-marital adventures you embark upon, and I assume there must be at least one to compensate you for the disqualified conjugal member, I require only that you keep them from the press and allow me the secondhand pleasure of hearing what I want to know about your exploits. Should children ensue from any such alliance I shall be prepared to turn a blind eye to their genetic endowment though not to their education, which must include the classics and French. I should like, though this is not written in, you to share one meal in three with me, lunch by preference, that pivotal hour around which the day rotates. Anything else? she asked, fixing me with an eye whose precise hue currently eludes me. Well, I said, and proceeded to enumerate the remaining items, counting them off on the fingers of both hands, until I was stuck with a sole thumb stuck up, as if attendant upon the beneficence or lust of a passing motorist. That, she said, what's that one for? Strangely, I couldn't remember. I can't remember, I said. In that case, she said, as the band launched into a sugary Blue Moon, you'll permit me to specify it for you? Do, I said. A pen, please, she demanded, and I held out my hand for the next miracle, completed in a record-breaking ten seconds. There, I said, and passed it to her. She wrote, beneath the last ornate paragraph of legalese, That all above be null and void. Sonia, I exhaled, shocked, this renders you liable to exploitation. I am a simple girl, she said, and wish to live unconditionally. Amen, I said, and seized the beribboned wodge, tore it in half, and half again, thrust the drawn and quartered pieces into the ice-bucket.

To us, she toasted, touching her glass to mine. The champagne fizzed, as in my head our future.

*

The two women did not seem surprised by the news of his intended departure. For a while neither spoke, but regarded him steadily and gravely.

'We knew you would decide to go,' said Julie at last, breaking the silence. 'We have been expecting it since the new moon, and it is now full. Therefore what we are about to say is in accordance with our heartfelt wishes, and should not be assumed to be a passing whim. You explain, June.'

June moved a little closer to Mesmer, and took his face between her hands. Gazing at her, he was overcome as always by the luminous crescent caressing her face, by the irises whose colours told him so much. Now they were the deepest green, like a Northern sea.

'I shall come with you.'

'But why?' Mesmer gasped, caught between the joy of her continued presence and the thought he might be the one to come between, however briefly, two such as her and Julie.

'Not only because your aura complements mine, but also because we understand more than you do about the nature of your Journey.

Remember we have both travelled the path you take. Remember too New Stoke is not without its special wisdom, gleaned over the centuries of making merry with magic.'

'What is it you know that I don't?'

Julie placed her hand upon his, and continued, 'It concerns the old one, with whom you arrived, and with whom you will also depart.'

'Very? But he's busy with his training project. You should see the high wire he's strung up over the Trent.'

'We have,' said Julie, 'and know full well the good he's doing. Nevertheless we are not mistaken.'

'And April and May. They've been gone on him ever since he told them he was Vladimir Illich, my first day in New Stoke. They'll be terribly upset.'

June said, 'The winkies are getting too old to play with the gerries all the time. They'll soon be leaving the clitoral-littoral, and will become interested in girls and boys nearer their own age. They'll get over him in three days flat, don't you worry.'

Julie said, 'Listen to us tell what we know. Are you ready?'

Mesmer nodded, and looked from one woman to the other, the one so fair, the other so dark, Julie who had borne May, June who had borne April, his day and his night, so wise and so tender, his darling youknow-duo.

Julie began, 'That which he bears shoulder-perched across a time-fault.'

June took up the refrain, 'An entity malcontent with what and where it is.'

Once more Julie, 'Intent upon restitution to a world of its own choosing.'

Again June, 'Attached by karmic threads to your own person.'

'Feeding on energy that it once more may be free.'

'Has it a name?'

'Has it a sex?'

'I have an idea,' said Mesmer, 'from what Very told me by the penta-centre my second day in New Stoke that it has both, the first Candle, the second female.' He looked from June to Julie and back again, wondering whether he'd elucidated or merely intruded.

June spoke in turn, 'Candle Light, queen of the circus, high-wire artiste, tumbler and trapezist.'

'Who fell into a tank of gasoline, putting herself out with a greater flame.'

'In order,' Mesmer explained, 'that she might go out like a Light.'

'Self-extinction,' said June.

'Auto-destruction,' said Julie.

'Not without its karmic risks,'

'Whatever your after-politics.'

'Requiring return to restore the balance.'

'What if she was pushed?' Mesmer asked, never having thought such a thing before. 'What then?'

'If,' Julie emphasized.

'Then,' June went on, 'the same rule would apply.'

'Return.'

'To exact restitution.'

'At the place of her extinction.'

'At Wick.'

'In the circus.'

'But how?' Mesmer asked.

'Through the agency of the dragon's tooth.'

'Talisman to which you are evidently susceptible.'

'And the power of a youthful Journeyer.'

'Flux,' said Mesmer. Then as an afterthought, 'But if so who on earth could have pushed her?'

'No one on earth,' said June.

'Because impervious to the noble-global,' said Julie.

'Therefore from another time.'

'Pre-historical.'

'One for whom Candle is but a disguise.'

'Behind which to enact her purpose.'

'Or his, I suppose,' Mesmer put in. 'What can it all be about? And why should it have anything to do with me?'

'Questions,' said June.

'For which there are no easy answers,' said Julie.

'But this we can say.'

'That Very seeks to rekindle his Candle.'

'That you are the one to show him how.'

'But how? I don't know,' Mesmer protested.

'Nor us.'

'The Journey will take care of that.'

'One way or another.'

'But further.'

'Whatever is behind Candle.'

'Of which Very knows nothing.'

'Is what has drawn Very to you.'

'And will make him seek to take you north.'

'To the circus.'

'At Wick.'

Mesmer felt drained of purpose by all these seemingly unavoidable indications. He said nevertheless, 'But I am set on going south. To Bright On. And thence to Medi Terra. What's to stop me?'

'Arriving, nothing.'

'But not leaving, that may be different.'

'There being forces that increase with distance.'

'Like those binding quarks together.'

'Or conjured up in spells.'

'Ah, yes,' said Mesmer to June, with all the certitude of recently gained experience, 'that I can understand. To be away from you now would exert a terrific pull. And the further, I feel sure, the greater.'

'For me too,' said June, simply.

'You?' said Mesmer, taken aback.

'You are not without charm yourself. And no spell binds without interaction.'

'She's as hooked as you, you foolish boy.'

So saying, Julie put her arms around June, and continued to address Mesmer. 'You see, not only to help you master the vicissitudes of the flux, but because you are a peach. She must go with you, to be able to return to me.'

In the hearth a log crackled and a spurt of gas from its interior ignited, causing the shadows of the trio by the fire to dance on the walls.

'Tonight,' said Julie, 'we must celebrate, starting here and now with the three of us. Much energy must be released to send you on your way.'

*

Our nuptials have been arranged for six weeks hence, at Martinmas.

Of possible invitees and among my co-clinicians, Beanbag is at least amusing, with his ingrained propensity to exaggerate, and his wife bears a reputation among the junior hospital fraternity for her unparalleled orgonotic streaming, a veritable Nile in flood, goes the word in the corridors. But Beanbag means Toegrind, most unamusing of men, for ever on the lookout for converts to his faith in therapeutic massage, while his wife has recently taken to hypnosis in addition to pills and hysterical pregnancies. And Beanbag and Toegrind would entail the Satyr of the Tavi, the goat-reeking Dr Murgatroyd, whose initial examination of the female mind requires the body unadorned upon the couch and whose only other known pastime is the trumpeting of his enviable rate of cure. I think Murgatroyd's forepaw groping its way into bridesmaids would not set the seal on what Sonia means when she says, Not a big one, Gulliver, but a proper one. Sonia, my treasure, I reply, it will be as you have always dreamed it should, allow me to shave the guest list a fraction closer to the bone.

My acquaintances of ex-wives, past mistresses, bosom pals, accountants, lawyers, Nobel Prize winners, ministers, gillies and the grateful cured who renew their severance gift with cards of remembrance every Christmas, contains fewer candidates than might be supposed, for many of them are dead, and are not therefore the company they once were.

Of those currently in my care, Mrs Minceberger would choose to see design of the most malevolent kind behind the random movements and impassive masks of the waiters waiting. Baroness Tree would not content herself with eyeing said Claridges minions, other more active senses would be called into play. And, to take but one further example to establish the hypothesis beyond fear of refutation, Mrs Skywide's poodle could not be left off the list were she to be on it, and I have not yet reached the stage of senility where I am indifferent to having my Krug lapped up by hounds.

Sonia, I remarked after one such list-constructing session, this is going to be a lop-sided affair, what with your West Country multitude hiring coaches and sportscars for the occasion, perhaps we should have it in a registry office after all. You promised, Gulliver, she said with what I can only call finality, and indeed I had, having made a considerable donation to the Restore The Spire Fund in the parish I deemed suitable for our betrothal, thereby to rid the admittedly progressive priest of any late doubts concerning the marriage of one already twice divorced to another fifty or more years his junior. Indeed I have, I reassured her, there will be no backtracking from me, and if it means that the pews to the right of the aisle be under-subscribed, I shall not be looking over my shoulder, but only into your eyes, my darling.

Who's to be the best man? she asked suddenly and apropos of nothing. I haven't given the question much thought, I replied, truthfully enough, having entirely forgotten the existence of the office in my haste to make her mine. Don't you think it's time you did? she asked. It was a question whose implications I debated before replying, Beanbag, I suppose, better him than Toegrind. Better, Gulliver, she said, is hardly best. But better, I managed to rejoin, than the merely good.

On that inconclusive comparison we abandoned the subject to parley of the repast we would put on, where I sensed I had once more the edge.

*

The farewell revel didn't take long to spread from the thatched house by the Village green, aided as it was by April and May's excited departure with the news, after they'd arrived and had shed a tear at the prospect of one of their mommas being away. 'But I shan't be long gone,' June had said.

At that April had begun to dance a jig, was soon joined by May and together they'd danced out of the door. Neighbouring children were the next to join in, bringing with them instruments and the odd adult, always that much slower, even in 2411, to respond to changes in the body-atmospheric. By midnight a great bonfire was blazing on the green, with children dancing round it chanting negentropic spells to keep the hot drinks hot and the iced ones icy. The bandstand from then on was never quiet, as many a band climbed up and performed, with songs composed for the occasion and lyrics wishing Mesmer and June flux speed on the morrow. From the vantage point of the old oak next to the pub named after it, up which at some point he was hoisted, Mesmer could see the outline of the pentacle glowing in the night, with each of the gates as the brilliant apices of the star. Even as he watched the fountains began their fiveplay, and with amazement he realised all of New Stoke was in on the party. Fireworks shot high along the length of the Trent, and from the other fifths of the city the sounds of revelry wafted through the night. Rare wines were brought up from cellars, huge soufflés were baked. In the swirling patterns of dance he lost sight of June and Julie, and when he descended the tree to find them he was caught up in a general movement towards Downtown and the river. A while later he found himself on one of the terraces of the Flaming Flamingo, wondering whether to take a dive fully clothed into the Trent below him, until he was dragged into a debate about the effects upon the body-symbolic of certain herbs and fungi for which the Flaming Flamingo was renowned. What potions he imbibed in the course of the conversation he was unable later to recall, nor how he got from there to the broad back of an elephant, seated next to June, while the great beast sprayed them with rose-scented water from its trunk. When someone suggested a gondola race within minutes fifty of the craft were jostling down the river, their occupants struggling with oars and gasping with laughter, Mesmer himself next to April and May, adding his weight to their skill, a combination such that when they passed beneath the winning bridge, no-one was in front of them. For a brief interlude he was cycling around the cobbled streets of Old, with Julie, discussing separation equations and sewerage aesthetics. Later, he was lying on his back in soft earth, between two late-flowering shrubs, listening to the thump of rock music from the direction of Downtown overlaid with the pensive lilt of a violin trio from a balcony in Town, conversing with the moon. It is possible he dozed off in this comfortable position, for the next thing he was aware of was a lightening in the eastern sky and the excited chatter of children. Sitting up, he saw not twenty yards from him the figure of Very Light urging on Bert with one winkie in the saddle and a dozen more queueing up for a ride.

'Bright morning to you, sprout,' called out the trapezist. 'Rumour has it you're on your way, and since so far our paths have run parallel, it would be a shame to allow them to become otherwise.'

'Flux, Very, you do look fresh,' said Mesmer, feeling far from it himself. And indeed, the old timer was decked out in newly laundered gear, with his silken wraparound crisp, and his pantaloons fairly glistening.

'As I am, dear lad, having given myself over to sleep while all around they surrendered to the grape and other gifts of nature. As is Bert, also. We are ready to go whenever you are.'

'Have you seen June?' said Mesmer, wondering perhaps whether he might postpone his departure for a day in order to recuperate.

'Indeed I have. She said she'd be outside the Village Gate at eight prompt. It is now seven.'

One hour later, thanks to the foresight of the landlord of the Cheery Wryneck in preparing Golden and to the assistance of a good many other New Stokers in other respects, Mesmer was able to ride through the Village Gate, with Very jogging along behind on Bert, to find June waiting where she said she'd be, astraddle a snow-white palfrey, looking as if she'd slept through the night instead of dancing till dawn.

*

I have managed, in the intervening days, to relay by word of mouth, before the embossed invitations are loosed into the infinite void of the mail service, my intention to ask, among those whose paths have intersected mine, and have received positive indications. Beanbag has accepted the role of homo optimus with an alacrity that inclines me to reassess the roots of the Reichian will to pleasure, could it be a sublimation of more primal symbolic bliss? Thus fortified, I reneged on my promise to exclude the unreliable, and have extended the paw of hospitality to the lot, co-healers, the mad, my surviving retinue, not least among them Mesmer himself. That he has répondu oui without equivocation I put down to Sonia's phrasing of the invitation. She conducts this business with an acumen it is a joy to behold. I only hope I don't let her down by dying before the day.

Enough now of our party, still in the future by a month or more, and return to the aftermath of his, this dawn departure along doubtless yet another post-mechanical highway, rabbit strewn and pearly with dew, ah me, how happily would I convert it to macadam and re-introduce the internal combustion engine, as he this morn, I'd guess, if he has anything like the hangover he deserves. While they get set for a lengthy trudge through the shires, all a-drip with autumn, I shall take the opportunity to reveal a slice of my life, those years wherein and whereby I became what I am, a permanently shrunken shrink.

My trainer was a gentle intelligent man, given over to matching socks and ties in primary colours, and formed in the first explosive years of our science by one formed by Freud himself. During the fifteen hundred hours I logged on his couch, mumbling, cajoling, threatening, stammering, whimpering and telling stories, his silences spoke volumes more than my own ravings and his few words rang unutterably true. It would be nice to recall what essential verities he did convey from behind the couch to the prostrate student upon it, but transference and repression since have taken their toll of such accuracy. In the place of definitive history I can only offer the questions I would put now were I where I was when I failed to put them, and continue to associate with panache. Like, with Sonia in mind, that old acorn, What does a woman want?, a teaser I must put to Mesmer on my wedding day, if his revolutionary guard is not up against a fruity reply. Or, attributing omniscience to the interlocutor, When, precisely, will my toecap make contact with the bucket?, Will then the composite grammar of my self follow my constituent atoms down the terminal plughole, never to flow again freely from the silver tap of discourse?, and, mesmerising God entirely, What, in a word, will be the future of the human race, fifty, five hundred, five million years from now? My memory jogged by anthroposophy, I did in fact put a series of queries to my real mentor beyond the couch concerning pricks and nipples, following on from his pointing out that I'd transposed the n and c in the word 'principle' in a letter I'd sent him on the subject of analytic integrity. A tissue of lies, had been my first response to this intelligence, until he'd produced the offending text, and I'd had to admit the truth of it. Quite often I loathed him as much as I gave him reason to grow weary of me, and once spent two weeks determinedly saying not a word, figuring quite wrongly it would hurt him more than me. Only when I detected a stifled yawn behind me did I resume speech, and then only after a bout of crying that could only be stemmed by his offering me a stick of barley sugar he kept in a tin on his desk, presumably for just such emergencies. Thinking of him now, I do so with nothing but gratitude. Such power as I possess I owe to him, and for all my ill-mannered irascibility, my thoughtless pre-occupation with pleasures I'm in no state to enjoy, and my heartless treatment of the symptoms of our times, I can still use it to give help to those in need, and in pocket. I know full well my cure fails the wider criterion of health, that one should not become ill in the first place, but then I am a representative of my class, bound by its historical mission, now nearing its end by the signs I read in the wind, and am therefore unable to countenance the greater prophylaxis Mesmer and his ilk can lay claim to. There is much in his vision that is attractive, but as well as classbound I am bound by the discipline I am heir to and can only treat his ultra-world as symptomatic and continue to dog him through its vales and byways.

Yerse. These amateur philosophic nights close in around me whenever I think of my guide and trainer, dead now these forty years. Better that I drive him from my mind than let more such self-indulgent fancies invade the case. I deal in what is strictly necessary, no more.

*

As the days shortened and the trees of the Great Midland Forest took on the brilliant shades of autumn, the trio wound their way through the shires, towards South England's most populous city, Bright On. They passed through the industrial complex of Brum, with its termini and auto-factories visible now and then in the Sitka spruce and sequoia of the region, turning out the basic products for the sifting-shifting, with not another human in sight, apart from a party of children and their teachers discoursing on maintenance. A week later they were riding beneath the Cotswold edge, through the Vale of Evesham, visiting some of the mobile communes gathered as they were for a Romany festival. Then up through the old stonewall country, where grazed the semi-wild sheep used by the toiler-soilers in the making of their fabulous cheese, the dizzying Cotswold blue. The change from limestone to chalk was matched by the heightened astral tension of the Wiltshire downs, so that as they passed close by Avebury ring June's strobe pulsed incessantly, and when they reached Stone Henge, even Very's beard began to curl. They kept going at a steady pace until they reached Salisbury, where the solido studios ensured there would be action of a kind not found in the villages they'd stayed in so far. As luck would have it, the whole town, save the spiritualists who lived only for the flux and rarely left the Cathedral precinct, were engaged in a period reconstruction of the films of Genre-Look Godard, always a favourite among the Wessex intelligentsia. But the threat of Christmas snows moved them on, through the backwoods of the Hampshire plain, where they saw bear and the fleeting shape of wolves through the trees. By the time they joined the beaten track of the South Downs Way, the temperature was dropping fast into the traditional cold of the midwinter festival, and flakes of snow were beginning to blow into their faces. Away to the south the sea looked grey and wintry, with barely a sail to be seen. They rode three abreast, thankful for the heat generated by Mesmer's allcock and projected into their underclothes. There were few fellow-travellers now, most preferring the buses that left their trails overhead, or the tube which could be heard whistling through the treetops, a flash of silver against the brown of the woods below them in the valley.

Bright On, when it appeared over the brow of the down, was in spectacular contrast to all the rurality they'd enjoyed since leaving New Stoke.

Architecturally, the city was constructed around the principle of change within continuity, so that from month to month whole sections of the town would be altered, from the foundations upward. The architectural revo of the twenty first century had coincided with the original rebuilding of the town, after the Great Rage. It was said that no two buildings were alike, nor was any given building the same for more than a week. Yet what in the Californian Redoubt had led to anarchy, in Bright On resulted in what all were agreed was the most satisfying of cities. The rate of change was such that no sensibility was affronted by the difference between today's Bright On and yesterday's, for the sifting-shifting was directly linked to the regional pressure from the noble-global. At the same time the past was preserved in a continual reworking of its traces, so that the Pavilion in August 2411 might have been just as

Mrs Fitzherbert would have remembered it, while now in December it might sport a chinoiserie history's accidents had never allowed to develop.

It was said too that this city of half a million, cupped into the interface between downland and sea, enjoyed a complexity of culture consonant with its architecture. The various levels of production, admin and maintenance, while responsive to the noble-global, provided local solutions to regional requirements, so that the body-social was both universal and unique. Those who migrated to Bright On did so in the knowledge that their lives would thread through the multiply interlocking rings of the city giving them experience impossible to imagine beforehand, and for those born and raised there the curious simplicities of the remainder of the region held out an equal though different potential. Bright On had no centre, only a balance of interests, forever changing as new desires entered the body-symbolic, calling forth new projects, new enterprises, new social groupings, new art, new knowledge. And its relation with the region was such that each provided what the other lacked. The region supplied the supportive strength without which Bright On would have disintegrated into chaos, and it originated change to feed through the regional grid, preventing it from settling into cultural stasis. New Stoke's magic, the bucolic life of Stock Port, the intellectual ferment of the Wessex villages, all these and more might have become ingrown and petrified without the influx from Bright On. All this, of course, was elementary algebra from the theory of regional difference.

But to remain within the boundaries of this marvellous city was not the intention of the mounted three, for Mesmer's sense of what was right required that he at least travel on beyond the shingle of Bright On's famous beach. And where Mesmer wanted to go, his two companions were happy to follow. They would find a boat, therefore, either a three-crewer to sail themselves, or a larger vessel if any were setting off to their destination, fabulous Medi Terra, greatest city of the West, sea-city extraordinary, matched only by that mighty air-city of the East, Ching, floating like gossamer above the basin of the Hwang-ho.

*

Never has it been my policy to offer premature interpretations, on the principle that the good analyst is the one who takes his time, or hers, yet I cannot help pass comment on the changed tempo of his travels. From Stoke to Brighton in one session, covering most of a session from the tell-tale meteo traces, has me panting to keep up. Can it be he is eager to have this over and done with? He has promised me a year and a day, and I have promised him nothing, explaining that analytic time is not to be measured in anything except hours, and even those are suspect. Five weeks, five years, who knows? I said. Sure, was his laconic reply.

Limited case space presses me towards a solution of current problems, of which the most pressing is the distribution of my flock among the ragged shepherdry to hand. A three month honeymoon I have told them all is not excessive when one considers the ages I have had to wait, and the danger I may not return from it alive. My mad cannot be left to their own lethal devices during the long months of winter, arrangements must be made. The Baroness to Murgatroyd, I think, their libidos should find sufficient in common to while away the hours, and Spein-Chiller for Toegrind, another deserving pairing, that may even do one or the other of them some good. Beanbag has nobly offered to take on Mrs Skywide, and any others I may have trouble disposing of, such is his devotion to me since the gift of best manhood. I told him he'd find one woman and a dog quite enough to fill his schedule, without overloading it, and with thanks, that I'd leave the rest to the locums. Only my fear that his wedding present will prove to be a hand-tooled-leather-bound edition of 'The Function of the Orgasm' prevents me establishing with him that full rapport that is the test of true friendship. Or from handing Mesmer over to him. He, Mesmer, is the most intractable of my current difficulties, when all around I see nothing but the hamfists of my confrères, whereas what is needed is kid gloves. Nor can I leave him to wander unaccompanied all those weeks, he might get anywhere, somewhere I might never find him. One plan, far from satisfactory, would be for him to send his slabs of narrative to our hotel in Cannes, where I would peruse them, scrawl annotations in the margin, and return them posthaste. Though the pen and eye is a poor second to the tongue and ear in such things, there would seem to be no better solution, unless Sonia can come up with an idea, which is possible.

Actual events have proved me wrong then right, for between the possible and the actual there has been a phone call, from Sonia, from the Rolls, wherein she has had a radio phone installed, much to Michael's discomfiture. It's not that I'm against the instrument itself, sir, it's just that when you're driving along you don't want . . . Quite so, but I am not the one to reproach, Miss Petersen I think should be the object of your objection, and it may well be she who desires a word in my ear, if you would be so kind as to hand her the receiver. Yerse, because he has his hand forever on the wheel he imagines he has a right to invade . . . Sonia, I am indeed listening, no narrative device could ever obtrude between the vibrations of your dear larynx and those similar of my tympanic membrane.

Her suggestion is as simple as it is predictable, all things considered, which I've been scrupulously avoiding doing so these past weeks of pre-nuptial bliss. She wants to bring him with us, install him in a room adjacent to our bridal suite, and have me continue the analysis among the potted palms. You know you won't be happy unless you've got something to do, she said. True, Sonia. And you know what an important case this is for you. True again, my plum. And you've said if you can crack it it'll rank alongside Wolf Man and Senatspräsident Schreber. I've said that? And you've got to consider him, you know what you think of the rest of the street. I coughed. Well then! May I think it over?

And so I am, weighing up a preferred orthodoxy against the inspired heterodox, balancing the hard looks of my colleagues against the hard facts Sonia's enumerated, considering the practical implications of such a shift of venue and the arrangements that would have to be made, to my financial detriment, not that that matters when one is hot on the scent of a resolution. Finally, there is the suspicion concerning the one I love and the one I treat, these two in my life whose liaison blends with all the exquisite texture of a well-made mayonnaise, never forgetting the dash of vinegar, so essential to its perfection.

*

'There's a chance,' said June, as they rode down the prosaic-mosaic of the sea-front, 'if we head for the ultramarina, we'll find an old friend of mine, a real seabitch. She runs a mean sloop, and moors it in Bright On, or at least she used to. She was always ready to go anywhere for a good sail with an inexperienced crew.'

At her suggestion they broke into a canter, making a merry clatter over the unread text beneath their feet, until they reached the far end of the front and the beginning of the ultramarina.

'How shall we find her, even if she's here?' asked Mesmer, as they rode on to the first quay. In front of them were more ships than he'd ever seen, from great clippers, hulls freshly painted and rigging perfect, their decks bustling with folk eager to be off on the tide on some world trip, through schooners, sloops, cutters, ketches, luggers, yawls, junks, sampans and outriggers, down to the tiniest dinghies with five year olds at the helm, all clustered together along the quays, in endless profusion.

'If Beth's here,' said June confidently, 'we'll find her.'

And indeed, a couple of enquiries later, they were making their way in single file down one of the furthest jetties, with the sea sucking and smacking beneath them and the hooves of their beasts sounding hollowly on the wooden planks. Very, Mesmer noticed, kept casting uneasy glances downwards. He was about to make the suggestion that if perhaps Very was not the best of seafarers it would be the easiest thing for him and Bert to hop on the bus, to meet up later in some prearranged spot in Medi Terra, when the high flier said, 'Air's me element, sprout, I'll admit, and I have no deep longing for the briny like some I could name, but I wouldn't leave you now, just because the wind's picking up. I am a Light, remember, not as bright as Candle, tis true, but just as courageous.'

Some way in front of them now, June came to a halt and dismounted. In the gathering dusk of the late afternoon her pubic strobe was pulsing the cheeriest yellow, a sure sign of greeting.

Seated on a capstan at the end of the jetty, smoking a cheroot, crooning a shanty, was a fine figure of a woman, no less than six foot four and two hundred and fifty pounds, blue-black in colour, and at seventy or so in the prime of life. As June approached she leapt to her feet, or as Mesmer saw, foot, in that her right leg below the knee consisted of an intricately carved wooden shaft.

'Splinter me good one,' she cried, 'if it's not my old mate June.'

With a shout of laughter she cracked the capstan with her wooden leg and enveloped June in her embrace.

A quarter of an hour later, all four of them were seated around the table in the galley of the Loaded Parrot, as Beth's boat was known, drinking rum, while below them in the hold Bert and the two horses munched hay.

'Hands,' said Beth, surveying Mesmer and Very a stern but kindly eye, 'is what I need. Can you both sail?'

Mesmer explained that he'd spent time plying a gondola in New Stoke the previous summer, not that it was the same thing at all as an ocean-going ketch.

'Sloop,' the seabitch corrected him.

'Sloop. And I am a fast and willing learner,' Mesmer concluded.

Beth reached out and ran an appreciative hand over Mesmer's upper arm and shoulder before slapping him heartily on the back and saying, 'You'll do. From now on you're crew if that's what you want.'

She now turned to Very and said, 'How about you, aged one?'

'As handy in the rigging as any you'll find,' said Very, 'despite me years. And me knots are the talk of the knotting fraternity. Ten seconds to tie and all day to unravel.'

'How are you in the hammock?' said Beth with the straightforwardness of one who'd spent her life before the mast.

Gathering up his beard in both hands, Very laid it on the table in a great mound and said, 'Madam, before you you see me beard. So much hair on me chin and so little on me head bespeaks me virility as well as me age. The only thing that worries me is balance. I might need a hand to steady me.'

Beth thumped her mug on the table. 'Spoken like a seadog. Barring accidents, we sail on the first morning tide.' To Mesmer and June she added, 'Excuse us, both. When the double hammock calls, the double hammock calls.'

'Candle,' said Very, 'couldn't have put it better herself.'

Throughout the remainder of the evening, as they cooked and ate a meal Mesmer and June were entertained by a whole symphony of sounds from beyond Beth's cabin door, including nautical expressions, circus cries, odd sentences in Russian, grunts of satisfaction, gasps, farts, the creaking of the hammock, the sound of wood on flesh, and of wood on wood, and on several climactic occasions, drowning out all else, a bout of braying from Bert, evidently responsive in the hold to the cavortings of his master's body-actual.

*

No word is innocent, that much I have learnt in my hundred years before the mast. Apart from my Olympian disregard of the antics of the buffoon and his belle, I shall not ask why it is that when 25th century prosthesis has presumably advanced way beyond its 20th century forerunner the seabitch must be lumbered with a wooden limb, knowing full well that the answers are to be found in the most elementary textbooks of my art, which Mesmer has no doubt been swotting up. Instead I remark the Loaded Parrot, subsequent to the Cheery Wryneck and the Flaming Flamingo the third of our feathered friends, revealing a general tendency to flight quite consistent with the appellation Partridge. Further, I note the field marks of this latest, a brilliance of hue and raucousness of voice appropriate to present company. Only the specific Loaded has me temporarily baffled, but that too must surely yield its meaning in the richness of time.

Tonight is my wedding night, and I write in a hotel room in Beauvais, having won my argument with Michael as to whether it was going to be the RN1 or the autoroute on condition it'll be the autoroute tomorrow. It has been a busy day, but one happily devoid of violence or untoward incident. No guests were set upon by security guards, the band played relentlessly on, Beanbag recited his lines without stammering or vomiting, even to applause, Murgatroyd made no obvious ploy for Sonia's fourteen year old cousin, delectable in russet organdie, and Mrs Spein-Chiller and Toegrind took to each other from the moment their adjacent knees hit the hassocks in the third row back on my side of the church. The Petersen legion turned out to be less legion than I'd imagined, less rustic too. Sonia's Dad, as she calls him, young Wilfred to me, ran a restaurant in Weston-Super-Mare for a number of years until staff problems and French menus drove him to other fields, I forget where. Her Mum was indistinguishable from the crowd, for which I was glad, having no wish to confront a mother-in-law, with all its attendant risks. Sonia and I converged on the altar without noticeable disapproval emanating from her front benches, thanks to the reek of sanctity and aftershave pervading the place from choir to bell-ringers. Sonia herself was transcendental in shantung, tulle and pearls, a triple rope reaching nearly to her knees, each silvery globule matched and taken only from the moistest of oysters, while her perfume concocted for the occasion and wafting from her in gusts as we stood before the priest was truly the invention of a mighty nose. We do, we intoned in unison, until death do us part.

Not least among the sitting, standing, quaffing, praying guests was he who at this moment I assume to be dreaming in his room at the end of the corridor, the object of this case history. The more I thought about Sonia's suggestion, the more practicable it became, given a certain amount of discretion in regard to my other patients, to avoid rivalry and charges of favouritism. He slipped out of the reception before us, made his way around the side clutching a bag I wouldn't care to live out of for an afternoon, let alone a season, there to meet up with us after we'd made our honoured exit.

I think I'd better sit in the front, I said, we've got a long way to go and I like to see where I'm heading, you get in the back with Sonia. Thus ensconced, we set out à trois, or quatre if one includes the driver, which in this demotic age I suppose one must. Our conversation en route was as merry as any I can recall, helped along by the two iced magnums Michael had foresightedly stowed in the boot. Mesmer proves to be something of a wit away from the couch, as well as so informed on the state of the world and nation as to consign me to another age. To Sonia, I said, after one amusing account of some Whitehall scandal entailing a short war in some farflung corner of the Empire and some enrichment of arms dealers and politicians, not all of them belonging to the Party I support, Are you too on the side of the oppressed? On and off, she said. Ha! I cried, a Red in my bed as well as under it. She then murmured something about bread and butter, Mesmer added something else about guns and butter, Michael damn him made a remark about driving on the left, and I was left wondering if the general hilarity was at my expense before concluding it couldn't be, not if I was paying. I accept, I said, that I am a member of a class in decline, what I cannot accept is that any prole futurity could rescale the heights of our once great culture, can anyone persuade me otherwise? Does it need to, so long as people get what they want? said Mesmer. What, I said, warming to this exchange of questions, if people want precisely the privileges your Leveller's regime would deny them? May I ask a question? said Sonia. Do you ever need to ask? I said. Wouldn't you say, she said, privileges were just a compensation for something else? Such as? I asked. How about good sex, good housing and an assured income? she said. Good Lord, Sonia, I said, have you been reading when you should have been receiving? May I see your passports, please? said a voice from nowhere. Why, said Mesmer, as we made our way towards what passed for the bar on what passed for a boat, do you assume tomorrow's wants will be the same as today's? Since they've always been power, wealth, fame, I replied, how can you imagine they won't be for ever? Shall I have champagne, said Sonia, or shall I have brandy? Why not have both, mixed? I suggested. Precisely, you can have all those mixed when you've solved the problem of scarcity, don't you see? said Mesmer, somewhat imprecisely, I thought. Power? I demurred. Try it? said Sonia. No thanks, said Mesmer, but don't you think I'm right? He's into a power trip, said Sonia, giggling. Aren't you, Gullie? Gullie? I said, shocked, Surely not the way to address your groom, my sweetest and ripest of nectarines? Are you patronising me, Gulliver? she said, giggling no more. Christ, this isn't going to be a matrimonial row, is it? said Mesmer. Will car passengers please return to their vehicles? said the voice from nowhere. Passeports, S.V.P.? said a heavily accented voice from elsewhere. Aren't you forgetting the State? said Sonia, surprisingly, to Mesmer. Sonia, I said, this is getting out of hand, an inkling of pink is one thing, a revo red altogether another, has he been indoctrinating you? Would you say your lot haven't? said Mesmer, with a truculent edge to his voice that I must in fairness attribute as much to the drink as to any vicious wish towards his analyst and friend. Do you think, I said to him, it's going to work, this experiment in cure? Is this Beauvais, so soon? said Sonia. It is, madam, said Michael, and drew to a halt outside our chosen hostelry.

Where room service is non-existent after eleven. Should I after all have taken Michael's advice on the matter of route and given us all over the far tenderer mercies of the Meurice? One last unanswered question before addressing myself to the pillow, next to my bride, this most precious of nights.

*

Waking to the warmth of June beside him and the swirl of her graft through the hair partially covering her face, he thought for a moment he was back in the Cheery Wryneck until the slap of wavelets nearby reminded him it was the Loaded Parrot that cradled him and his enchantress. Gently he disengaged himself from her limbs, clambered out of the hammock and made his way up on deck, thinking to take a quick plunge in the waters of the ultramarina before breakfast. As his head cleared the hatchway, he was surprised to see, not the forest of masts all around he'd expected, but the openness of the sea. Beth, it seemed, had set sail at first light, while her crew slept on unawares.

The sound of her wooden leg clumping along the deck made him turn.

'Morning,' she called, and threw a mop in his direction. 'Up in time to swab the deck.'

He set to with a will, and in no time had done that and a half dozen other seafaring tasks.

'Clean some herrings and then we eat,' said Beth.

So he joined her at the bucket she sat by, unhooked his allcock and pulled out the laser-sharp blade.

'Like this,' she told him, and with an old-fashioned knife slit the fish from end to end, throwing the innards high in the air over her shoulder, to be seized by a swooping gull. 'Easy.'

While they ate Beth yarned, punctuating her stories with emphatic taps and scrapes of her wooden leg on the deck. Listening to her, watching the sun break clear of a line of cloud, savouring the smell of fish, tar and hemp that characterised the Loaded Parrot, Mesmer could easily understand the lure of life on the ocean wave.

But of all the yarns she spun, none fascinated him so much as those concerning her Ponce, who'd sailed with her for thirty years before retiring into bee-keeping in the mountain fastness of the Sierra Nevada.

'The best cet-setter as ever whaled the seas, was Ponce, bar none. You should have seen him, sitting cross-legged in the bubble, with the cet-set on his head. Take it away, Ponce, I'd say, open it up, no crinkles on your cerebellum. Wipe his brow, I would, while the cet-set flashed every colour you've ever seen, and his mind reached out into the deep, every synapse jumping. Oh yes, those big cets love to play hooky on the time-line, inventing serialities just for the fun of it, trans-global counterpoint, even the baby whales not so dumb as they can't add a note, and Ponce's body shaking and sweating, and me checking the cet-set didn't overload and leave him stranded out there. He took them as they came, all across the sensory range and way out of it, with a smile tickling his ear lobes. Three days and three nights one trip lasted, and I kept dowsing him down, feeding him a sugar drip and holding his head when things got heavy. Girl, did I see energy, and did Ponce use it, when he was out there in the deeps with the humpbacked blue right grey killer white krill-eating lot of them.'

'Flux, seabitch,' said Mesmer, caught up by the feel of what she was saying, if not entirely the sense. 'I'd certainly like to try it out myself'

Beth laughed uproariously. 'Blow your cerebellum clear out of your arse. No chance.'

'Oh, well,' Mesmer said with resignation, 'you can't do everything on a Journey.'

'You a Journeyer?' Beth exclaimed, dropping her knife on the deck. 'You should've said so. Ponce always said nobody's readier for the cet-set than a Journeyer. Come on down. I'll show you around.'

The seabitch made her way to the bows of the boat and opened a hatch. Looking down, Mesmer could see a ladder leading to a transparent bubble, a hemisphere of glass, slung underneath the keel of the boat. There was just room enough for one person to sit inside it. Following her instructions he climbed down and settled himself cross-legged on the floor of it, which somehow moulded itself around him to provide a comfortable cushion and support. The pale aquamarine light permeating the bubble was immensely pleasant, and it would have required no effort to sit there for hours, watching the fish swimming along on the other side of the glass, peering in at him peering out.

'Ready?' came Beth's voice from the gloom behind him. 'For anything,' said Mesmer.

From above his head there descended into his field of view an apparatus of quite astonishing intricacy.

'The cet-set,' Mesmer breathed.

'Designed by Ponce himself.'

Its primal construction was evident enough, and consisted of a circular base designed to fit around the cranium surmounted by two arches intersecting at right angles. However, because of the armature of diamonds encrusting both base and arches aligned in such a way that each facet reflected other facets, each of these reflecting yet more in turn, the basic structure decomposed into an infinitude of mirror images. It was this complexity of reflection that would enable it, when empowered and placed on his head, Beth explained, to amplify and broadcast the endlessly changing fields of the body-electric, and to receive too those of the great cerebrating mammals of the ocean deeps.

'Can I try it straightaway?' Mesmer asked.

Before the seabitch had time to answer, Very Light's voice wafted down the hatchway behind him. 'Hold hard, sprout. Tisn't time methinks for whaling yet awhile. Wait till we get to Medi Terra, and your sealegs harden. If you want to take it, that's me advice.'

*

And mine, when the anagram ECT is so inescapable from the deplorably foreshortened cet that my snout is forced beneath the lexemic soil in the search for semic truffles. Mesmer, I protest, is this the gratitude I deserve after so many months of analysis, a barely understated preference for the barbarisms of my less fortunate colleagues? If electricity is what you want I'll turn you over to Dr Gridwort and his electrodes, though the resultant convulsions would end your story all too precipitously, without the climactic dénouement you doubtless have in store for us. And us, dear boy, is no editorial nicety or regal delusion, but the necessary corollary of analysis in the back seat, Sonia having kindly agreed to sit up front, next to the driver, whose ear also cannot be assumed to be utterly unhearing. Us, then, for the moment, it is. So speak not of premature termination, lest you deprive us of a good ending and miss out yourself on the bouillabaisse my Medi Terra so deftly concocts with her fish.

Paris is already some little way behind, and by the lick we are passing these Burgundian hills we should have no trouble in reaching the roadhouse in Roanne I have in mind for lunch, after which analysis will give way to digestion for the remainder of the day. Before that, and while still stimulated by the peripheral view of the city I love more than any other, excluding Rome, some memoirs are perhaps called for, and if perhaps not, are on the agenda nonetheless.

It was no accident, I am sure, that had me staying with a maître of renown when the cobblestones began to fly in May '68. We were debating the criteria for the termination of training analyses and letting loose their objects among the unsuspecting sick, when a whiff of tear gas clawed at my mucous membrane. Jules, as I shall call him, closed the windows of his comfortable apartment overlooking the Boulevard St Germain and poured me a glass of marc. It is a symptom, he said. Signifying? I said. Precisely, he said, and would say no more until we were down and out in the street below, where a torn jacket, some spilled paint, a few abandoned placards and a litter of gas cannisters were the only traces of the scene we had witnessed. Is it finished? I asked. Is it ever? he replied, and led me to a café where the waiter told us how three flics had clubbed a pregnant woman to the ground, not six paces from the outermost of his terrace tables. The woman? Jules asked. Taken away, the waiter said, by her friends. By the flics, the patronne insisted from within her cage. Shall we continue our stroll? Jules suggested.

Up past the Odéon a battle was in progress, one whose opposed forces have since exhausted the image-makers and wordsmiths, but at the time I snapped away with my Leica and spoke of two insect orders, the free-flying short-lived lepidoptera, tatterdemallion and flamboyant, versus the massed ranks of coleoptera, shinily blue-black, encased in armour. As we two huddled in a doorway, referring to the former order, I said, Amazing, their resistance. That which resists, Jules said, speaks. My job is to overcome resistance, I said, but policeman I refuse to be. Your resistance does you credit, he replied, but you would do well to analyse your own implication in the regime the flics make possible. And you? I said. Am elsewhere, was all the clarification he would give me at this juncture, though when we were advised by a towering sergeant to be on our way lest misadventure befall us, he commented further, There are other regimes.

The friendly sergeant was dealing out justice by banging a boy's head against the wall of the Ecole de Médecine. Is there nothing we can do? I stormed. You wish, said Jules, to straddle the line between repressor and repressed, an impossibility, and very English. Whereas you, I replied, mustering a semblance of my native wit, wish to rub it out altogether, another impossibility, and very French. Touché, he conceded, and walked over to the representative of the law, with myself hard on his heels, to roundly curse him for his brutality. From the look on the sergeant's face, together with his raised club, it seemed as if we also, despite our age, would fall prey to his ire, but mercy or prudence prevailed and with a final crack of bone on stone he abandoned his victim to the blood bespattered pavement. Said victim, far from being unconscious, as I had assumed, hurled abuse at the departing policeman, thanked us for our timely intervention, and confided in us the adage that society was a carnivorous flower, before dashing off to join his beleaguered comrades. Not unmoved, I said to Jules, Carnivorous indeed, but I currently fail to detect its floral aspect. Jules shrugged the incomparable shrug of his nation, and said, Violence made manifest, and the liberal who grows fat on its latency begins to weep. It is the gas, I protested, wiping my face, and fat I have never been. Ask that student, Jules said, what he thinks of your sentiments. But I could not, for he was otherwise engaged in struggle. So it must be to Mesmer I turn, these dozen years later, if I want an answer, which I am not sure I do.

The only coda to my story is that I later discovered my treasured Lagonda had been fired by the mob. Fortunately, neither the French state nor myself were substantially out of pocket after our adventures, for the CGT got the workers back to work and my insurance coughed up handsomely. But for me at least, not being in a position to pass judgement on the French State, life would never be quite the same again. That

Lagonda was the last vestige of my youth. No more would I change down into howling third with the wind blowing in my face, my companion of the hour caressing the leather of the passenger seat with her silken bottom, urging me faster or beseeching me slower, according to temperament, which in the end came to the same thing, the immeasurable content of a warm cunt on a cold night.

And now, up in front, sits Sonia, endowed with one beside which others are but copies of the Original, and here sit I, in the back, as useless as a strip of chewed-over biltong. Beside me sits he whose illness leaves me baffled, when all that I have ever wanted from the world is diagonally opposite him, ready for the taking. And diagonally opposite me is Michael, driving. Mother of mercy, is this what Reed has come to, the redundant D in a quartet in C?

*

During their sea-voyage to Medi Terra Mesmer spent more and more time in the bubble beneath the prow of the Loaded Parrot, familiarising himself with the cet-set and its bejewelled mysteries. Even Beth's enthusiasm for ports of call, where as often as not she had an old seadog waiting for her, failed to turn his attention.

'You go,' he'd say, when the option of going ashore arose. 'I'm quite happy here.'

Then, with the Loaded Parrot gently rocking at her moorings and nobody on board, the animals as much as folk enjoying a walk on dry land, he'd finger the jewels, coming to know in time their every facet, placement and flaw. He yearned to put the cet-set on his head and let the power flow, but he'd taken Very's advice, and Beth's too on second thoughts, that he'd best wait till Medi Terra. For one thing, she said, the city cets were that much easier on a body-mental than the wild mothers of the deeps and trenches. And for another, when he did launch himself outward, she, June and Very should be present to service him and give him support.

He spent many hours as well on his allcock to Ponce in his bee farm half a hemisphere away in the Mexican mountains, posing questions and relishing the answers. But for all the gentle cet-setter's recollections and willingness to talk, Mesmer was left with the impression he could only find out for himself what cet-setting was really like.

'For each it's different,' Ponce said, 'for no two are it the same.'

When at last the Loaded Parrot sailed jauntily through the Pillars of Hercules all were on deck to get a first glimpse of the marvels of the sea-city, with Mesmer doubly excited now that the prospect of being be-cetted was imminent.

Medi Terra was held to be the most perfect of Western cities, and was therefore the most populous. Since the far off days of garagism, when the sea had been declared dead to all life forms except the human, the inheritors in their wisdom and sensitivity had chosen to restore it to all that it had ever been at its best, and to make it more besides. From now and for ever, it was decided, art and nature would be in harmony, life would be as it should. With the exploiters, polluters and arms racists gone, with nations discovering that their own interests were compatible with those of others, and all finding out that the late garagist technology conferred only blessings when used for good and within reason, it was only a matter of years before the best-terrest were achieved. Once again the sea seethed with fish and the olive groves marched down to the shores. The old towns of the littoral flourished, and new ones sprung up as architecture was restored to its pre-eminence among the art-sciences. Only in the museums could the wretchedness of the past be found, just so folk wouldn't forget. There one might see crushed car bodies, wage-labour factories, battery housing, war machinery and other souvenirs of the way it had been. No wonder then that for all those living in the old towns like Venice, Bar Celona and Alex-and-Ria, or in the island villages of the central waters, or in the plains, groves, mountains and submarinas, Medi Terra provided the conditions for the fullest, happiest and longest of lives. From the Pillars of Hercules to the Golden Horn Medi Terra supported the fully grown civilization it had once cradled.

*

We four too have arrived in Cannes. But again he is at me.

*

Three days sail into Medi Terra Beth announced there were cets about, and indeed they could be seen not a hundred metres off the starboard bow, lazily turning in the water and spouting from their blowholes.

Mesmer stripped naked as instructed by Beth and made his way down to the bubble housing the cet-set. In front of him Very was symbolically cleansing the floor with his beard, and on either side June and Beth held his arms. There was room in the bubble itself only for two, so after Mesmer had settled himself down cross-legged June eased her way round so that she was framed by the greenish blue of the sea just beyond the glass of the bubble. Kneeling in front of him, she leant forward with the crescent of her nutrient graft filling his field of view. Her eyes were pulsing violet, and he could detect a fragrance of roses on her breath.

'Are you ready, Journeyer?'

Filled with excitement and apprehension, Mesmer nodded. 'Then we shall begin.'

With both hands June reached up to the cet-set, held it briefly some six inches above Mesmer's head, then with a single downward movement lowered it until it made contact with his temples. Immediately the ring of diamonds around the base began to glow with the colours of June's strobe, now flickering faster and in a constantly changing spectrum.

Such consciousness of his surroundings lasted only briefly, before he entered a realm such as he had never known, and of which he could not speak.

*

Let it speak for you. The tiniest intervention, entirely justified, I think, under the circumstances.

*

He was without speech, dumb, yet part of an order that required no speech, as he sensed the plays transcribing the waters of the globe, each cet a focus of harmonies, each movement an element in a game that had been going on for millennia, since the days when Mesmer's ancestors had roamed the sub-Saharan scrub in search of grubs, a game that had no beginning and no end, for itself, a repetition with variations that might take a millisecond or might take a century, through births and deaths, incorporating the life of other species, other beings real and imaginary, other times future and past, logics with no known key, cyphers codes and glyphs, senses without organs, emotions without names. Be-cetted, with the waters streaming past in diatomic brilliance, he knew he'd only returned to what he'd always been a part of, unknowingly, something of which his Journey was the minutest fraction, his lifespan of a hundred and twenty years no more than a hundred and twentieth, and his lives past and future comprising a thread wound round a spool along with a million billion others. And with one of these he knew he was knotted, in a topological intricacy such that a single cut in the right place would restore both to their right alignment. For this reason alone he must return, that finally and for no other, not even the enchantment of his nights with June or the power of Golden beneath him bearing him along joyously over wet grass after a shower in the clear air of Peak at dusk.

*

It has said enough, and I not nearly enough. Most of the details, however, of our sojourn to date must perforce give way to what can be squeezed in before the next session and nowhen else. A footnote, then, before he's back with more.

My own contribution to this tri-dimensional ontology, one that has not seen daylight for many a year and has never been committed to print, is a tract I have provisionally entitled 'The Psychopathology of Everyday Flies'. It is my sole addition to the discourse of the Other, and bears the marks of an obsession, that I know full well.

I first became aware of the beauty of the beasts at an early and impressionable age when one alighted on my father's hand, drawn no doubt by the smell of money. I watched it enjoy its last second and a half of life before being consigned to eternity by his absent-minded swat. Thereafter my ruling passion was the study and conservation of the order of dipterans, save those individuals destined to form part of my collection, of which the first and still preserved item was the crushed corpse of the greenbottle I retrieved from the floor beside my father's chair. While others of my age and sex were engaging in quite different adventures, I would sneak off with net and killing bottle in search of *Calliphoria vomitoria*, of the silky blue bristles, or *Haemotopota pluvialis*, whose utterly silent flight makes it as difficult to capture as its bite is painful. I even devised the motto 'Chitin is thicker than skin' to mark my allegiance, an apt enough formulation in view of the thrashing I got for inscribing it in permanganate across the lintel of Matron's boudoir. In later years, between marriages and mistresses, I would return to my cabinets, make corrections and additions, remount the shabby and discard those fallen prey to lice. Later still, partly in response to fashion and partly because of my gleaming new mentality fresh from analysis, I preferred to examine the creatures on the wing, or sucker, whence the preliminary observations for my magnum opus.

Flies, like whales and infants, cannot speak. Their analysis, and the founding principles for the possibility of their analysis, had therefore to be derived rather than induced, reasoned rather than experienced. My 'Psychopathology' had to be deduced from axioms, of which the prime concerned the dualism between air and land. In the air, the fly is supreme, aerodynamically unsurpassed, capable of feats that are the envy of aves and aviators, untouched by material constraint. By contrast, on land, though passably agile in its sexapody, it is much as any other creature, doomed to defer to the lumps and bumps of the tabletop. Such a being, then, marked by alternate transcendence and immanence, by utter freedom and dull contingency, one it would not be too far-fetched to claim bears a resemblance to the human, encounters, after launching itself from the shit-pile, a window-pane. Where air was, and appears to be, is brute matter. No longer can the dipteran be sure of his or her right to liberty, for at any moment, out of the blue, might come the eye-smashing crash of fused silica. Is it any wonder that the fly, by nature's right the happiest of mortals, is prone to madness? Its frustrated buzz is the least index of its confusion.

Thus, in a nutshell, my thesis, and now, in a moment, my tisane, poured as always by my bride. Thank you, Sonia, your concern for my welfare knows no bounds. As, I think I can fairly add, does mine for Mesmer's.

*

On the mighty grooved flank of the whale passing not ten yards from his be-cetted eyes, inscribed in yard high letters was the word RETURN. With a flick of her fluke she turned about to expose the other flank, and with it, unmistakably, TRANSFORM.

*

No more can he impart at this juncture, on grounds that he does not understand, he says. I, too, am at a loss, when it seemed everything was going swimmingly. In compensation for his silence I shall take the opportunity to render the next case fact, perhaps already overdue, and when rendered, take it as good enough reason to round off the third of these seasonal divisions.

(9) Surreptitiously, one morning, when all the other Partridges were out of the house, Mesmer removed Grey Dagger from its cocoon of cotton

wool and took it downstairs to the cellar, where he drilled it through with his father's Black and Decker, ruining three vanadium steel bits in the process. He inserted into the drilled hole one end of a hundred foot length of flexible co-axial cable that he had purchased the previous day at the DIY superstore in the shopping precinct, whatever they may all be. Carefully he stripped off the insulating plastic, then peeled back the outer copper webbing of the cable and folded it back over Grey Dagger, giving it a lustrous striped appearance. Next, with a length of fine copper wire he bound the ends of the webbing to the outer circumference of the cable, making a join secure enough to stand up to any likely eventuality. Back in his room, with the door locked and a chair underneath the knob, and a Leave Me Alone notice tacked onto the outside of the door, he checked his inventory of glucose solution, vitamin tablets, pain killers, plastic bucket, box of tissues, multi-purpose penknife, cable plugs, junction box, and treasured single volume 1934 first edition of Trotsky's 'History of the Russian Revolution'. Then, pausing only to bid Grey Dagger a speedy passage, he swallowed it together with the first couple of feet of its attached flex. Throughout that day and night, and into the following day, he lay on his bed reading, with only brief periods of sleep, all the while paying out the line inch by inch as Grey Dagger coiled its way through his system. It was important neither to feed in the cable too quickly and risk an internal tangle, nor to delay the moment of emergence. Through a combination of calculation and the sensations from his abdomen he was able to judge Grey Dagger's whereabouts and rate of progress. When at last, with him squatting over the bucket, a particularly energetic bowel movement ejected it he wasted no time in celebration, for he was now in some pain and was suffering from rectal bleeding. As firmly as he dared he pulled through some half dozen feet of cable, an operation that took the best part of an hour, even aided by the now violent peristalsis brought on by the laxative he'd taken earlier. After wiping the cable clean, he cut Grey Dagger loose, with the vow that he'd return it to a shore where it might be washed by the eternal ocean, whenever circumstances permitted. He cut the other end of the cable so as to leave an equal length extruding from his mouth as from his anus. Threaded now like a bead on a wire, Mesmer was ready to begin the final stage of his project. To each of the free ends of the cable, he attached, with some difficulty, for it was delicate work, an aerial plug. One of these he inserted into the junction box he had already sited on the wall in preparation for this, which in turn led out to the TV aerial on the roof, the other he pushed into the socket on the back of his portable colour TV. He had considered in advance the correct way for him to be facing, and had concluded that the mouth end of the cable should lead to the TV, and the far end to the outside aerial. With trembling fingers, a consequence not only of too little sleep and internal bleeding, indicated by traces of red on his 'our avian friends' duvet cover, but also of excitement at the approaching culmination of his labours, he switched on the TV, or television as I prefer it. When the screen stayed resolutely grey, he didn't give way to despair on the assumption that his gastric juices had proved too much for the insulating plastic, but revealing a presence of mind which persuaded me his was a case worth taking, he rechecked the connections at both ends of the cable, and found that he had mistakenly transposed the In and Out leads at the junction box. This corrected, there straightaway swam into vision the head of one Anna Ford, reading the News At Ten headlines, a presence conditional, he well appreciated, upon there having passed through his body the electrical impulses from which it was constituted. For the first time in his life Mesmer felt entire. With utter joy he watched the succession of news items—a plane crash, a violent confrontation on a picket line, an announcement of interest rate changes, a bomb explosion in Northern Ireland, a winning goal in a football international, a royal baby on a pony. The News over, he immediately fell into a deep and dreamless sleep.

This penultimate of case facts finds me strangely moved, as I write it up from my preliminary notes seated in a wicker chair at a glass-topped table in the sun-lounge of the Majestic, and a single sail braves the Mistral-flecked waters of the Mediterranean beyond the window. It is also raining.

IV

WHITE HEAP

The approaching Spring finds the littoral in a ferment of new life. At random I remark the swelling buds of the hibiscus, the swelling buds of the children so soon to be young women, the young women each year more desirable parading the Boulevard in front of the hotel, where I can spy them through the glass of the sun-lounge, at last justifying its hyphen after an unusually overcast winter. From the direction of the port, basso profundo shouts and the smell of freshly caught fish fall upon my ears and nose, as no doubt will their bearers upon the throats of the girls flocking in droves in the direction of the port. How easily might Sonia be among them had she not my wealth and Mesmer's health to busy herself with, the latter so much more elusive than I'd hoped when we set out from London. Sonia is blooming, like the rest of her gender along the Côte, and if her attention to Mesmer did him as much good as it evidently does her, I'd have no grounds for complaint. But he has shown a reluctance to get well, manifesting itself in a refusal since our arrival three months ago to do anything other than freely associate. Are you not dreaming? I say. If I am, he says with dangerous lack of concern, I can't tell it apart from the real thing. Which is? I ask in a low tone. Well, life, of course, he laughs. Whereupon I make the decision that if he is not to be cured he must be killed.

*

Little did Mesmer know, when he read the words on the sides of the whale, that his companions had been watching over him for two days and a night, feeding him a sugar solution intravenously and drying his sweat-soaked body. Nor did he know, until his return, that the cet-set had been signalling a cycle of repetition in the complex variations of the encircling rings and arches of diamonds, such that Beth despaired of ever getting him back. Nor would he have ever known, had it not worked, that it was only through Very's suggestion his dragon's tooth might break the stasis they were able to get him back at all. Afterwards they told him the full story, how the old trapezist had taken off his dragon's tooth, passed it to June who re-threaded it with a hair from her head and tied it with great care beneath the flickering intersection of the overarching diamonds, so it hung freely just over the top of his head. When it had begun to spin, slowly at first but with ever-increasing velocity, until it had become a blur of shimmering energy in the centre of the crown, Beth had thumped her wooden leg on the side of the Loaded Parrot and had announced the breaking of the cycle.

Later, after twenty four hours sleep and a tasty meal, Mesmer felt none the worse for his experience and quite the wiser.

'I hope,' he said, 'I haven't hurt the cet who hosted me.'

'Not a chance,' Beth said. 'Those big mothers could take two dozen jammed Journeyers and they wouldn't even fluff a note. She'll still be chuckling you got so hung up, that's all,'

'That's good,' said Mesmer. He turned to Very, who was just behind him, leaning over the rail of the Loaded Parrot as it bore through the crystal clear water at a steady eight knots towards the neighbourhood of Medi Terra known as Ma Sails, one of the seabitch's favourite ports of call.

'I've got you to thank for this,' he said, indicating the dragon's tooth, now hanging on its thread of hair around his neck, 'and return it to you, now its completed its restoring task.'

Before he had time to lift it over his head, Very stayed his hand.

'Keep it sprout. 'Tis yours, no longer mine.' Very coughed embarrassedly, and spat into the sea.

'But why? You were the one to summon the dragon. Surely it's yours whatever.'

Very looked even more embarrassed, and began to polish the already gleaming handrail of the boat with his beard. To June, who was sprawled on the cabin roof sunning herself and writing a letter to Julie and the winkies, he said, 'You explain, dear lady.'

June pushed her writing pad to one side and smiled at Mesmer, who as ever was spellbound by her charms, most noticeably on this sunny day her dark brown nipples with their flickering star-maps.

'It's a gift, from him to you,' she said. 'He wants you to have it, and to keep it until you're called on to pass it to another.'

'Gosh,' said Mesmer, and was unable to find the words to continue.

'You see, sprout,' said Very, 'me days in the circus are numbered. Time was when me balance was the talk of the north. Lately it's begun to go, and I'm not the high flier to cling to the rope when I should be on the ground, or under it.'

'But there's no reason to suppose you'll soon be for the flux,' Mesmer protested, disturbed that his friend should be talking of such things. 'Old Jack's been thirty years in happy retirement, taking up horseflesh when admin got more than he could handle, and he and my dear breast-mother have never been better, in or out of the sack.'

'It's not the sack as worries me, sprout,' said Very, 'but me balance. I've even had spells of vertigo. For a high flier that's a sure sign the end is nigh.'

Mesmer found Very's prognosis almost too much to contemplate, so fond had he grown of the old timer. 'Is there nothing I can do? With or without the tooth.'

'Well, with it you might. Without it, nothing.'

'Do go on. I'm game for anything. After what you've done for me. Or before it.'

'In that case be prepared to come north with me, when the time is ripe, to the circus, in Wick, where with that tooth around your neck and a disposition like your own, there's no telling Candle may not be coaxed back out of the flux. If I could go out with her, doubly flickering in the Northern night, I couldn't imagine a happier ending.'

Nor Mesmer either, if ending there had to be. It was agreed then, when the time came, he would go with Very, and June would come too, to see if they could help.

*

Once the machinery is in motion there's no stopping it. I have made my decision, and even if I wanted to I could not revoke it, such is the logic of contemporary plotting. His decision to dream on cannot save him, though it should add interest to a case history that was in precipitate danger of becoming a mere catalogue of facts. Interpretation can at least while away our final hours.

This gift of tooth is a happy invention, and one I'd have taken as a sign of hope in earlier days, before we left the security of my consultancy, before I was wed, before he and Sonia made a habit of taking late evening strolls along the Boulevard de la Croisette. Its quid pro quo, the task of rekindling Candle, was not unexpected under the circumstances, which throughout have heavily favoured some such pyrotechnic adventure. If and when she comes flaming in, I shall be pleased to make her acquaintance, but before that some narrative is called for.

I found Brand under Hit Men in the East London Yellow Pages, a text Michael materialised from beneath the dashboard of the Rolls. His fees are convincingly high and his record impressive according to the brochure he's sent me, no fewer than a dozen natural deaths of what he calls celebrities attributable to his expertise, ranging from salmonella in the salmon at the Clochard to a pencil in the kidneys in the Commons bar, the consequence this latter to all the world of a perfectly ordinary parliamentary tumble. Who's the smear? this personage asked when I put through a phone call to the number in Leytonstone. Your pardon? I begged. The smear, the blob, the kneecap, for chrissake the fly. His entomological metaphor saved me from utter incomprehension, and I told him, Partridge, M. Don't worry, John, the voice leered in my ear, when I've finished with this bird there won't be a tailfeather to pick your teeth with. I didn't rebuke him for his nominal familiarity, possibly because John sounds well in contrast with the label my father's malice contrived to tie on me. Such travels as I have enjoyed have been well within the boundaries of West Europe, though I once toyed with the idea of visiting Rio before deciding deck quoits and widows blowing their inheritance on one mad fling might be more than I could stomach. And Shanghai, whose cuisine and brothels were unsurpassed before the spirit of revolutionary puritanism consigned the chefs to the factories and the girls to the fields. Yerse, always the tendency to drift, floating forever down rivers of association, in the punt of the mind, beneath the crack-willows of recollection, ah me. Brand, are you still there? He was, and his price was ten Ks, five in advance, five more on completion. I told him I wanted him to be ready for action at the drop of a hat, and he me in words of his own choosing that such preparedness would cost me. Put it on the bill, Brand, I said, and one more thing, the choice of weaponry, that's my pigeon, I understand you're versatile? He was, and would adjust the budget according to a system of weightings calculated on comparability and productivity. When I replaced the receiver I did so with a sense of relief at having found one so conversant with the spirit of capitalist rationality. Had he not taken to crime Brand would have made an excellent captain of industry. Whereas I, I am pleased to imagine as sometimes I lie in my bath, could have been a credit to a Conservative front bench, had I not taken to analysis.

*

Throughout the final months of 2411 Mesmer and June celebrated their passion from one end of Medi Terra to the other, with Very their constant companion, or nearly so. They left Beth holed up with a savoury crew in Ma Sails, where she wanted to rest up a while before taking the Loaded Parrot across the Atlantic to join Ponce. Mesmer was glad to accept her standing invitation to hop on a bus and visit whenever he felt like some honey or a change of air. He thanked her cordially for taking them on board, and for initiating him into the mysteries of the cet-set.

'Anywhere, anytime,' Beth said, with a playful dig in Very's ribs with her wooden leg, 'ain't that right, ol' timer?'

'Your hammock, madam,' Very replied, 'was an education in itself.'

But now, with the Spring equinox a month behind them, and the New Year only a matter of days away, Very kept glancing at the clock and looking North, until Mesmer took it upon himself to suggest it might be the time to go.

Very looked up from the lobster pot he'd been inspecting on the end of a pier, and said, 'Couldn't say it meself, sprout, but 'twouldn't be a bad idea. If Candle's flicker is ever to be seen again, the night of the great celebration's the time to do it.'

'New Year's Eve,' Mesmer exclaimed.

'Precisely,' said Very, lifting up a lobster by the tail, 'when 2411 is no more, and 2412's born at midnight.'

'Leaving me May Day to get back to Stock Port.'

'All the time in the world,' said Very, 'if you take the bus.'

And the bus too they'd take from Can to Wick, that same afternoon, if there was space on board for the three of them and their respective mounts.

*

This last hour has been conducted in flight aboard the Nice-Inverness El Al service, with Sonia draped around Elle, myself keeping an eye on Al the pilot and Allah the co-pilot, have I got the religion right?, and Mesmer with no trace of the fear that plagues me between runways chattering on about his greater improbabilities. Analysis, I heard myself remark to a passing stewardess, more like a, before my simile was lost in a wicked pocket waiting for us over the Grampians, that and the contents of my stomach, which I shall not itemise, breakfast being nothing out of the ordinary.

Of my consorts only Mesmer has been amenable to the move from the Midi to my Scottish estate, acquired, for the record, in a burst of Reed expenditure between the wars from an impoverished laird dying of consumption and whisky. Sonia said, when I put it to her, But whatever for? In order, I explained, that I may discourse with my gillie. On what? she said. Oh, on grouse, I said, vaguely, then as an afterthought, and partridge. Can't you do it by phone, she not unreasonably wanted to know. I'm afraid MacQuarrie has an aversion to the instrument, I improvised. Why do I need to come? she went on. And him? pointing at Mesmer. As to your presence, Sonia, I cannot insist, only plead, but as to his, it is essential to his treatment, now entering a critical stage, I speak as a medical man. Mercifully she conceded, on condition it would be for no more than a week, and then London.

Next came Michael, hanging around the lobby of the hotel as usual, in quest of whatever it is chauffeurs quest. Michael, I said, here our ways part, we'll be flying, you'll be driving back to London alone, unless you can find a clean hitchhiker to enliven your transit. He didn't argue, that being more than my tolerance could permit, but managed with a shrug and a peculiar trick of tossing his car keys into the air and catching them unseen behind his back to convey the impression that he thought I'd taken leave of my senses, and moreover that without his hand on the wheel there was no guarantee we'd arrive anywhere near our destination. Consider yourself lucky, I said, in order to mollify him, a week off, no responsibility, and all the mileage your expenses can cover. Wordless, but whistling, he departed.

*

In Wick, after an uneventful bus ride, Very introduced June and Mesmer to the circus folk, as bonny a crowd as one might wish to find, and none more so than Viola Fortini, Very's onetime rival on the highwire, and Angus Bar-Higgins, lion tamer, both of whom Mesmer had met in trace on the ring speakers a year before, on the first day of his Journey. To meet them at last was a pleasure indeed. These two agreed to show the newcomers around Wick and its circus, while Very made some vital preparations for the coming performance.

The circus itself was hewn out of the bedrock of the town, with the greystoned houses tiered up around the ring, in such a way that from every house a view could be had, either from a window or a roof. Overhead the fabric of the Big Top was at present invisible. Only when a performance was in progress would the laser discontinuities come into action, blocking out the stars and stilling the wind, giving a traditionally hermetic closure. All the houses were festooned with bunting in celebration of the coming New Year, and along the streets and over the interconnected rooftops the bustle of Wick life went on apace, getting ready for the influx of folk from Shet Land to Harris. In Wick, it was said, nobody ever wanted for a bed, a meal, or a dram, even if all the world were to land on their doorstep.

'Do you know,' said Mesmer to Viola, as they stood on a roof high above the ring, 'what it is Very intends to do to restore his Candle?'

'All he's told Angus and myself,' said Viola, a lady of middle years and the high-browed mien of circus performers, 'is that we should have our beasts to hand. The rest will be taken care of by himself and those he has been travelling with these past months, of whom none so important as yourself, it seems.'

'Flux,' said Mesmer, wondering what he might be called upon to do. 'What beasts?'

'A lion,' said Angus. He was a man of few words but immense courage, as could be seen by his relations with the pride, each one of which jostled to be at his right hand, and therefore chosen for the performance.

'And my squirrel,' added Viola, producing from the pocket of her amethyst-studded tracksuit a red squirrel, which bounded up her arm to sit on her shoulder, perkily nibbling a peanut.

'And Golden too, I suppose,' said Mesmer.

'And Scheherazade,' said June, indicating her palfrey.

*

At last a name, and one that could have opened up a thousand and one nights had we had it earlier. That there will always be something left out is one certainty in a world of long odds.

With MacQuarrie to collect us it was but a short run up the glen to the ancestral home. MacQuarrie, I hissed, when I got him on his own, Sonia and Mesmer having been engulfed by the welcoming apron of Mrs MacQ, you haven't by chance seen a stranger hereabouts, have you? None but your wife and the lad, he replied. Excellent, I said, and if you do, pay no heed, for I have found it necessary to hire a detective to keep an eye on the boy, his family being of a mind to see kidnappers behind every rose bush. Especially say nothing to him, for he is sensitive. Aye, the gillie said, Sir.

Brand must be hereabouts, if he's followed my instructions to the letter, wielding the honest blade I insisted must be his weapon, ready to plunge it between the aorta and the left ventricle, if Mesmer should stray from the safety of the hearth and towards the gloomier corners of my manse. The method is dictated purely on aesthetic grounds, so that his going may bear as close a relation as possible to the heartland of the case, in my opinion Grey Dagger, soon to be succeeded by White Heap, in the terminal case fact, yet to be rendered. Ah, but here comes Mrs MacQ's famous tea, resplendently sconed and haggised, which Sonia and Mesmer throw themselves upon with the gastronomic indiscrimination of youth. I think I shall partake of a wee dram of MacQuarrie's treasured malt.

*

'And Bert,' said Very's familiar voice fractionally before his berry-brown head appeared over the low parapet of the roof they stood on. But where once his magnificent beard had billowed there was now a short-cropped goatee and comparably neat moustache.

Before anyone could speak, Very held up a hand. 'Say nothing please. It wasn't easy, but it had to be done.'

'But why, Very?' Viola said. It took no great experience of life to see she had a softish spot for the old timer, and her demeanour was one of getting used to whatever he might get up to, however difficult that might be. 'It suits you though.'

'Doesn't it just?' said Very. 'In the mirror I had me doubts, but now I can feel the breeze on me face I can tell I did right.' He rubbed his thumb over his cheek, pink after its lack of exposure to air for so long. 'It seemed only proper I should pay homage to me past life when I'm on the point of rekindling Candle.'

'Vladimir Illich,' cried Mesmer, comprehending why it was Very's new look seemed familiar.

'Precisely, sprout. The beard, the brow, the piercing gaze, the stern but kindly curl to me lip, and all the rest. Only I couldn't bring meself to abandon me wraparound, nor me pantaloons, nor me ropy sandals. There are some things you can't give up.'

As if to emphasize Very's point, the dragon's tooth around Mesmer's neck suddenly felt weightier than normal, like it was affected by an increment of gravity.

*

Ha! Even at this late hour he seeks to wage class war. So be it. When we are driven into a corner we are prepared to defend our rights with anything to hand, and six inches, no, eight inches of cold steel is hardly the thing when faced with the rabble howling for that which legality and their own dereliction does not entitle them. Dynamite, Brand, are you listening? Out with a bang, eh? No pissing about with niceties, get what I mean? The smear well and truly smeared, all right? His silence at the other end of the line proves his approval of my revised method, and no doubt too of my speedy acquisition of his criminal vernacular. Does Mesmer really imagine that the belated re-appearance of his tarnished hero can deflect the band-wagon of contemporary history? Again, no answer, which is all to the good, when the fuse to Brand's dynamite winding inexorably along the contour of the glen through the dead trees and parading capercaillies of the Old Caledonian Forest should already be lit.

At eight in the evening the laser network filled the sky with its composite tracery, and the audience gathered in windows and on rooftops, so that not a space was to be seen in any of the tiered surround. For the next three hours a succession of bareback riders and stilt walkers, animal tamers and flea trainers, clowns and tumblers, acrobats and jugglers delighted the crowd, until the ring mistress cracked her whip and announced the impending attempt on Candle's restoration.

Mesmer felt a pang of nervousness in his stomach, for he still did not know how Very intended to do it.

June said, 'Shall we enter the ring? Old Very will be waiting for us.'

Leading Golden and Scheherazade they made their way into the ring to thunderous applause. Instead of the tank brimful of gasoline that Mesmer had half expected to encounter, in view of Candle's chosen means of departure, the ring was empty but for three upright chairs some fifteen feet off centre, arranged in a semi-circle. Seated on them were Viola, Angus and Very, each tuning their instrument, respectively viola, violoncello and violin, the same, Mesmer remembered, as he'd heard them play in trace his first day out of Stock Port on the greenway. Only Candle's first fiddle was absent.

When Very saw them he leapt to his feet and rushed over.

'Welcome, madam, welcome, sprout. Couldn't tell you what I had in mind before, in case word of it should leak flux knows where. Shall I tell you the programme?'

It was, Very went on, simplicity itself. He and his two companions in the strings would be playing Beethoven's Opus 130, a piece much loved by Candle, on their depleted quartet. With them would be their beasts. Bert was standing patiently as ever, behind Very's chair, stock square, with his head lowered and emitting no indications that anything was out of the ordinary. Behind Angus's chair there lay a lion, keeping one eye on Bert and the other on his master. Mesmer hoped he had been recently fed. On Viola's right shoulder there perched her pretty red squirrel.

'Why the animals, Very?' Mesmer asked.

Very considered the question for some while before saying, 'Not entirely sure about that one, sprout. I could hardly leave Bert out of the final act, seeing as he's travelled with me for so long. And if Bert's to be there, it seemed only fair for Viola and Angus to have theirs too. Company for Bert at any rate. But I hope me reasoning on the quartet's clearer.'

This last was accompanied by questioning looks at each of his listeners. It struck Mesmer that his beard had already begun to grow after its severe cropping.

'Definitely,' Mesmer said, keen to reassure him on this at least. 'It'll give Candle a motive to return.'

'Couldn't have put it better meself,' said Very with satisfaction.

'What would you like us to do, Very?' said June.

'You, dear lady, I'd like to stand opposite our little trio, with Golden and Scheherazade on either side of you, making sure the astral route's free of traffic, if you wouldn't mind.'

June smiled at him, displaying her filmic tooth long enough for Mesmer absently to notice the film The Magnificent Obsession—the original version—playing on it. 'I shall be pleased to do what I can. And shall need to compose myself.' So saying she led the horses to where Very had indicated, and closed her eyes.

'And me?' said Mesmer.

'You, sprout,' Very replied, 'play the most important part of all, being a Journeyer.' He put an arm around Mesmer's shoulders. 'Look up there.'

Mesmer looked, and saw, high up above the ring, picked out as a thread of silver in the glare of the spotlights, a tightrope.

'But I've never walked a tightrope in my life, not even when I was a winkie,' he blurted. 'What's to stop me falling?'

Very chuckled and said, 'Your dragon's tooth, dear boy. Whirl it around your head as you walk, and its gravity will keep you steady as a rock. No risk at all so long as you don't stop doing that. When you're half way over, above us playing and June astralling, Candle, if she's coming, will come. That's me reasoning, sprout, fault it if you can.'

*

All this, and Walpurgisnacht to boot? I'd call up half the street and have them in on the climax were they not so damnably far away, and were not my own revisions demanding all the attention I can spare from the need to listen.

Brand's absurd suggestion that we employ explosives and risk the eggs of the ospreys nesting in my back garden has been suitably quashed. No, Brand, what we need is a little imagination. Strangulation is the only conceivable technique. Cast your mind on to the Argentinian gaucho, striding the pampas in search of game, a lone vicuña taking water, a jack rabbit about to crap. Hark at the whistle of his bola as the weights fly through the air before their centrepetal moment creates a throttling vortex around the neck of the victim. Note how the cardiovascular responds, with the dormant organ limp between unsuspecting legs jerking to terminal erection before the gopher croaks. A fitting end, don't you think, Brand? One I am sure Sonia will appreciate. Oh, yes, my nose may not be a sightly object, but it can still detect a vintage year at two paces and a woman's heat at twenty. When she departs for just a short after dinner stroll by myself Gulliver smelling of one thing and returns after midnight reeking of another, it is not difficult to draw my conclusions. And if further evidence is required, there are his own nightly peripatetics, with their all too blatant-latent constructing the overly sexed-text.

*

Below him the ring seemed perilously tiny, and in it the figures of folk and animals even more so. The sound of the depleted quartet wafted up to him, as it entered its last movement, the signal for him to begin his walk. With an impulsive glance downward at June, whose pubic strobe was pulsing colours he'd never seen before, an old-gold shot through with sky blue, and with the dragon's tooth whirling about his head, he stepped forth. Tentatively at first, but with increasing confidence, he placed one foot in front of the other. He felt no sense of imbalance, only now the hope that all would go according to plan, as the dragon's tooth gave him all the stability he could wish for. Already he was a quarter of the way across. Another few feet and he'd be in the middle. Without warning, his allcock began to broadcast the sound he'd first heard almost a year before when Very had fallen in the Trent, a cacophony of cries, grunts, whispers and giggling that was unlike anything in 2411, so soon to be 2412. Mentally he commanded it to cease, then when that had no effect, by word of mouth, but still to no avail. Forgetting in his concern Very's instruction, he brought down his right hand to apply to the manual, his right hand from which the dragon's tooth whirled. Too late did he realise his balance had gone. Flailing his other arm to restore it, his foot slipped off the rope. Unsuccessfully he grabbed at the tightrope as he began to fall, faster and faster, down towards the centre of the ring, the space demarcated for Candle's return.

*

I hear a knocking on the door of my manse, it must be Brand, it can be none other at this late hour, it shall be I who lets him in.

There remains only in this interval of free fall the requirement to record the last fact of the case.

(10) Upon waking, although in distress from internal bleeding, Mesmer felt able to construct his White Heap, the end and apotheosis of all he had been through. This curious document, titled I am sure as a compromise formation from heat and hope, subtitled Terms For A Better Possible World, consists of a sheaf of pages, each one headed by one of the doubles he's littered his future with. My presumption that these should be read as a premature intuition of the analytic situation, with each word spoken by the analysand inwardly interpreted by the analyst beyond the couch, was contradicted by his own version of their genesis and significance. With the TV aerial passing through him, hence, he says, at once being shafted by the world and spewing it forth, he knew he could begin to think his Utopia. Accordingly, with an ear attuned to every cadence, he listened to the string of words It was speaking, finding every now and then one among them, when accompanied by a telling image, that found an answering echo within him. Two hours of latenight television was sufficient to give him what he needed, twenty double terms, to which I myself have been unable to resist adding another three. When it was complete Mesmer switched off the set, placed his White Heap beneath the pillow, and called loudly through the wall to his sister Vicky, who trying Mesmer's door and finding it barred woke her father and persuaded him to break it down. It was also she who rode with him in the ambulance after their shocked discovery of his condition, a white heap upon the bed, and urged upon her parents the need for him to undergo analytic treatment with the best there was to be had, by reputation the healer whose last gasp cannot be far away. But not before I've put pen to paper to draw the conclusions any reasonable lexicographer might expect from a list so tantalising as he's laid before me. With the help of his narrative it's been possible to derive a contextual sense, and where that's failed I've had to invent. May he forgive me for any errors of judgement that have crept in.

White Heap

CLITORAL-LITTORAL. What in other climes has been known as childhood, richly innocent, takes on the enviable status of satisfied libido, a beach whereon one basks, with the ocean of the flux behind, and the great continent of adult life in front, variegated by regional difference.

SPINAL-VAGINAL. Here, I assumed Mesmer to have been reading Reich, except he swears he's never done so, much to Beanbag's dismay, and my rule is to accept as true what my patients believe. A process, then, vouchsafed to all, involving the full biological works, from earlobe to womb.

NOBLE-GLOBAL. This, glossing Mesmer, finest flower of Communist Matriarchy was inaugurated in the fiftieth year of the Revo and combines the then worldwide Bell Telephone System, the software underlying the SIFTING-SHIFTING (q. v.) and what had once been known as female intuition, now understood as the fluxional ground of all communication. Its purpose is to ensure the BEST-TERREST (q.v.), given the state of knowledge and the development of the productive forces. If any person or collectivity or region feel themselves hard done by, they merely have to make their way to the nearest kiosk or pick up the nearest allcock, and register their complaint. The NOBLE-GLOBAL assesses the possibilities for change consistent with maximal satisfaction all round, and puts into motion the necessary changes via the SIFTING-SHIFTING (q. v.) .

SIFTING-SHIFTING. The descendent of what was once known as the economy. Production having been fully rationalised after the Revo, with currency and commodities discontinued, and with the enormous capability of hitherto unproductive labour taken advantage of, the BEST-TERREST (q.v.) in production and distribution were soon achieved. The SIFTING-SHIFTING also incorporates individual requirements, so that all may contribute as much or as little as they wish to the total social product, in a manner that gives satisfaction. With energy needs taken care of by solar transformations and, with a few exceptions (see SHIT-COMMIT), drudgery by automation, no-one in three hundred years has done anything other than what in earlier times would have been recreation. I find these notions curiously attractive, as one who is disinclined to do any work at all other than sit behind the couch and listen.

CRYPTIC-ELLIPTIC. Of which I cannot speak, and thereof must be silent. He may have his ideas on the subject, but he's kept them to himself.

OEDIPAL-SCHMOEDIPAL. The residue, in a matriarchy, of the cornerstone of my science. How the other concepts have fared he refuses to let on, so too the question of its practice, though if I had my way all would undergo it as the groundwork of their education.

BROTHER-OTHER. The amicality that exists across the boundaries between people, and the boundaries within it, contained in a fraternal salutation.

QUICKER-FLICKER. I, like the grizzled programmer on the bar stool in the pub o'erlooking the gondola-strewn Trent, am a bleakist, conceiving of my life as a brief spark between two eternities of blackness. This, the spark, is it.

DUSKY-MUSKY. Belonging, as I recall, to little April, a brunette. Some things will never change, thank the flux, even though I all things considered prefer the seventh veil a lighter shade, like that unnamed of little May.

VERBAL-GERBIL. One of my few contributions to his lexicon, coined in a fit of pique to refer to the clown from Wick.

TOKEN-UNSPOKEN. An entry for which there is no textual evidence.

CLONING-ZONING. Availing myself once again of Mesmer's explications, human reproduction. With the success of genetic engineering in the years leading up to the Revo it became possible for any numbers of individuals to contribute to the genetic endowment of a foetus. For the most part, after the abuses of the garagist class in attempting to eliminate discontent by suppressing certain inheritances, post-Revo society limited the contributors to those involved in the

CARING-SHARING (q.v.). The persistence of distinct sexes, while no longer necessary from a biological point of view, was a consequence of the application of the theory of regional difference to the CLONING-ZONING, with most children opting for one sex or the other when departing the CLITORAL-LITTORAL (q. v.).

CARING-SHARING. An ensemble of relations involving displaced quanta on to the BROTHER-OTHER (q.v.), most often between two people. This is what Mesmer says, though I'd have no hesitation in placing it in the CRYPTIC-ELLIPTIC (q.v.).

YOUKNOW-DUO. June and Julie, a title acquired during a hot summer at the Flaming Flamingo.

SHIT-COMMIT. A committed committee, making sure everything's as it should be in Under-Stoke, even in 2411 a malodorous place.

PENTA-CENTRE. Point of access to Under-Stoke, not a short hair's distance from that to the MOISTER-OYSTER (q. v.).

MOISTER-OYSTER. What I in my weariness would call a womb with a view, but Mesmer insists is a universal index, sensitive to everything that occurs.

TOILER-SOILER. A farmer, dedicated to right ecology and organic methods. Interrogated as to the productivity of such archaic agriculture, Mesmer replied that the industrial production of protein-bearing cultures had arisen out of the agri-business of late twentieth century garagism, and still provided a proportion of total food requirements. TOILER-SOILERS should be thought of more as gardeners, producing an aesthetic as well as food.

PROSAIC-MOSAIC. What the streets are paved with. One walks on a text cobbled together out of centimetre squares of coloured minerals.

CET-SET. A lexicographical anomaly this, being formed on graphemic rather than phonological opposition. Referentially, a device worn on the head enabling the wearer to communicate with the higher ocean-going mammals. It works, according to Mesmer, through the properties of certain crystal lattices of amplifying the electrical fields associated with mental activity. He says the theory was developed with the twenty first century discoveries of the importance of quantum effects in neurological processes.

BEST-TERREST. Derived from the theory of regional difference, the complex parameters defining global optima, says Mesmer.

SEXED-TEXT. A Reed contribution, and therefore self-explanatory.

BLATANT-LATENT. So too this.

*

The dragon that saved him from being dashed to death on the floor of the circus ring was an entirely delightful creature, some fifteen feet from nose to tail, with sky-blue wings, a body covered in old gold scales, and bushy green eyebrows. One moment he had been tumbling head over heels, the next he found himself astraddle her back, seated in the space between her wings and with his arms around her neck. Down she had swooped, then, through the laser tracery of the Big Top, summoned by the rites of recall Very had initiated, materialised by the energy of a youthful Journeyer, and guided in along astral highways through the pentacular skill of June. Only the chatter on his allcock remained unexplained, and perhaps always would, for as soon as the little dragon had zoomed through the roof, it had gone silent. He was to think later that maybe it was a residue from a world intersecting with his and mediated by the dragon. If so, he was glad it was a world he knew nothing of, for it was frightful indeed by the sound of it. But these thoughts didn't occupy him as the dragon descended towards the circus floor, with wings beating powerfully, and with flame belching from her nostrils. With a final flutter of her wings she came down in the very centre of the ring, in the space demarcated for Candle's return, in a perfect four point landing. Wrapping her diamond-tipped tail about her as delicately as a cat, she turned her head and fixed him with a weimaraner eye.

Mesmer slid from her back, and embraced her with profound gratitude for his deliverance, even as June's arms encircled him.

She said, 'You've mussed your eagle's feather. Here, let me fix it.'

*

Ha! One mussed eagle's feather. The upshot of my attempt at cure. And my attempt to kill in this other world he finds so noisome has been an equal failure. Brand, following my latest instruction that the definitive instrument of death should be a poison my researches on flies led me to invent through many hours of extraction, ebullition, distillation and condensation, blew it. Not into Mesmer's cup did the toxin find its way, but into mine, either through incompetence or treachery, I cannot decide which. Already I feel its numbing effects making themselves felt, or unfelt, at the extremities of my corpus. Sonia, most inestimable of friends and wife extraordinary, be so kind, if you would, as to guide my fingers across the page. The last rites of the case shall not go unperformed as long as there's an analytic ear to hear. Thank you, thank you, but let's not waste ink, seeing as it's become so precious.

*

Very's voice rang out in the stillness of the Northern night.

'Saved the sprout, alright, she did. But where's Candle?'

Whereupon he began stamping with his foot and tearing at his beard, already half grown back to its former magnificence. It was all Viola and Angus could do to stop him falling on the ground and beating his head against it. Mesmer had never seen anyone in such a state.

'Flux, Very,' he said, but could not go on, because nothing he could say would alleviate his companion's distress.

June, meanwhile, was tickling the dragon above her glorious green eyebrows. This evidently pleased her enormously, because the fire belching forth from her mouth had been replaced by no more than the odd puff of smoke, and she was making a sound that Mesmer could only assume was the dragon's equivalent of a purr. He became aware of a warm sensation at his fingertips, and found he had been holding the tooth throughout his fall and ride, quite unknowingly. If further evidence was needed that this was one and the same dragon Very had stolen it from it was provided that instant by her opening wide her jaws and exposing two formidable rows of teeth, of which the lower revealed an unmistakable gap. As unmistakably, as she did so, she favoured Mesmer with what was nothing other than a wink from her pale green eye.

'It's me dragon,' cried Very, 'come back for her tooth.' Impelled by a sense of what was necessary, Mesmer unthreaded the tooth from the strand of June's hair. To Very, who supported by Viola and Angus had come up to the dragon's head, he said, 'I'm quite happy to give it back, if that's what she wants. I'm awfully sorry about Candle though.'

To his surprise, however, just as he was about to insert the tooth into the gap, the dragon shut her mouth. Thinking perhaps she had understood him to have already put it there, Mesmer waited for her to open her mouth again. When she did so, he tried a second time, but again she snapped it shut as his hand approached. When, on the third attempt, he almost lost his fingers in the process and a snort of flame made him leap back to safety, he concluded that it was not her tooth she was after.

'But what can she want?' Mesmer asked, quite baffled by her behaviour.

'I think,' said June, who was still tickling her above her eyebrows, 'you'd best put the tooth back around your neck.'

Mesmer rethreaded the tooth on its strand of hair, and put it back over his head, noticing as he did so that the initials at its base had changed from V.L. to M.P., a substitution he found rather moving, if hard to understand how it had come about.

'It's Very she wants,' June announced. She was clearly in a position to know, Mesmer could see, because her pubic strobe and irises exactly matched the dragon's colouration.

'I, dear lady?' Very croaked. 'But what for?'

'I believe she wants to take you with her.'

'But where?'

'I can't say for certain, but it's decidedly elsewhere, not of this earth at all.'

Excitedly, Mesmer said, 'Do you hear that, Very? If you go with her, maybe you'll find Candle.'

'Me balance has gone,' Very replied morosely, 'ever since Candle snuffed it.'

It occurred to Mesmer that the combination of shocks Very had recently suffered, first his own fall after the old trapezist had assured him of his safety, then the appearance of the dragon, then her refusal of the tooth, now this suggestion he should fly off on her, had been too much for him. It looked like his mind was beginning to go.

'Thinking I'm past it, eh, sprout?' Very said suddenly, with something approaching his usual vitality. 'Gone a bit gaga?'

'We-ell,' Mesmer admitted.

'Not a bit of it. Just resting me brain, that's all. Get me a sandwich from Bert's saddlebag, I've decided to take me chance in the flux with this here beastie.'

The dragon, who'd been regarding Very unblinkingly, gave a snort of fire from her nostrils, and a little flutter of her wings.

'Well chosen, Very,' Mesmer exclaimed. 'You've obviously pleased her. Do you want a leg up?'

'Not so long as I can cock me leg over. I may have lost me sense of balance, and I may have lost me cause in Candle, if you get me meaning, but that still doesn't mean I can't get in the saddle. Ask Bert, who's borne me all these years.'

So saying, Very bowed low to all those gathered around him in the ring and tiered up around leaning out of windows and perched on rooftops, embraced Bert who'd ambled over, took a huge sandwich from Viola, and with a short run leapt on to the scaly back of the little dragon. Once there, he wiggled himself around a bit, and slid up and down, and said, 'Not so comfy as I'm used to, but then I dare say we'll be travelling a mite faster.'

The dragon beat her wings vigorously and fire belched forth from her mouth and nostrils. She was ready to take off, it seemed. June stepped back a pace and took Mesmer's hand. 'Is there anything you've forgotten?' Mesmer asked Very.

'If there is, sprout, there's nothing I can do about it.'

'It all seems so sudden.'

'Doesn't it just? But best I go quickly, lest I change me mind.'

'Bye, Very,' cried Mesmer. And from June, and from Angus and Viola, and from all the Wickers, the same cry rang through the Northern night. 'Bye, Very.'

'Take good care of Bert,' said Very.

With wings beating furiously and flame gushing forth, her tail lashing and Very waving from the ridgeline of her back, the dragon took off. As she climbed steadily in an expanding spiral, towards the laser tracery, and beyond into the starlit sky, everyone waved back and shouted flux speed, and none more so, if a trifle sadly, than Mesmer who'd enjoyed the old one's company for a year. Even when the last glint of gold from the dragon's body and the last flash from her diamond-tipped tail were indistinguishable from the constellations, he continued to wave, for even though he could no longer see Very, it was possible Very saw him. He only stopped when June put an arm around him and said, 'Tomorrow is the last day of your Journey and the first of 2412. It is May Day. Listen.'

And indeed, on the night air could be heard the peal of bells from the Jeanne o'Groats pluri-kirk ringing the changes of the Internationale, so ending the old year and bringing in the new.

*

I too note the haste with which he disposes of the buffoon, and wonder whether he'll linger longer over my funeral pyre. Already I hear the dark wings of extinction beating, closer by the minute, as this last hour draws to a close. Only the reluctance of my labio-linguistic zone to succumb to the poison and Sonia's willingness to transcribe ward off the terminal silence. But I'd better not push my luck, devilish though it has always been.

*

June said, 'They'll be pleased to see you, back in Stock Port.'

Yes, thought Mesmer, to play with his dear sisters Lois and Marushka, to discourse with Elmsfootloose III and sport with Mandy Rocket, to ride with Old Jack and be bathed by his breast mother, these and more were the delights that awaited him when he got home, after so long on the road.

'When will I see you again?' he asked.

'Whenever you wish. I'll be in New Stoke, with Julie and the winkies, and there'll always be a place for you.' With her nutrient graft swirling, and her irises deep amber, June embraced Mesmer, as they stood in the circus ring in Wick.

Mesmer could only say, so choked was he with emotion, 'It has been a rare enchantment.'

'For me as well, dear Mesmer.'

'I feel there should be something else, I don't know why.'

'There is still the coming night, for my bus doesn't leave till ten in the morning.'

'Something more still.'

'Perhaps you should cast your eyes downwards then.'

Thus it was he saw, where the dragon had stood, next to the four imprints of her feet, a series of marks that could only have been made by the diamond tip of her tail.

'What do they mean?' he said.

'Go around the other side. You're looking at them upside down.'

*

Yerse. There will always be a last word. Not mine, but the future's.

*

There, in the dust, was written the word

Supplement

I

Hardly a satisfactory conclusion, this missing last word, yet one not dictated by authorial whim, nor by some kind of postmodernist refusal to allow the narrative closure associated with the 'good' read, rather something determined by the logic of the text. How much less satisfactory would have been any conceivable single lexical item. Whatever the dragon may have written in the dust of the circus at Wick, it would be certain to fall short of the expectations of resolution, finality, explanation engendered by the convergence towards a conclusion. The chain of words Mesmer encounters in his travels, variously inscribed on the sides of fish and marked by capital letters, is, to put it another way, an unfinished and essentially unfinishable series, being no more or less than the word presentations thrown up by the unconscious. To have specified another, under the pretence it was the last, would have been to betray the sense of incompletion that dominates throughout. The penultimate sentence, 'Not mine, but the future's', is in its own way not far from the mark, the implications being that the radical incompleteness of the text, any text, is a condition for the emergence of meaning through reading. What it means at any one time is not determined solely by what is written, but also by how it is read. Each reader supplies his or her own array of association. Each reader interprets the text as the analyst interprets the dream. Unread, the text is nothing, marks on a piece of paper, scratches in the dust of Wick's circus's futurity.

Having said that, a supplement deserves an explanation, tempting as it would be to suppose it fills the place of the missing last word.

If the reader is the complement of the text, the supplement is something else, an intervention that subtracts as well as adds, in any case changing that which has preceded it. Even the existence of a supplement affects the text, marking it out as unfinished, in need of something it itself doesn't have, a possibility of interpretation, revision, emphasis or explanation that will make a new text through backward superimposition. At the limit, what has been read as a novel may come to be seen merely as the pretext for the supplement, that which enables the supplement to be written and to be read. The supplement refers to the text, the text is what the supplement is about, but in finding its precise object it can begin to speak of that which the text could only approach in a veiled or allusive manner.

Together, text and supplement constitute a novel, *The Utopian*. Already the supplement begins to say what the text could not, in referring to the whole of which the text is a part, a metonymic move that opens up the question of the role and function of the novel without calling into play extra-novelistic discourses. Such an enquiry into the conditions for its own project releases the possibility of establishing levels of coherence beyond that of 'the fiction'—such a notion being something of a fiction itself, in that no fictional discourse can exist without a measure of interpenetration with the factual. Not self-reference for its own dubious postmodernist sake, but in order to pose serious, even deadly serious, questions in a way that neither 'fiction' nor 'fact' could do alone. The 'play' of the text and the 'work' of the supplement—such terms being understood as already under erasure, since even the most frivolous of discourses redistributes cathexis and the most leaden is not without its measure of pleasure—together cause a tremor in that to whom and to which the novel is addressed, as along a geological fault-line when rocks move in opposed directions. Such radical incompatibility descends down into the substrata of the novel as well as up into the atmosphere of ideology. We live and think, all of us, astraddle such fault-lines. In activating one of them, *The Utopian* relies upon no more than recognition.

The text opens with an awakening, from a dream of pre-history, on the first of May 2411. May Day: international distress signal, date of celebration of the workers' movement and, in its sound image, a forerunner of those doubled terms that recur throughout the text and finally undergo a degree of explication in Reed's rendering of Mesmer's terms for a better world. The implications of doubling are already present from the first in the suggestion of both sickness and health, of individual distress and social well-being. And in a continual exchange of meanings around a dialectic of sickness and health, the text makes use of doubling as a figure that will generate many variations, the most notable of which is the doubling of the text itself, on the one hand 2411, on the other the present. Apparently and initially a commentary upon the dream of his patient, Reed's byzantine first person narrative is played out in a different form in the narrative of 2411. Again, the status of the two worlds varies according to one's position within the text, 2411 being a dream from Reed's standpoint, and the present from Mesmer's being no more than an intrusion from a nightmarish pre-historical past. The notion of the dream, too, has a double aspect, both as aspiration towards an ideal and as something in need of interpretation. Each part of the doubled text, therefore, in these and further ways seeks to contain and explain the other, expressive of a dialectic that refers back to the oppositional structure of the world we live in, whose inevitable development according to the principles of its own inner contradictions cannot but generate a future we know nothing of.

In 2411 Mesmer sets out on a journey whose function, though not precisely stated, is to secure the passage from childhood to adulthood, the entry into society proper. Its symbolic 'year and a day' is redolent of the world of childhood, peopled by giants, dwarves, maidens and dragons, subject to the arbitrary law of magic, and of course as the 2411 narrative unfolds so such creatures make their appearance, enchantment holds sway, magic operates. Mesmer's journey, then, partakes of the logic of another world, that of infancy, and expresses that other journey we all must take in order to enter society, the passage from the pre-history of the young human animal to the history of the gendered, structured, socialised, human subject. The cautionary tale of Oedipus, with its figures of patricide and maternal incest, is the shadow of this passage, haunting it with the consequences of what must happen if symbolic castration, that is to say, recognition of the limits of desire, is not acknowledged. At the core of myth, fairy stories, Greek tragedy, popular melodrama, genre fiction this story lies in wait, generating the source of our pleasure, the knowledge that we as readers have successfully negotiated that dangerous passage, have entered the realm of the symbolic. It is even suggested that Oedipus is the structuring principle of all narrative, resting as it does upon the disruption of one particular order, the working through of the consequences of that disruption, until a new order is established (typically through death, marriage or departure) and the story can end. If so, then the introduction of the pseudo-patriarch into the maternal idyll of 2411 in the form of Very Light can seen as a condition for narrative to occur. The implicit contradiction entailed by such a move is part of the problem the text sets out to articulate. If Mesmer's journey is a recapitulation of Oedipus, he must in some sense get back in order to begin again. The chosen method here has been to incorporate into Reed's interpretative commentary the story of Mesmer's backward passage from young adulthood to a form of madness that symbolises the pre-Oedipal pre-linguistic world of early infancy, enumerated through ten 'case facts'. In it Mesmer successively fails to achieve the socially sanctioned goals presented to him, refuses the positions offered, whether as lover, graduate, party cadre, until alone in his room in his parents' house he embarks upon the strange and cryptic behaviour that will result in his finally being strung out on the TV wire, TV on, constructing his White Heap, his terms for a better world.

Mesmer's forward journey through 2411 is paralleled by a backward journey in the present, which in turn, however, contains implications of progression. His regression can be read in a diametrically opposed way, so that his withdrawal from women becomes a necessary separation from the mother, and the stringing of himself up on the TV wire running through him from mouth to anus (and vice versa) becomes submission to paternal rape, or less concretely, to the law of the father, the symbolic order (including language itself) which pre-exists him and through whose acquisition he is (re)inserted into society.

The journey forward is the journey back, a continual exchange of meanings between becoming and forgetting, between progressing and regressing. So too Mesmer's 2411 journey, inaugurated by a departure from the maternal home, continued via a series of encounters with and detachments from mother symbols (the moister-oyster, the whale, the dragon), completed with an expulsion of 'the father' and a return to Stockport where he will be able to choose a woman other than his mother, is also a journey back. The succession of literal words he meets may be understood as expressive of that realm where they have lost their transparency of meaning, have become pure signifiers, things in themselves, until finally, with the marks in the dust of the word that is unrepeatable because in the last instance it doesn't exist, Mesmer has regressed beyond the limits of the symbolic, into the pre-linguistic imaginary world of the mother-child dyad.

One of these two double movements, the case history as told in the case facts, is embedded in another narrative, that of Reed's infatuation with his receptionist Sonia, his marriage to her, and his subsequent murderous jealousy concerning a putative affair between her and Mesmer. It soon becomes clear that this narrative also explicitly doubles that of 2411, in the correspondence between the antics of Very Light and those emotional of Reed, between the geography of the two converging in the twin visits to the Mediterranean and to Scotland, and in the finale where Reed's attempts to dispose of his patient are matched by the impending threat to and last minute reprieve of Mesmer in Wick's circus. Equally explicit is the converse of this from the point of view of 2411, with Very Light identified as harbouring a 'temporal succubus' from pre-historic times, one whose interest in Mesmer is at best ambivalent, at worst hostile, who can be none other than Dr Reed.

The two narratives then double each other throughout, complexly and with many a variation, the signs of the one modified but ever-present within the other. Each world, 2411 and the present, contains the other in trace, by implication. 2411's matriarchy cannot escape the sign of the father, even relies upon it for its narrative, as equally the present cannot escape the image of the mother, variously presented as the lure of an ideal future and as the shadowy memory of an ideal past. So the terms for a better world—the noble-global, sifting-shifting and the rest—doubled as they are, reside within a text whose other elements double and redouble, an endless mirror game of reflections ad infinitum. But the seeming symmetry of these two facing mirrors is doubly marred by a structural incompatibility between their two discursive modes. Such are the strategies irrealism invokes to do justice to the real.

Instead of a simple oppositional mirror structure, the text is radically decentred by the use of third person narrative in 2411, first person narrative in the present. A mirror structure would certainly decentre in that neither part of the text could achieve that hegemony of meaning that is claimed to order the so-called realist text within which all discourses are hierarchically arranged. If both 2411 and the present text were either first or third person narration then neither could achieve the dominance necessary to ensure realism. Put another way, both together would not offer a stable position for the reader to judge the 'truth' of the text. But the use of the different person narration imposes a twist that eliminates even the possibility of a centre as the point of balance between the two, a kind of averaging out that would permit a 'statistical truth' wherever they conflicted. 2411's third person narration and the present's first person narration entail that the two part-texts occupy different narrational territory. While the 'he' of 2411 is consistent with the 'I' of the present, from the standpoint of 2411's 'he' the present's 'I' is radically elsewhere. At the same time the 2411 text resists subsumption within the present text as a hierarchically lower discourse, as for example occurs to direct speech within inverted commas in classic realism, because the narrative refers to and seeks to subvert the world of the present text. Reed's world belongs as much to pre-history as Mesmer's 2411 does to the uninterpreted dream. Neither can irrefutably contain the other; and no midway point exists where a balance between them is established.

The first-person narration of the present text, as well as setting up this asymmetrical relation to 2411, introduces and acts as the textual vehicle for the redoubtable Dr Reed: analyst, interpreter, commentator, wordsmith, inflated ego, would-be and ex-womaniser, plutocrat, attempted murderer, accidental suicide.

The formal structure of the text finds itself reproduced in the transference, that by-product of the analytic relationship, initially thought of by Freud as a hindrance, later conceived as the essential condition of cure. Through re-enactment of infantile dependencies, desires, phantasies and emotions, transferred onto the neutrality of the analyst, who listens, occasionally interjects a question or interpretation, but otherwise does nothing, the patient, or analysand, rediscovers the force and form of those infantile roots to his or her neurosis, then, most importantly, is able to use the positive side of that transference to provide the authority needed to release the neurotically bound energy. When the crypto-parent has heard it all, and has been understood to confer his or her blessing upon what the discourse of the other reveals the analysand to be, the guilt that underlies neurosis can dissolve.

But transference is not simply uni-directional. The analyst develops a counter-transference in relation to the analysand, just as infantile, charged—for the unconscious is never exhausted, but is merely comprehensible, and this only through analytic self-knowledge—and, because the analysand is vulnerable, potentially dangerous. To ward off this danger, to prevent the analyst possibly doing irreparable harm to the analysand, it is a requirement of the psychoanalytic profession that all analysts undergo a training analysis. In this way they are able to recognise and deflect their own potentially counter-therapeutic impulses.

Reed's deplorably unchecked counter-transference finds expression not only in his veiled homoerotic advances towards Mesmer, in his jealousy and his descent into murderous psychosis, but also in the increasingly insistent presence of the destructive 'temporal succubus' in 2411. This, Very Light's dark side, which is Reed's own unconscious, may be conceived as a perception on Mesmer's part of the danger he is in, or, at a different level, as an effect of the narrative structure of the text. For the question arises as to who is the narrator of the 2411 text. If Mesmer, then his perception of Reed's unrestrained counter-transference will be incorporated into the narrative; if Reed, then the introjection of his unconscious into what he is reporting cannot be ruled out; if some intra-textual third, one candidate would be Reed's chauffeur Michael, 'an excellent raconteur', who might ally himself with truth rather than his employer. However the 2411 text is read, Reed's not exclusively disinterested concern for his patient makes itself felt.

Finally, the decentred oppositional structure of the text functions to fracture the imaginary unity of the 2411 narrative. The possibility of commentary, even if rarely fulfilled—Reed having problems enough of his own to find time in those precious ten minutes between hours to interpret— introduces an element of distance into its reading. Instead of entering into the diegesis as a kind of secondary dreamer, the reader is offered the position of the analyst, whose ear is attuned to those botched notes through which repression signals its operation. The transparency of the prose style of the 2411 text turns out therefore to be as productive of the modernist stance as the more obviously 'signifier-oriented' utterances of Reed. Indeed, if there is a moment when modernism earns the prefix 'post', it is at the point where the obsessive tendency to foreground the materiality of the sign gives way to a concern with the deeper structures of narrative and the complex ways in which reader and text interact. This latter focus reintroduces history at the point where formalism tends to evacuate it. For the production, distribution and consumption of meanings takes place within a social and psychic economy every bit as historically mobile as that other economy in which texts become books become commodities. Nor is the one economy independent of the other.

II

2411's Utopia is both communist and matriarchal. One reading of the text is that it is a meditation upon the compatibility of these two.

A minimum condition for the social ideal of communism is the transfer of the means of production from private to collective ownership. Over and beyond this, the principle of transfer from 'private' to 'collective' can be extended to include personal property, money, housing, dwelling space, the choice of work, health, education, the raising of children, sexuality, and mental possessions like speech and thought. (The scare quotes indicate the many and various difficulties in different instances. For example, it can be argued that much of what is generally thought of as private, like opinion and belief, is in any case social; that 'sexual communism' is a specifically male phantasy with little appeal to women in the forms usually envisaged; that de-privatisation of education and health can and does take place within capitalist societies; and so on.) Utopias with a socialist/communist basis are to be distinguished largely on the nature and extent of this redistribution.

The utopian vision associated with the marxist conception of the proletariat as that class able to universalise the conditions for its own emancipation has, in general, perceived communism as something on the far side of socialism, possible only when common ownership and rational use of the means of production has abolished scarcity and as a consequence the State has withered away. This specifically marxist conception of history, fraught as it is with a notion of stages inevitably succeeding one another, has had an uneasy and ambivalent relation to utopianism. On the one hand Engels pointedly contrasted utopian socialism that merely articulates the hopes of a particular class with scientific socialism based on an understanding of the working of society and thereby given the possibility of realisation. On the other hand even Marx was not above projecting his ideal day into an imagined communist future, when all would be able to live as he would lie to himself.

If any single thing has tended to discredit the marxist promise it has been the notable failure of the State in soi-disant socialist countries to do anything like wither away. Critics of socialism point to the centralised, all-powerful bureaucracies and to the ruling elites which can be just as self-serving and even less accountable than the ruling class they've replaced, and claim, not unreasonably, that history itself has refuted the marxist dream of prosperity, freedom and democracy.

There are two general lines of defence against such charges. One is to take further the anti-utopian tendency within marxism and say that not only was talk of the withering away of the State immature and ill-conceived, but that a strong State is a necessary condition for the safeguarding of the Revolution and the human gains it made possible. This is the Stalinist (some would say Leninist) response. The other, which Mesmer evidently supports, is to say that the ideal is not marred by the shortcomings of reality, that socialism if it is to fulfil its promise must be international, must be brought into being by a politically and socially advanced working class and must be sustained by a far-reaching democracy, conditions that have nowhere yet been met.

The world Mesmer conjures up in his Blue Prints is one of inconsistency, waste, stupidity, irrationality, aggressivity, cruelty, exploitation, betrayal and decline. The world he dreams of, the world he inhabits in 2411, has relegated all of these to the dustbin of pre-history. 2411 is truly 'the negation of the negation'. Even the charge that such a society would suffer from crushing uniformity is met by 'the theory of regional difference'. As to the rest, technology has been harnessed to satisfy needs without converting humans into adjuncts of machines or despoiling the environment, labour has ceased to be alienated, the State has been converted into a world-wide thoroughgoing democracy, the causes of social conflict have been eliminated, all, in short, is as it should be.

Though, by and large, the argument holds up that utopianism tends towards totalitarian politics because the overall end will dominate all means to achieve it, there are nevertheless elements of utopian thinking in even the most modest of piecemeal programmes. The usual contrast is between, on the one hand, the utopian project with its clearly conceived blueprint and, on the other, a negatively utilitarian emphasis on putting right what is wrong without concerning itself too much with what's going to go in its place. But every move to put something right implies at least a notion that a potentially better alternative could in principle exist, and usually contains a notion of what that might be. It is not so much, therefore, a contrast between a politics that has a clear conception of ends and one that wants only to remedy evils, but is a question of totalities. Utopianism in its insistence on getting everything right all at once, rather than letting the effects of particular changes work themselves through the social system, is, in effect, undialectical. The irony is that much anti-utopianism is wedded to as firm a hostility to marxism, a system of political thought that more than any other stresses the inseparability of any single element of society from the rest. The further irony is this sense of the interrelatedness of the social, which is marxism's most potentially anti-utopian feature, can both by its friends and enemies be simplified into a dogma of the ultimate blueprint.

Whether or not Mesmer is a marxist, there's no doubt he's a utopian, though by a characteristic twist, his Blue Prints are not equated with 2411, but with those aspects of the present that drive him into the future. This catalogue of wrongs is the reverse of 2411, where each one of the elements of the Blue Prints has been righted or abolished, making for a utopia that is in a curious way an effect of an aggregated piecemeal programme, a sort of anti-utopian utopia.

Alternatively, Mesmer's sickness, his insanity, is a response to the 'sanity' of a world of which the Blue Prints are a factual record. Mesmer's complaint, like Portnoy's before him, has both a medical and a protesting sense. Reality sickens him, phantasy lures him with its vision of sanity.

Like Mesmer, the Left, by which is meant all those whose political project consists in changing the world rather than exploiting it, suffers from a characteristic 'sickness'. Reality, the way things are, is the cause of the sickness, either through its direct effects or, more attenuatedly, through a capacity to identify with the sufferings of others, and the cure is to be found precisely in changing that reality. The corresponding 'health' of the Right consists in an acceptance of and maximising advantage from the way things are. Unpleasant aspects of reality are avoided rather than confronted, the suffering of others is ignored rather than alleviated.

These reflections can be made sharper by considering them in the context of the analytic situation and its criteria for health and neurosis. At root the analytic cure is unconcerned about the social consequences of its resolution, except in so far as these impinge upon the psychological functioning of the analysand. Adaptational therapies, to whose ranks in the United States psychoanalysis tends to have been recruited, by contrast conceive of cure as happy conformity of the individual to the social norm, health under these criteria being defined in terms of the relation of the individual to society, whereas for psychoanalysis it is defined in terms of the resolution of inner conflict within the psychic apparatus. The one's healthy individual may be the other's sick individual, and vice versa, a point that stands out most starkly, but by no means uniquely, in the Soviet State's practice of treating dissidents as insane. Adaptational therapies equate health with social conformity and, by and large, such conformity is incompatible with the project of trying to change the world. The psychoanalytic notion of health has nothing to say about social conformity one way or the other.

Mesmer, then, and the Left more generally, is indeed sick by the criteria of adaptational therapies, as equally Reed and the Right are healthy. But by psychoanalytic criteria, of which Reed is the guardian despite everything, Mesmer's refusal to take the world as it is may or may not be crazy. It is not Mesmer's sickness at the world that is his problem, Reed intuits, but his retreat into phantasy. And from this psychotic detachment from the real, Reed is quite right to try and cure him.

While not competent to produce even a sketchy history of utopian thought, I would propose, by no means originally, that utopias take on the colouration of the aspirations of rising classes and other groups. Utopian visions may be seen as the ideal expression of such aspirations, conceived before the full potential of the class or group in question has emerged in reality and rendered such dreams open to the critique of dystopia, the nightmare every dream can become. Thus More's *Utopia* presaged the actual requirements of the bourgeoisie—legal equality, private ownership of property, contractual freedom, and so on—and gave them an ideal form over and against the existing hierarchical feudal social relations. When, in time, the acquisition of power by this class brought into existence a world very different from the ideal, one in which a ruthlessly exploited proletariat was an integral part, a new utopian vision could emerge, expressive of the struggles of these newly dispossessed. In William Morris's scientific utopia *News from Nowhere* we find a characteristic blend of romanticism and marxism, extolling the communal and collective and projecting them into a realm of non-industrial, even pre-industrial, rurality that seemed the only alternative to the horrors of urbanisation under capitalism. Now that the various socialisms, a century later, functioning in the name at least of the working class, have brought into existence new forms of oppression and have done nothing to dispel such aspects of the old order as racism, nationalism and male domination, the newly or still oppressed continue to write their future histories of how things ought to be.

Of these, none is more forceful in industrial capitalist countries than the women's movement. As well as articulating hitherto invisible forms of oppression and engaging in a variety of specific struggles at different levels within the social formation, the movement has re-thought the terms in which their oppression, and hence society, is conceived. Just as the rising bourgeoisie invented a discourse of universal moral responsibility, the rising proletariat a materialist notion of historical change, so the women's movement is developing a theory of patriarchy that while drawing upon prior work in anthropology and psychoanalysis is transforming both these into a new conceptual field. As a corollary of such thinking, the existing order of social relations can be contrasted with one that is its ideal non-patriarchal counterpart.

The text of *The Utopian* was written under the impact of such a discourse. Its influence extends throughout the text to an equal, in some respects greater, degree than that of socialist thinking.

III

The theory of patriarchy points out that all existing societies, including the socialist countries where the promise of women's emancipation has been only partially fulfilled, are dominated by men in fact and ruled by the law of the father in principle. The actual dominance of men is mirrored by the symbolic dominance of the phallus, under whose sign women enter society as suffering a lack, to be made up in derivative form only through the acquisition of a baby. Further, the patriarchal order is founded on the internalisation of the incest taboo, that feature of all existing human societies which Levi-Strauss has shown permits the exchange of women and the extension of social life beyond the biological family. This also takes place under the threat of castration for the boy-child, symbolically expressed as the limitation of desire for the mother in order that other women may subsequently take her place. For girl-children, the more complex Oedipal passage involves not only a transfer of libido from mother to father before repression occurs, but also a prior process of opting for one of several positions in relation to the clitoral/penile comparison. The forms taken by the various agencies within the psyche—superego, ego and id—thus all bear the differential marks of their bearers' entry into society, of which none more pronounced than those relating to desire. The specification of those forms of oppression of women deriving from the different structures of desire in men and women, coupled with and in addition to those economic and political, has been an accomplishment of the women's movement.

The first section of the 2411 text indicates that the phallus has ceased to occupy the prime place it had under patriarchy, has been replaced by a new index of sexual difference, that of the vulva, and now occupies a marginal position as the allcock and, more problematically, as the clitoral-littoral. Mesmer's utopia is evidently an expression of a wish to know female sexuality and force it into the confines of his own desire, at the same time as his desire seeks to find its own object. The allcock compromises the matriarchy with the ineliminable trace of phallicly defined gender difference, introducing a certain instability, later amplified, into the 2411 text. So despite its concern to placate an imaginary castrating mother with such supposed sops to feminism as the absence of the incest taboo, the supremacy of the mother, the downgrading of the role of the father to mere biological intervention—and that only as one possible means of procreation—Mesmer's utopia moves, narratively and figuratively, across a phallicly constituted slippage of signifiers.

The introduction of Very Light enhances the tension already present and provides a condition for the narrative to develop. Mesmer's journey, unspecifiable as to its aim and object within uncompromised matriarchy, whatever in fact that might be, is co-opted into the much more pressing need Very has to restore his mother Candle to life. The account of her death, wrapped up in a series of puns and metaphors, is given laconically enough by Very but leaves Mesmer deeply troubled. However, Very's apparent lack of concern masks his deep-seated wish to return, and to take Mesmer with him, to the site of her 'snuffing it', of her 'going out like a Light'. The metaphoric density of the text at this point resists analysis, but since a well-known principle of psychoanalysis has it that the point of greatest resistance is potentially the place of greatest advance, certain indications are called for.

The most obvious component is the regressive wish to return to the mother-child dyad, when the flame of infantile desire burned brightly. Mesmer is caught up in Very's, that is to say Reed's, project, and this is consistent with what takes place later on in the present text, as Mesmer becomes made progressively an accomplice to Reed's schemes. Thus Mesmer's wish to escape from the madness-inducing reality of the present into a world where all is sweetness and light is caught up in Reed/Very's darker, more arcane desire, which turns out in the end to be for death. But before that, much takes place on the borderline between the Imaginary world of the mother and the Symbolic world of the father. The extinction of the flame of infantile desire under the threat of castration finds expression in a veritable explosion of phallic objects and signs: Wick (that which is dipped), Candle, the taper (which little Very lit before his mother took her last dive) and Very Light himself whose beard and baldness suggests pubic hair and the retracted foreskin of the erect penis. The implication is that Very/Reed wishes to be the phallus, specifically, to restore his mother to life (= wholeness) by being her phallus. This position is, we know from the double perspective of the psychoanalysis of women and of all of us, one the baby enjoys. Mesmer, in so far as he is party to Very/Reed's regression, partakes of this wish to become the penis of the phallic woman, but parts company with his analyst when Reed calls in Brand, preparatory for the greater and final regression to when he was in no way distinguishable from his mother, to before his birth, to death.

The most striking free-floating detached phallic object in the 2411 text is the dragon's tooth, which bears Very Light's and ultimately Mesmer Partridge's initials. The Oedipal import of this is suggested straightaway with the intertextual associations of dragon's teeth, which legend has it were the foundation stones of the city of Thebes, where the drama of Oedipus took place. Rather than the phallus Very might wish to be, the dragon's tooth signifies the phallus Mesmer can have, the acceptance of which from the father denotes his accession to the patriarchal order and acknowledgement of incest prohibition. When he first touches it in the pub overlooking the Trent he experiences desire in relation to April and May, little girls such as a post-Oedipal pre-pubertal boy might be interested in, at the same time as Very/Lenin is recounting the story of the Russian Revolution. This recapitulates and reverses the order of socialist first, man second, his priority at the time of his sexual initiation by Miss J. S. IV, the first event in the series culminating in his mental breakdown. Subsequently the dragon's tooth marks in its special way the displacement of his interest from girls to women, June and Julie, then later, on board The Loaded Parrot registers his acting out of the phantasy of the engulfing mother, after which he becomes its bearer. Finally, having acquired its symbolic re-inscription MP, it is refused by the dragon where it originated, leaving Mesmer in possession of both it and the knowledge that women are not missing anything. He can now return to Stock Port without Very, there to begin his adult life as a man in 2411's matriarchy.

While this far from exhaustive account of the role of the phallus in 2411 indicates that the imaginary matriarchal order is permeated by the existing patriarchy—how could it be otherwise?—it is not thereby reduced to it. Mesmer's working through of his Oedipal resolutions via the analyst's stand-in of Very is but one component of the 2411 text.

Mesmer's matriarchy, though compromised, acts as a critique of the patriarchal order he finds himself within in the present, in particular through the close parallel between Very and Reed, and the continual counterpoint between the 2411 text and the present text. The patriarch as trapeze artist who has lost his balance, as the father who never knew his son, as Don Juan unable to get an erection, as the analyst who goes insane, as the baby in search of the mother, as the murderer who succeeds only in self-destruction—these are the figures the text makes play with. The one-time star of the circus ring, Christ, Lenin or whoever else has held the crowd's upward gaze and bated breath, becomes the cheery saddletramp, the decrepit punster. If, finally, Reed's uncontrollable aggression rebounds upon himself and he is consigned to an overdue termination, his 2411 representation lives on, diminished and harmless it is true, having exchanged his trapeze for a donkey and his donkey for a dragon, to travel on to some unknown destination at the dragon's whim. The end of patriarchy does not signal the end of the male gender, and the figures of Reed and Very, as broken-down patriarchs, have their helping roles, Very as fellow traveller who gives Mesmer somewhere to go, Reed as analyst who hears Mesmer out. Each in his different way and from his different position within the text provides Mesmer with what he was missing, Very the full membership of his 2411 society and Reed the power to act where before he could only dream. The extent of the cure Reed can provide is limited by the nature of Mesmer's complaint, in that it is the world that drives him insane and the only cure for that is social change.

While the narrative is dominated by male figures in one respect, in terms of sheer numbers they are considerably outweighed by the women. First though, a word about the question of characterisation. With the exceptions of Reed and Mesmer, who are respectively overblown to the point of caricature and highly schematised, none of the characters are offered as points of identification. They are not rounded, full or believable, are not, in short, the products of realism, and they should not be treated as if they were.

In the present text the significant women, that is to say those who contribute to the narrative's economy and could not be removed without repercussions elsewhere, are: (from the case facts) Mesmer's mother Esme, his sisters Vicky and Rose, Miss Junior Stockport IV, Dr X, and 'a dour nurse'; (and from Reed's commentary) Reed's unknown mother, his first and second wives, Sonia Petersen, and his patients Mrs Minceberger, Mrs Spein-Chiller and Mrs Skywide. From 2411: Mesmer's breast-mother, his sisters Lois and Marushka, Elmsfootloose III, Mandy Rocket, April and May, June and Julie, the sea-bitch Beth, and, by repute, Candle Light.

Rather than considering these individually and finding only eccentricity, a more productive approach treats them as elements within certain structures. Generally speaking, the notion of repetition and doubling is once more to the fore. There is a close parallel between Mesmer's case fact series and his 2411 series, with the mother and two sisters present in each, and Elmsfootloose III and Mandy Rocket together matching up with Miss Junior Stockport IV—Mandy Rocket, recall, designed Mesmer's allcock and Elmsfootloose educated him about sexual difference. Beyond that there is a doubling of doubles with Mesmer's two case-factual sisters matching first Lois and Marushka, then the equally young but non-related April and May, then their mothers June and Julie.

Reed's over-evaluation of Sonia doubles Mesmer's enchantment with June. Candle is comparable with Reed's long-dead mother, whom he never knew.

The other main axis of significance apart from doubling is that of opposition, which may be thought of as a kind of negative doubling. A series of pairs may be constructed, effectively demarcating a number of potential places the women of the text can occupy. Notable oppositions, together with the characters each term most pertinently fits, are: desired(able) (Sonia, June)/ undesired(able) (Reed's female patients, his ex-wives); working (2411's women, with the exception of June)/ non-working (Reed's women, with the exception of Sonia initially); familial (mothers and sisters)/non-familial; mutilated (June, Beth)/non-mutilated; child (April, May)/adult (June, Julie); phallic (Elmsfootloose, Beth)/non-phallic; and, to extend the notion of character, animal (the moister-oyster, the whale, the dragon)/human.

Mesmer and Reed's passage through the text can be considered in terms of the encounters they have with the various positions women can take according to such a schema. Each in his different way has to negotiate the range of relational options that the text and, since the individual imagination is in the last instance always social, our existing social order permits men toward women.

The occupation of positions over a series of oppositions is one way of articulating the obsessions and phantasies pertaining within a particular social order. One particular emphasis the series allows and indeed foregrounds is that relating to mutilation and violation.

Men's typical phantastic fear of women resides in the threat of castration they represent. The perceived 'wound' of the female genitalia, the 'loss' of the penis they can be imagined to have had, the castration anxieties around the Oedipal passage which are linked to perceptions of gender difference, the symbolic significance of erectile potency and the fears attaching to its loss, the myth of vagina dentata—all this and more attests to the scope of the phantasy. The corresponding female fear concerns violent penetration by the penis—and so far as phantasy is concerned all penetration is violent—most extremely yet paradigmatically by the 'impossibly' large paternal or adult male organ as projected back on to the perception of the little girl.

These phantasies are asymmetrical in at least two respects. Firstly, castration involves loss, and loss of gender definition, but does not transform the imaginary body in its topology, which remains the topological equivalent of the closed sphere. Penetration, on the other hand, does not entail gender change but does alter the topology of the body from a closed to an open sphere, that is to say one that can be turned inside out. Different aspects of the self are therefore threatened by these two phantasies. For the male it is not his 'humanity' but only his sex; for the female her very bodily being is transformed into something unknowable, is threatened with otherness. Secondly, and importantly, women's fears are consistently and with much publicity realised, while men's are not (except in the minor variant, not without its attendant trauma, of loss of erectile potency). Women do get raped by men, men don't get castrated by women. A part of the horror of rape derives from the rupturing and transformation of the bodily self which takes place without any of the countering force of a wish 'to take inside'.

Rape, then, by no means exhausts the 'violence' of penetration. The moment of transformation from the closed surface of clitoral pleasure to the open one of vaginal discovery is a charged one in most (all?) cultures, guarded by ritual and hemmed in by taboo. It is held in the West to mark the symbolic transition from girlhood to womanhood, the recognition of which, incidentally, is not to concur with the sort of moralistic essentialism that demands the 'true woman' be receptive to penetration— no more than its converse that the 'true man' resists (anal) penetration.

The complex play of meanings relating to the psychoanalytic figure of castration has been touched on, without yet speaking of it with regard to the women of the text. Sufficient here to say that Mesmer's utopian women are inscribed within the same symbolic order as that in which he is dreaming, that is to say, such figures of castration, mutilation and so on are carried over into his utopia to co-exist alongside the countering figures of a matriarchal primacy. Reed is right therefore to treat it as symptomatic, though what he cannot conceive is that it is symptomatic not so much of individual neurosis but of social contradiction. Mesmer's girl-children April and May, penetrated in phantasy, speak of an obsession with the lower age boundary of the girl-to-woman transition that is a feature of our culture. His symbolically castrated June, object of his 'enchantment', with her nutrient graft and star-map nipples, is the fetishized woman whose lure is so consistently powerful. Phallicised Beth is the 'man-woman' of the male imagination whose clitoris successfully competes with the penis. And so on.

Considerations of topological transformation are not, however, limited to the women of the text. Mesmer himself undergoes a transformation which in certain respects represents an even more radical reconstruction than that of penetration when he swallows Grey Dagger and the TV lead. This effectively transforms him from a closed sphere to a torus (doughnut), with a hole running right through him. Where he thought he was, safely centred, he is not. Instead there is an absence at the point where all ideologies of the unified subject would put presence. Through that missing centre can run the thread of the TV lead, linking him irredeemably to a world not of his own choosing, making him part and effect of the social order rather than an indivisible psychological whole within it.

Such a decentring of the individual subject has been the effect of the discoveries of both Marx and Freud, the join at which these two explanatory systems meet. The text's debt to both these ways of thinking is explicit, and the investigation into the compatibility of the communist and matriarchal dimensions of 2411 may also be conceived as one into the continued compatibility of Marx and Freud. Both systems invoke the idea of structure, in common with the natural sciences, although the structures here are non-physical, in the one instance social, in the other mental. At its simplest, marxism says that 'people' occupy places within economic, political and ideological structures, and psychoanalysis that 'people' are themselves structures. The ideologically given object 'person' is thus bracketed, but in question, as is the concomitant baggage of essences, innate characters and transcendent morality, to the embarrassment of those whose political, cultural or even literary projects requires them to be irreducibles. Such anti-humanism does not, as its detractors suppose, lead to a criminal indifference to people but to the far from utopian project of the betterment of the human condition via an understanding of its social and psychological origins.

IV

All texts have their origins in determinate conjunctures, whose effects are therein inscribed whatever pains the author may take to achieve something not of his or her time. Such attempts at disguise are not generally called for, of course, except when the world of the fiction is to be radically different from our own, as in some science fiction or a utopia. But these too, however imaginative, even in proportion to their apparent otherness, are inescapably of their time, as a quick glance through yesterday's futures shows. Jules Verne, H. G. Wells, Huxley, Orwell, Bradbury, Ballard have their times as surely written across their work as any writer using everyday settings. To imagine that one can escape the present is an illusion. All that can be done is to release the currently conceived range of options the future seems to hold, which never finally says anything about real futures but only about the working of ideology in the present. Yet in achieving this more modest end such fiction can have a better grasp of the present that that which consciously and specifically addresses itself to the existing order of things. Our hopes and fears may be a more accurate measure of current reality than our sense, always inherited from the past, of the way things actually are. The present always eludes us, is invisible to us, because the understanding the present produces is not until later available to interpret it. The present therefore is in excess of our capacity to make sense of it, in the same way as texts are in excess of the meanings they offer at the moment of their production. Future readers discover what makes the text of its time. They uncover its unconscious, of which the author more than anyone is ignorant, even innocent. (While the supplement, by positioning itself an iota further down the march of time than the text, may be able to elucidate meanings unapparent at the moment of the text's conception, the text plus supplement, that is to say *The Utopian*, cannot but be ignorant of its own unconscious.)

In reaching out from a patriarchal capitalist order and invoking one that is neither, the text must bear the traces of all it negates. Its conscious vision owes everything to the struggles of those classes, genders, nations, groups, ethnicities the existing order oppresses, but whose voices, however muffled, are nonetheless heard, at least by Mesmer strung out on his TV wire, delving in his encyclopaedia. His vision, constructed from the hopes, demands and needs of those whose voices he hears, awaits the reading that will consign it to a past as a moment of utopian history.

The terms of Mesmer's oppression are inarticulate, conceivable only through his identification with that of others. His final silence in the case facts, following on from his fall from speech to writing, indicates that for all his successful journeying they remain undiscovered. Instead we are left with the traces in the dust, the last of the line of signifiers he encounters, language in search of an object. The fiction, with its supplementary metafiction, continually falters on, skirts around, toys with its constituent material, as if the answer to the question of the utopian vision is to be found within language and nowhere else. In a sense it is, if only for the truistic reason that both questions and answers, facts and fictions, are verbal entities. In a deeper sense too the text's concern is fundamentally with language, as Reed twists around on the tortuousness of his own chosen prose, its unconscious erupting through it in a welter of slips, hesitations, gaps and forgettings, in short all the material which he as analyst should be working on to produce the cure for the analysand. And though the reporting of 2411 is classically transparent, with the signifier neatly containing and contained by its signified, the world so rendered is by no means an imaginary untroubled by the symbolic order it exists within. The symbolic lurks just beneath the surface of the text, ready, like the significant fish and their successors, to present a word for inspection, complete with the chains of association leading away from it to unknown conclusions. Very Light scatters signifiers around like a cloud of virtual particles around an atomic nucleus, indeterminate, undefinable, and fleeting, but beyond this quasi-analytic presence the 2411 text continually threatens to tear apart the language it's made up of. Even the place names—Stock Port, Bright On, Ma Sails—mock the solidity of the objects to which they purport to refer. Here we approach the crux of the matter. For the attempt to write a matriarchy, communist or otherwise, in which the law of the father has been superseded, in which the symbolic order ushered in by the function of paternity and the incest taboo has been irredeemably altered, nonetheless relies upon the language of such a precedent order. That language, as much as anything else, is of its time, even makes its time. If the represented is unspecifiable apart from the means of its representation, and if such means necessarily are inadequate, then it is quite simply impossible to say what one wants. This is not merely a failure of the imagination, even of well-judged foresight, but is in the very nature of language and its objects, and of desire and its. In so far as a utopia is a consummate representation in language of a certain object of desire, one in which all desire would be satisfiable, it is an impossibility. Having said one thing, having held in place in language the condition for satisfaction, desire, that is to say, the beyond of what has been written, begins its own work of disruption, of putting in process what had momentarily been fixed. The specification of the object of desire is to already open the way to the pure signifier whose chain of attendant meanings leads on to newly constituted objects of desire, more, better, yet more desirable. Utopia as an object flees away from the pursuer along chains of signification.

This said, the position that language is language is language, with no possibility of saying anything about anything, is a formalism that itself is ultra-leftist and utopian. While it is true that utopias devolve upon desire and language, it is also the case we live in a real world and that something can be done about it. Visions of what might be, as well as specific struggles against what is, empower all social movements committed to change. While what will happen is unknowable, being an effect of a complex array of forces which includes as yet unknowable future knowledge as one of its determining elements, the material force of such aspirations should not be underestimated. 'To each according to her desire' is not exclusive to 2411.

What is/what is not, fact/fiction . . . It would be tempting to align the two dichotomies and set up equations between fiction and the imagined future, between fact and the existing present. Quite apart from the indubitably factual but equally inexistent past, the dichotomies won't align for the reason they occupy different conceptual territories, the one ontological, the other discursive. Nevertheless, having said this, and without getting into philosophical technicalities, there is a sufficient overlap between the two to make the correspondence worth pursuing a little further. Certain discourses within the fiction refer not simply to an imaginary world but to objects, which if contextualised differently, would be held to be real. Harley Street, Wilhelm Reich, Tammy Wynette and the gluteus maximus are potentially inscribable in a factual discourse in a way that Wick's circus, Old Jack, Viola Fortini and starmap nipples are not. The extra-textual, albeit textualised and fictionalised, exerts a constant pressure on the text, as it gets caught up in the tension between the conceivable and the actual, between Mesmer's Utopia and the world of his Blue Prints. This pressure is nowhere more pronounced than at those points where current anxieties about the future of humanity are counterpointed by the seemingly unlimited benefits offered by the good use of a similar technology as that which threatens us with destruction.

The second millennium approaches with hopes and fears in a precarious balance, one in which the long haul towards peace and global prosperity may be overtaken at any moment by total annihilation. On the one hand a technology which offers the prospect of unlimited energy, computer-controlled production, rationally planned use of resources, the progressive elimination of disease, in other words all the material conditions for a life of ease and freedom, and on the other the instant

Armageddon offered by the arsenals of the superpowers. This contrast, more than anything else, numbs, terrifies and bewilders not just Mesmer Partridge, but presumably most people in the world.

In despair Mesmer wonders whether he should give no more than a blind monkey's fuck in a snowstorm. To which Reed, recalling his days as a walker in the Black Forest and a conversation with a philosopher some may have identified as the existentialist Martin Heidegger, replies in effect that though this is no bad expression of the human condition the fact of care is also a structuring principle of our existence. Care, in its dual sense of both solicitous concern and of burden, runs through us, makes us human. If there is anywhere within the opposed discourses of Mesmer's 2411 and Reed's case study where they meet, if there is a single instance of Reed's capacity to care overcoming his narcissism, if there is a moment at which Mesmer is rescued from an incipient nihilism, it is this. Without Reed, Mesmer would never have completed his year and a day of journeying. Reed's own deteriorating ability to tell reality from phantasy and his own engulfing dark side render him deaf to the nuances of Mesmer's tale beyond this point. The crumbling facade of patriarchal authority reveals a chaos of confusions, conflicts and a desperate last-ditch attempt to ward off the loss of his power by enlisting the services of the thug Brand, who characteristically, or at the unconscious behest of his master, fucks up. A metaphor, is this, not surprisingly, for the planetary ruling class, most precisely the owners and controllers of international capital, whose remedies for the increasing instability of their regime and mounting protests of the multiply oppressed rely more and more upon the threat of violence, upon the build-up of assorted weaponry. If, flux forbid, the hand of the professional killer cannot be stayed, then our white hope must be it falls on its hirer, leaving Mesmer free to complete his journey, whose last day is 2412's first.

The text offers no conclusions, except the negative one that change cannot be halted. There are no final solutions, no utopias, no points at which all desires are satisfied or all conflict ended. But far from being grounds for despair this endless unfolding of history's text, written and re-written, read and re-read, is the condition for making a few as yet indecipherable scratches upon it. The future is open, despite pessimisms which see annihilation or the iron heel as the only options—though these cannot be ruled out. It may be the combination of social movement and bioengineering will indeed stimulate a move towards matriarchy, even towards the elimination of the male gender, unflattering though that is to my male self-esteem and (consequently perhaps) on form so far unlikely to improve things much. The international proletariat may yet find its way forward after the impasse of the last half century and provide the conditions for the emancipation of us all, as the founders of dialectical materialism thought it would. Maybe fractions of humanity as yet unthought of will emerge to guide us into a safer and happier future. Perhaps another global war will take place, then others out of the ashes, an endless recapitulation of death and desire, of destruction and construction, under the name of the symbolic father for ever. Maybe we live under orders of reality as yet unsuspected, so that our understanding of history may turn out to be as misconceived as that of the millenarians of a thousand years back. We know only that history is unfinished, like analysis, like the text. The last word is still unwritten.

Afterword:

The Interpretation of Political Dreams

ANDREW COLLIER

The text of *The Utopian* alternates between the words of Mesmer Partridge, the utopian, comprising a narrative of a journey through England and thence via France to the north of Scotland in 2411, by then part of a worldwide libidinised communist matriarchy; and the words of Dr Reed, the psychoanalyst to whom this journey is recounted by way of 'free association'. Dr Reed is a figure such as might be played Fernando Rey in a Buñuel film: he is bourgeois to the bones, aging, lustful, impotent, sexist, an obsessive gourmet. He is the 'master of suspicion' from whom we learn of Mesmer's garage-owning father ('From infancy the gurgle of the pumps, the hiss of the sprayguns, the whine of the salesmen'), Mesmer's own brief career as a sectarian revolutionary, and of his 'crisis of militancy' alias schizophrenic breakdown. At one level, the credibility of Mesmer's utopia as politics is undermined from without by the uncovering of its neurotic origins, as well as from inside by its mythological features (e.g. the dragon's tooth, of which more later). For Reed's 'case facts' do not leave any doubt that Mesmer's breakdown is no mere 'labelling strategy' on the part of family or doctors.

At the same time, 2411 is a seductive utopia, combining the attractions of several classic utopias: nature conquered as in Bacon's dream, yet culture integrated into nature as in Morris's—and hedonism even more rampant than in the mediaeval poem *The Lark of Cokaygne.* Mesmer's prose has an undeniable charm about it, though slipping now into sentimentality, now into adolescent sexual fantasy, as Reed is quick to point out. Reed's prose is tougher, he gets some of the best lines, but in the end that is about all he gets. For Reed, notwithstanding the confidence borne of wealth and a training analysis, is a man taken over by the death drive; while he is an unrepentant bourgeois and phallocrat, he is as ready to see the passing of his class and sex as Wagner's Wotan to submit to the twilight of the gods. Just as the name 'Mesmer Partridge' suggests a certain misfittedness,[1] the name 'Reed' evokes biblical images of culpable weakness: 'The broken reed . . . that pricks and pierces the hand of the man that leans on it' (Isaiah 36), or (bringing out the contrast with the revolutionary) 'Hanging your head like a reed' disparaged in favour of the injunction 'let the oppressed go free, and break every yoke' (Isaiah 58). But I must return to the question of the mutual critique of the narratives—what they debunk and what they leave—when I can do so with more concreteness.

To précis a narrative is always to do it an injustice, and for the purposes of the present essay I can be excused recounting Mesmer's Journey. Instead, I shall sketch the social structure which is the background of it.

The 'base' of that structure is easily outlined: science and technology have become gentle giants, yielding a massive increase of human power over nature, which power is exercised with restraint and respect. The motorways inherited from 'garagism' (Mesmer's word for modern capitalism) have been grassed over; a herd of roe deer watch Mesmer 'with a genetic wariness still not abolished by the absence of danger from Woman'. Scientific control of the weather has led not to bureaucratic predictability, but to variety 'in accordance with the theory of Regional Difference'. Genetic engineering has made it 'possible for any number of individuals to contribute to the genetic endowment of a foetus', but 'for the most part, after the abuses of the garagist class in attempting to eliminate discontent by suppressing certain inheritances, post-Revo society limited the contributors to those involved in the CARING-SHARING (q.v.)'. (The upper case phrase is the only familiar instance of a set of rhyming paired concepts which is Mesmer's conceptual apparatus for understanding society in 2411).

The socio-economic structure is based, like Morris's, on local communes, city-states in which direct democracy prevails. The relations between the communes are mediated by the NOBLE-GLOBAL, the pooled information and allocation system into which 'any person or collectivity or region' can register their complaints at any time. The name for the economy thus governed, the SIFTING-SHIFTING, suggests that the tunnel vision of commodity production, seeing only the exchange value of its intended product, has been replaced by an awareness of all the effects of human labour on people and environment.

The surprises come with the superstructure: its matriarchy, its sexuality, its language, and magic. In the first place, while classical communism has aimed at the emancipation of 'all mankind, without distinction of sex or race',[2] 2411 is explicitly said to be a matriarchy. Fathering is occluded, but the mother-child couple, uninterrupted by paternal intrusion and the consequent oedipus complex,[3] continues into adult life. This is reflected in language and symbolism. While some aspects of 'sexist language' have simply been evened out (the sailor Beth can be admiringly called 'a real sea-bitch'), others have been inverted (the generic feminine in the quote about roe deer). In place of the supposedly phallocentric Freudian theory of sexual stages (oral, anal, phallic, genital),[4] we have the CLITORAL-LITTORAL and the SPINAL-VAGINAL. The pairing of words itself (matched by the splitting of place names: Stock Port, Man Chester) suggests, with allusion to Irigaray, the replacement of the unity of the phallus with the duality of a pair of lips. Many, perhaps all, sexual taboos have disappeared; brother-sister incest, lesbianism, troilism, sexual relations across great age differences—none of these causes a raised eyebrow (male homosexuality makes no appearance, but nor do males, apart from Mesmer and Very, and their relationship, as we shall see, is pre-empted by the transference situation). At one level, this is wish-fulfilment for Mesmer, locked in his room in 1979 'LISTENING TO MY FATHER BULLY MY MOTHER DOWNSTAIRS/ MASTURBATING THREE TIMES A DAY', as he tells us in the second Blue Print. But the wishes might be regarded as regressive in two senses:

1. The traditional Marxist view (whether true or not matters little) was that matriarchy and 'group marriage' belong to primitive communal society, not mature communism. However 'regression' here has only a historical, not an evaluative meaning.

2. From a psychoanalytical point of view, on the other hand, an undisturbed libidinal relation to one parent may appear as regressive in a pejorative sense—as infantilising. Furthermore, it must occur to the reader, though Mesmer's narrative gives no intimation of it, that mothers might find such a continuing tie a bit of a strain. While it is possible to see Mesmer's 'Journey', which is clearly a recognised rite of passage in 2411, as akin to the 'end of mothering' in Marge Piercy's *Woman at the Edge of Time* (Antony Easthope reads it this way),[5] I can find nothing in the text to suggest any such loosening of this dyadic attachment.

But this aspect of matriarchy is the point of entry of a serpent into the Eden of 2411. Mesmer's companion of the road is one Very Light, trapeze artist, magician and reincarnation of Lenin.[6] His Mother, Candle Light, has committed suicide in the circus by diving into a tank of gasoline with a lighted torch between her teeth. Her son Very, at her request, lit the torch. Parallel with Mesmer's Journey (clearly a transference-symbol for his analysis) is Very's quest to bring his mother back to life—a quest which ends with his own departure, on the back of a female dragon, from the sublunary world. This whole subplot is infested with magic, which raises a number of questions, staging with Reed's 'Are there Marxist-Leninist magicians?' Yet Very's magic is no alien intrusion like that of the Devil among the Stalinists in Bulgakov's *The Master and Margarita*. No one in 2411 is surprised by the dragon's tooth that Very has acquired; June the female protagonist, has psychic powers; the children of New Stoke chant negentropic spells at a party to keep the hot drinks hot and the iced ones icy; New Stoke itself (built on the site of the Five Towns, destroyed by the garagists in the civil war) has the form of a pentacle. Yet magic—that prototype of all manipulative technologies—can hardly be said to occupy the niche of religion in the superstructure of 2411, about which all we learn is that the word 'flux' or 'the flux' (the paradigm of that which eludes manipulation) occupies the lexical if not the theological role of the word 'God' in modern English. And 'flux' after all has dialectical credentials, from the dictum of Heraclitus (an early dialectical materialist, according to Lenin) that everything is in flux, to Mao Zedong's idea that funerals should be joyful celebrations of the triumph of the dialectic: everything passes.

But before interpreting these images of nature in the ideology of 2411, a word is required on the psychoanalytical dimension of this. There is a somewhat loose parallel between the people in Mesmer's life in 1979 and those in his fantasy of 2411. Reed's alter ego is Very Light, whom he dismisses, in the spirit of Mesmer's rhyming pairs, as a verbal gerbil. Very is a focus of positive and negative transference; the transference must be worked through, and the 'progressive depopulation of the room' accomplished—i.e. the elimination of the super-ego figures projected by the analysand onto the analyst. Before his analysis, Mesmer's 'transference' has presumably been onto Lenin. Hence Very must 'be' both Reed and Lenin, and as such must be loved, revered, made ridiculous, and ultimately bidden 'flux speed'.

The focus of the magic—the dragon's tooth—is produced by Very in a pub in New Stoke. As Mesmer fingers it, dark doubts arise in his mind about Very's intentions. Then Very reveals his previous identity, and listeners gather to hear his tales of Bolshevism. Among them, two girls, April and May, sit and finger the tooth. Its magic transports Mesmer into an irresistible illusion in accordance with the girls' sexual fantasies. From then on, Very's Lenin narrative is interrupted as the acrobatically and geometrically extravagant fantasies alternate with it. This incongruous alternation cocks a snook at both super-ego figures: at Reed, who has just surmised that Mesmer has been influenced by the 'conceptual flatus' of his Jungian rival Dr Schwitzelstik, and goes on to align him with his

Reichian rival Dr Beanbag; and at the overserious and prudish Lenin. For it is not the same as if Very had re-incarnated Engels or Luxemburg; this is the Lenin who could not believe his ears when he heard that working women discussed sexual problems at party meetings—the Lenin who said that the Soviet State would manufacture everything 'except icons and vodka'.

At this point I may seem to be in danger of getting into a blind alley. I have focused on the mutually critical nature of the two narratives which constitute *The Utopian*. But the initial effectiveness of each narrative may be undermined if read under sentence of the other's critique. We would then have a replication at the imaginary level of the theoretical blind alleys of 'applied psychoanalysis' digging for the neurotic roots of the discontents of civilisation, and reductive Marxism dismissing psychoanalysis as the self-indulgence of a decadent bourgeoisie.

And indeed, at a seminar on utopianism at which this book was discussed, I have heard some readers suggest that the fantasy character of 2411 and the manifest neurosis of Mesmer, as revealed in Reed's 'case facts', thoroughly drain any political content from the utopian narrative; that the wishes it fulfils are oedipal or pubertal, the content distorted by subjective aversion to garages and sectarian politics, the images regressively evoking a culture far longer gone than Morris's fourteenth century England or tenth century Iceland. Reed is vindicated about 2411— though in 1979 Reed's own paranoid and probably true belief that his secretary and new wife Sonia is having an affair with Mesmer leads to his own destruction. This in turn has suggested to some that the *whole* text is to be read as Reed's fantasy, a fantasy not of Eros but of Thanatos, the death-wish of one bourgeois sexist projected onto his whole class and sex. It can of course be read that way. For that matter, Reed could be Mesmer's fantasy—the class equivalent of the Cokaygne geese that fly to you, ready roasted on a spit and dressed in garlic, crying 'geese, all hot, all hot!' But then, once one gets into the dubious business of assigning hidden intra-textual narrators, why not Reed's chauffeur Michael, an 'excellent raconteur' who at least shares a forename with the extra-textual narrator? But the serious point that this reading makes is the de-politicisation of the novel; the utopia loses not only its utopian but its Marxist political function. Here I want to defend the political import of the

First, the 'Blue Prints'. Utopias may be described as blueprints for a future society. Mesmer's Blue Prints, written at the brink of his breakdown and entrusted to his sister, contain no such proposals. The first two are stark lists of the evils of life in 1979. The first starts:

SOLITARY CONIFINEMENT
SPRAWLING SUBURBS
MINDLESS REPETITIVE LABOUR
URBAN MOTORWAYS
CONTEMPT FOR KNOWLEDGE
THE DOLE
COMPULSORY OVERTIME
FORCED RETIREMENT
PERMANENT ARMS ECONOMY
CHILEAN JUNTA
RAPE
OVERCROWDED CLASSROOMS
GUTTER PRESS
MUTILATION ON THE ROADS
RACISM

and proceeds for nearly six pages, through 'unwanted uniformity, diesel fumes, defeatism, urban decay, rickets, commercial vandalism, berufsverbot, overfishing, child prostitution', ending with nine verbs which 'sum up what people do to each other': 'ambush, crucify, flummox, grieve, muzzle, nauseate, outstare, vilify, zero in on'.

The second Blue Print, organised in hanging paragraphs starting with the letters of Mesmer Partridge's name, includes such entries as:

RIVEN BY CONTRADICTIONS,

LIKE FAMINES CO-EXISTING WITH FARMERS BEING PAID NOT TO GROW FOOD,

LIKE NOT   ABLE TO AFFORD NURSERY SCHOOLS WHILE LUXURY HOTELS ARE BEING BUILT,

LIKE HOMELESS FAMILIES OUTSIDE EMPTY OFFICE BLOCKS,

LIKE PUTTING PEOPLE OUT OF WORK TO ENRICH THE ECONOMY—and juxtaposes '£20 for a social security claimant, £20,000 for a Picasso sketch, £200,000,000 for a year's worth of dog food, £200,000,000,000 for a year's worth of armaments'.

The brutalities and stupidities of 'late capitalism' (and also of 'existing'—or perhaps I should now say, in a different sense of the word, 'late'—socialism) are presented as the inescapable reality of the world in which Reed makes so comfortable a living. These are not part of Mesmer's neurosis; his neurosis is part of *this* world. And 2411 is at least a world without these phenomena. Here we are on the same ground as classical Marxism: what we know about the socialist future, says Rosa Luxemburg, is what we must get rid of. The concrete particulars that are to replace it can be discovered only in the process of building them.

If Reed and Mesmer have undermined the credibility of each other's positions—the erotic fantasy of the schizoid ex-militant, the thanatic fantasy of the impotent rentier—we are certainly left with the depressing indictment of the status quo; but why then go beyond that indictment, to the images of a utopia? For the following reason, perhaps: the negative definition of socialism favoured by Luxemburg allows us an abstract sketch of the political and economic structures of socialism, but a great deal else is left indeterminate. These structures are the skeleton of socialism; we want to see its face. Many faces might be compatible with his skeleton, and that is part of the strength of the non-utopian style of socialist advocacy—it does not pre-empt the open future. But its drawback is that, confronted with the image of nothing but a skeleton, people expect the face to be a skull. That is to say they take the absence of a description of the facial characteristics of socialism to be a description of their absence. They fear that the socialism projected by scientific socialists will be a society obsessed with pig iron production and committee meetings, in which culture, tradition, personal relationships, carefree pleasure, environmental beauty—not to speak of such things as a sense of awe at the nature of things—would be devalued and marginalised. Some features of 'existing socialist' countries, in their race to catch up with the west technologically, lend credence to this image.

Any attempt to remedy this by predicting theoretically the details of a socialist future would be worse than the problem it aimed to solve. The openness of the future, the freedom of later generations, the diversity of creative solutions to particular problems would be constricted. But an imaginative experiment is a different matter—and all the better if it bears its dreamlike quality on its face, and is a return of today's repressed. Such dreams can be effective politically to the extent that the awakening from that dream to this reality leaves us with an enhanced awareness of the lacks in this reality. Some remarks about one, almost subliminal, theme of *The Utopian* will illustrate this, and for the remainder of the essay, I turn to the material world of 2411 and its symbolic character.

Reed's narrative includes four encounters he claims to have had with historical figures. Two are named: Freud's patient the Rat-man (or rather his ghost) who has determined Reed's choice of profession, and Stalin, whom he has 'psychoanalysed' (at a distance) for the benefit of British intelligence. (This idea is quite credible: the psychoanalyst Walter Langer was employed by the Office of Strategic Services to analyse Hitler in this way.) The other two are identifiable: 'Jules', the French maître in whose company Reed witnesses the Paris events of 1968 is presumably Jacques Lacan: and the unnamed philosopher whom he meets walking in the Black Forest is Martin Heidegger, for the 'fable concerning the origins of man, to the effect that whatever the claims of Jove on his spirit and of the Earth on his body come death, it was Care who first shaped him, and therefore possesses him as long as he lives' occupies a central place in the latter's *Sein und Zeit.*

The place of the first three in the book is easy to see: it was the Rat-man to whom Freud most clearly expounded his view of the dialectic of cure, of the undoing of displacement; Stalin stands for everything about the 'regimes calling themselves socialist' which has 'made socialism so much harder to achieve anywhere', as Mesmer's second Blue Print puts it; and Lacan's translation of psychoanalysis into the terms of classical rhetoric underlies much of Mesmer's linguistic innovation; but what of

Heidegger?

The most fertile of Heidegger's ideas is surely his alternative to the Cartesian model of human beings as minds located inside bodies, the latter clearly bounded by their skins. As against this, Heidegger argues that we are 'being-in-the-world', i.e. our physical being includes the world about us, bound together by our practical concerns, much of which is more intimately part of us than our bodily organs.

There is a basic and subtle contrast between the ideologies of the worlds of 1979 and 2411 in that the latter assumes this model of our relation to environment as an internal relation, while the former we are skin-bounded atomic individuals with only instrumental relations to what is outside our skins. It is this, I think, which gives Mesmer's utopia its charm, which survives Reed's deflationary quips and Mesmer's own self-parody. The place of magic in 2411 is best understood in these terms. Historically, magic played a role in the transition from the medieval world view to the modern instrumentalisation of nature. In 2411 it marks the replacement of the latter by a relation to nature which involves on the one hand its much greater subjection to our will, but on the other its no longer being perceived as external to us, but as making us what we are.[7] Our relation to it is more like our relation to our limbs and organs than our relation to the purely instrumental tools and raw material of 'garagism'. Once again, there are Marxist precedents for this: the young Marx referredrecycled as a birch tree.

But I need to document my thesis. The body in the bounded-by-skin sense is referred to on several occasions in *The Utopian* as the 'body-actual', and this is contrasted with body-electric (a notion, Reed might have said, which would appeal to Dr Beanbag), body-symbolic, body-social, body-atmospheric, and (a final stroke against Descartes) body-mental. These phrases are used in passing, without definition. But the 'obviousness' of our identification with our bodies-actual (with or without the addition of a 'mind') has been dispelled. The magic in 2411 is what, within a Cartesian world view, might be called the union of one person's mind with another's body, or with bodies outside us. April's and May's fantasies affect Mesmer's body directly; Mesmer's and Very's need for counsel is met by the appearance of 'signifying fish'. On taking leave of

Mesmer's utopia, the reader may resume disbelief in magic without re-entering the Cartesian world of merely external relations with one's environment.[8]

If the world about us is constitutive of our being, we must take good care what we make of it. Here the design of New Stoke is a paradigm. Not only is it part of the extended bodies of its citizens—it is itself modelled on the human body-actual. Its pentacular form may suggest the head and limbs, or, in accordance with the slip recounted by Freud, the 'five straight limbs' which are all a man needs. But for the most part as befits a matriarchy, its physical symbolism is female: 'a ripe fig of a town'—suggesting the Italian use of 'fig' for the female genitals. Before entering the town by the gate, one will be entertained by the 'fiveplay' of its fountains.

The town is said to be not only a pentacle, but a torus, with reference to the pipes of Understoke where the sewage is recycled. Understoke is entered at the Penta-Centre, a civic anus right in the central agora where the citizens assemble. A short distance from this is the Moister-Oyster, an oyster-shell-shaped cavern inhabited by a labile spheroid which is a 'universal index', sensitive to everything that happens. Or as Reed comments, 'What I in my weariness would call a womb with a view'.

If a town is an extension of the human body—as most people feel that, for instance, their home is—then the slicing up of our garagist cities by urban motorways appears as a violation in the same way as most people feel a break-in to their house would be. The somatic character of New Stoke does not have to be a feasible bit of town planning in order to do its work in sensitising us to the garagist violence that we easily come to acquiesce in. That is exactly how a utopian text ought to work politically.

Endnotes

1 On the significance of this name, it is worth mentioning that the appearance in the text of an inn called The Cheery Wryneck and a boat called The Loaded Parrot is a reprise of Westlake's earlier novel *One Zero and the Night Controller*, in which a disco called The Blighted Sparrow, scene of One Zero's humiliation, is referred to under the names of other doomed birds, e.g. Laggard Lapwing, Washy Wheatear. This suggests a mesmerised partridge, no doubt about to be eaten by a snake.

2 'Introduction to the programme of the French Workers' Party', in *The First International and After* (Pelican Marx Library, 1974).

3 Though the rhyming pair OEDIPAL-SCHMOEDIPAL does occur, alluding to the Jewish joke: 'The doctor says my son has got an oedipus complex', 'Oedipus schmoedipus, what does it matter as long as he loves his mother?'

4 I say 'supposed' since, if phallocentrism implies male orientation, this is a misreading of Freud. 'Phallus' in this context refers equally to clitoris or penis. The feminist use of words like 'phallocentric' and 'phallocratic' diverges from psychoanalytical usage, whether Freudian or Lacanian. For Freud, both sexes have a phallus; for Lacan, both lack one.

5 See his essay 'The Personal and Political in Utopian Science Fiction' in *Science Fiction, Social Conflict and the Threat of War*, ed. Philip Davies (Manchester University Press, 1991).

6 Very is also virgin born, i.e. cloned from one parent only, which, since he is male and she female, is presumably miraculous even in 2411.

7 I should mention that the converse of this de-instrumentalising of our relation to the inorganic world is June's technological transformation of her own body-actual—her star-map nipples, pubic strobe, irises modified to reflect her moods by their colour, and the nutrient graft that decorates her face. (I found this aspect quite disturbing—but then I even find ear-piercing a little ghoulish). This theme recurs in *Imaginary Women* in the story of Molly, who had her whole body covered with tattoos of fish, only to feel desecrated and devote her life to reworking tattoos that no longer pleased their bearers. The chapter on the results of this Kleinian reparation is one of the most powerful in the book.

8 The theme of the body-world parallels crops up in Westlake's other novels too—most notably in the Night Controller's idea of the spatio-temporal grid that is at once her body and the metropolis. In *Imaginary Women*, the impression is that 'our city' (Manchester) is the organism, within which the human characters move like Spinoza's worm in the bloodstream.

Biographical Notes

Michael Westlake's writing career has been paralleled by his work variously as a film teacher (at Manchester University), journalist and translator. After living in Paris some twenty years, he moved in 2012 to Scotland, where he is working on further fiction and continues to translate.

Publications:

Novels:
One Zero and the Night Controller, 1990, Routledge and Kegan Paul, London
Imaginary Women, 1987, Carcanet Press, Manchester
The Utopian, 1989, Carcanet Press, Manchester
51 Soko to the Islands on the Other Side of the World, 1990, Polygon Press, Edinburgh
The Triumph of Love and Other Paintings, 1997, St Martin's Press, New York
World Enough, Internet publication 2008 (Lulu) and forthcoming, Verbivoracious Press, Singapore

Non-fiction:
(co-author Robert Lapsley) Film Theory: an Introduction, 1988 and 2006, Manchester University Press, Manchester

Toril Moi was born in Norway. She teaches literature at Duke University in North Carolina. Among her books are *Sexual/Textual Politics* (1985), *Simone de Beauvoir: The Making of an Intellectual Woman* (1993) and *Henrik Ibsen and the Birth of Modernism* (2006). She is working on a book on literary theory after Wittgenstein, Austin and Cavell.

Andrew Collier (1944-2014) taught philosophy at Bangor University and at the University of Southampton. With an intellectual formation bringing together existentialism, marxism, psychoanalysis and latterly Christianity, his extensive output included books on Spinoza, the psychotherapist R. D. Laing, and the philosopher of science Roy Bhaskar. Long associated with the journal *Radical Philosophy*, he was, as his many books and papers testify, a staunch defender of reason against what he viewed as anti-rationalist trends in recent philosophy.